Shadow Guardian

Rebecca Deel

DEDICATION

To my amazing husband. Without you, none of this would be possible.

ACKNOWLEDGMENTS

Cover by Melody Simmons.

i

CHAPTER ONE

Mercy Powers stood with the rest of the funeral attendees and watched in silence as the casket bearing the body of President Enrique Soldado's grandson was taken from the church, followed by a procession of the president's mourning family. Her heart ached for the teenager's grief-stricken parents. Fourteen was much too young to die. Carlos had fallen in a hail of gunfire in the street outside his home a few days earlier, a message to his grandfather who cracked down on illegal gun trade between Mexico and the United States.

Carlos's mother wept in Mercy's arms before the funeral began. Helpless to alleviate the woman's pain, she held Maria as she grieved. There were no words she could offer to comfort Carlos's mother. Instead, Mercy held her tight and cried silent tears with Maria as memories of her own loss assailed her.

Once the processional cleared the church, the crowd dispersed. Some would follow the hearse to the cemetery. Others would return to their normal lives, eager to push the sorrow from their minds.

Roger Jones, head of Mercy's Secret Service detail, leaned close. "You have ten minutes before we leave for the airport. The restrooms are through that door." He inclined his head toward the right.

"Thanks, Roger." She slipped into the aisle and walked toward the door. Only a handful of people noticed Mercy didn't join the stream of humanity exiting the building.

With the security detail flanking her, Mercy walked down the corridor to the women's restroom. After using the facilities, she took a minute to decompress. On the whole, she didn't mind attending state functions in her uncle's stead. President William Martin rarely called upon Mercy unless other dignitaries or Charlotte, her cousin, were busy with other responsibilities. This was one of those times the other department heads were committed elsewhere, and Charlotte had a new baby and couldn't get away. That left Mercy to represent the United States at the Soldado funeral.

Since she had already offered the condolences of her uncle to President Soldado and his family, Mercy and the security detail would leave from the church to go to the airport. Her lips curved. She'd reach home much faster if she left the bathroom.

Mercy wadded the paper towel she used to dry her hands and tossed it into the trash can. With a quick glance in the mirror, she pivoted toward the hallway door. A peculiar coughing sound reached her ears.

She frowned. Was one of the agents sick? Mercy approached the door. Before she took more than a few steps, the door flew open and three men dressed in black and armed to the teeth rushed inside. One of the men grabbed her while a second moved in with a syringe clutched in his hand.

Mercy fought against the first man's hold. "Let me go. I'm an American diplomatic representative." Where was her security detail? This couldn't be happening. She wasn't anyone important. Why would someone want her?

The second man snapped something in Spanish at the third who then grabbed Mercy's head to hold her still. A moment later, the second thug plunged the needle into the side of Mercy's neck. She flinched at the initial bite of pain as the needle pierced her skin.

Mercy's terror faded. Her tongue felt thick, her vision blurred. Although she fought to stay alert, Mercy lost the battle. She wondered what her uncle would say when he learned she was dead.

Darkness closed in.

CHAPTER TWO

Nico Rivera rolled over and sat up before grabbing his ringing cell phone. "Rivera."

"It's Maddox. My office with your team in thirty minutes."

"Yes, sir." He glanced at the clock and sighed. At least he'd slept three hours this time. Nico called each of his teammates, then hurried through a shower. From the sound of his boss's voice, his unit would be deployed again. So much for enforced time off.

Five minutes later, he dressed in his work uniform of black cargo pants, black t-shirt, and combat boots. After he strapped on his weapons, Nico grabbed his Go bag and left his home. At three in the morning, he didn't have to worry about Nashville traffic. A good thing. Brent Maddox, Fortress Security's CEO, wouldn't call in Shadow unit unless the mission was urgent. His team wasn't schedule for deployment rotation for another month.

Nico arrived at Fortress headquarters with five minutes to spare. He swiped his card through the scanner and parked in the garage under the building alongside his teammates' vehicles. Trace Young, his sniper, leaned against the side of his SUV, waiting for Nico.

"Know what's going on?" his teammate asked.

"Nope. I hope I have time to grab coffee before we're briefed."

"I thought Maddox said we were off deployment rotation for a few weeks. We need downtime, Nico."

"He wouldn't have called unless it was an emergency."

Trace frowned. "Next time we're off rotation, I say we leave town for at least a week."

Nico grinned. "I hear you." He didn't have an argument with that. He wanted time on a beach to bake in the sun with nothing more urgent on his mind than shedding the stress that was his constant companion on the job and off.

As they exited the elevator and walked down the hallway. Nico glanced into the communications room, noting that Anderson, Zane Murphy's trainee, was working tonight.

The two men strode into the conference room where the rest of their teammates waited. "I don't know any more information than I told you when I called," Nico said, forestalling the barrage of questions sure to come.

"Next to nothing," Joe Gray, Trace's spotter, muttered.

"Can't be good, whatever it is," Ben Martin commented.

Nico's eyes narrowed. Their EOD man looked tired. His whole unit was exhausted. Trace was right. They needed downtime before they reached the breaking point. He didn't want to lose a teammate because of mistakes from fatigue.

Sam Coleman, Shadow unit's medic, handed Nico a mug of coffee. "It's fresh and strong enough to peel paint," she said.

He nodded his thanks and sipped the steaming liquid. Perfect.

Brent Maddox, a buzz-cut blond SEAL, entered the conference followed by Zane Murphy in his wheelchair.

"Take a seat," Maddox ordered. "Videoconference in one minute."

"What's the mission?" Nico asked.

"Hostage rescue. HVT."

High value target? His eyebrows rose. "Who and where?"

Before Maddox could answer, Zane said, "The call is coming in."

The large television on the far wall lit up and President William Martin's lined face appeared on the screen. Nico sat up straighter as did his team members.

"Shadow unit is here, sir," Maddox said. "As requested, they know nothing about the mission."

"I apologize for keeping you and your team in the dark, Nico," President Martin said. "Any breach in security would mean the death of someone I care for very much."

Nico stiffened. "Charlotte?" He hadn't heard of any threats against the president's daughter. Wouldn't Martin have called in Durango to protect Charlotte and her family? The Delta team had a special friendship with her. Their team medic had delivered Sam, Charlotte's son, while rescuing her from a terrorist.

"She and her family are safe. My niece, Mercedes Powers, was attending the funeral of President Soldado's grandson on behalf of the United States. Her security detail was murdered and Mercy was taken."

"Do you know who took her, sir?" Nico asked.

"The Scorpions."

His hands fisted. Not good. "Are you sure?"

"Unfortunately."

"Why call us?"

"They threatened to kill her if I sent in a Special Forces team." A scowl from the leader of the free world. "They claim to have contacts inside the Pentagon. I can't take a chance on word leaking that I've authorized a team to rescue my niece. I can't send in Durango since Alex

Morgan has a newborn and Josh Cahill's wife is due to have a baby any time now, and their team is on leave for another month. Plus, Durango has completed several operations in the region where you're headed. I'd prefer not to send them back in for a while. I don't want their families in danger."

Maddox stirred. "What else can you tell us about the abduction, sir?"

"I'll send you an electronic file with everything you need to know. I want my niece back in one piece, Nico."

"Restrictions?"

"None except I want it done quietly. When you bring her back to the US, I want to know you've returned, but not where you hide her."

Hide her? Usually when Shadow rescued a hostage, their responsibilities ended with a safe return to the family. "What's the Scorpions goal? Why kidnap Mercy?"

"They want me to release their leader. The group planned to abduct the person I sent to the funeral. It's a bonus for them the US representative they nabbed is related to me." Martin dragged a hand down his face. "Just the thought of those vicious killers getting their hands on Charlotte or my grandchildren makes me want to vomit. I want Mercy out of their hands yesterday, Nico."

"Yes, sir."

The president looked at Maddox. "I'll send the electronic file in a moment. I owe you one, Brent."

Nico's boss grinned. "Don't worry. I'll collect."

With a flash of a smile, the transmission ended.

Maddox looked at Shadow unit. "Grab whatever supplies you need. The jet leaves for Mexico in an hour. Nico, I need to speak with you."

After his teammates left the conference room, Nico waited in silence for his boss to speak.

"I assume you caught the president's reference to hiding his niece when you return to the States."

7

"Yes, sir."

"There are rumors on the dark web about Scorpion expanding their reach."

"They want to move into the US." Nico dragged a hand through his hair. Not what he wanted to hear. The members of Scorpion were ruthless. They didn't blink an eye at collateral damage.

"Martin wants Mercy off their radar for a while. The terrorist group should move on to another objective if they can't locate her."

A nod. "We'll make sure she's protected. Do we have a safe house set up?"

"I talked to Rod Kelter, the detective in Otter Creek. He's given us permission to use his cabin outside Murfreesboro for this op." Maddox smiled. "Fortress rebuilt his cabin with several new improvements. I'll send you a list of the safety features."

"Panic room?" he guessed.

"Among other surprises. Ms. Powers will be comfortable and Shadow will have backup if you need it." His boss handed Nico a set of keys and rattled off the code for the alarm system. "The jet will take you to a private airfield where you will have an SUV waiting for you. Take enough supplies to camp for a few days."

"Do we know where she's being held?"

"In the Chiapas Province."

Nico scowled. Fantastic. He hated that place. "That covers thousands of miles, Brent, some of it the Lacandon Jungle."

"I'm aware," his boss said dryly.

"I'll scour the dark web and try to narrow your search," Zane said. "By the time you have boots on the ground, I should have more intel for you."

"What about Charlotte, Griff, and the kids? If the Scorpions can't get their hands on Mercy, they might make a run at Charlotte and her family."

"They've been moved to Camp David. No one will touch them."

"Temporary solution," Nico pointed out.

Maddox inclined his head. "We'll stop the Scorpions in their tracks."

Easier said than done.

"If you need anything, let me know. You'll get it, no questions asked."

"Once this mission is finished, you have to give my unit time off. We're pushing the edge, Brent."

"Your team will have two weeks uninterrupted time off without training or mission prep. You have my word."

"I'm holding you to it." With a nod to his boss and Zane, Nico spun on his heel and left the room.

He took the elevator to the lowest level of the Fortress building, a subbasement with vaults of weapons to choose from. Nico restocked his Go bag with flashbangs, grenades, ammunition, another Ka-Bar, and two more handguns. He moved to another secured room at the end of the hall and grabbed medical supplies to flesh out his already well-packed first-aid kit, then added several MREs and a packet of wipes.

He started to return to the elevator and stopped, frowning. If Mercy was kidnapped at the funeral, she wouldn't be dressed for an outdoor trek through rough terrain. As he backtracked to the room filled with Fortress uniforms in all sizes, he texted Zane and asked him to find out the woman's sizes. Within two minutes, the communications tech sent back a reply.

Nico walked into the wardrobe room and grabbed two pairs of cargoes and long-sleeves t-shirts, one pair of combat boots with thick socks to protect Mercy's feet from blisters. He glanced at his screen again and turned to the shelves on the far wall. He wasn't exactly comfortable choosing women's undergarments, but Mercy would have to have foundation garments to change into in case they had to camp. Hoping he didn't make a mistake, he shoved a couple of each into a zipped compartment of his bag.

Hoisting the Go bag over his shoulder, Nico strode to the elevator and joined his team in the parking garage. "Let's move."

Thirty minutes later, Shadow parked their vehicles in the private parking lot near the airfield and boarded the plane. Once they were inside, Nico informed the pilot that they were boarded.

When the jet was airborne, Nico pulled out his laptop and checked his inbox. Zane had forwarded the file sent from the president. "File's up," he told his team. "Review it along with the second file Zane sent on the Scorpions. Once you've done that, we'll formulate a plan of attack. We need to grab Mercy and leave Mexico. Fortress doesn't have many friends in Chiapas Province."

As his team settled back to review the files, Nico opened the document the president sent. By the time he reviewed both files, his gut was in a knot. If Mercy Powers wasn't already dead, she soon would be if Shadow didn't get to her, fast.

CHAPTER THREE

Mercy woke to complete darkness with a massive headache, nausea, a dry mouth, and the bone-deep knowledge she was in deep trouble. She didn't know where she was or who abducted her. In truth, Mercy hadn't expected to wake at all.

Made sense to merely knock her out. What was the point of killing her when she was a valuable prize alive? But why take her? She wasn't important on the stage of world politics except to her uncle. William Martin loved her as much as he loved his daughter, Charlotte. But these clowns wouldn't know that. Mercy had intentionally stayed out of the limelight over the years. She wasn't a fan of the media, not after they ripped Uncle William and his family to shreds during political campaigns. No question, politics was brutal, and it was a blood sport she preferred to stay away from.

Besides, she'd learned to avoid the media and the spotlight when she was married. Her husband's safety had depended on secrecy. Old habits were hard to break.

Mercy became aware of dirt under her cheek and frowned. Where had the gunmen taken her? She listened for sounds to indicate her location and heard absolute silence. No traffic, no blare of sirens, nothing. As a city girl, this kind of silence wasn't normal for her, almost oppressive.

She rolled to her stomach and rose to her hands and knees. When she swayed, Mercy sank back down to her stomach. Man, whatever had been in the syringe had been strong. How long was she unconscious? With no windows, Mercy didn't have a way to estimate the passage of time.

While she gathered her strength to try rising again, she glanced around, hoping for a pinprick of light. Nothing. This was almost like being buried alive, Mercy thought, and shivered.

She shoved her morbid thoughts aside. Steeling herself, Mercy rocked to her hands and knees. This time, she was successful in staying upright. Good grief. She was weak. If she had the opportunity to escape, Mercy wouldn't be able to run far. Hiding was her best option because she would never outrun her kidnappers.

The utter darkness disoriented her to the point that she was afraid to stand up. Guess she'd crawl as she explored her prison. On all fours, Mercy moved forward, hoping she didn't pitch headfirst into a hard object. When her hand bumped against a solid surface, she reached out to feel the obstacle in front of her. Stone.

Frowning, she felt along the stone wall. It wasn't smooth like a man-made structure. This was natural. Dirt floor. Rock wall. Listening intently, she heard water running nearby, like a creek. She was in a cave?

Mercy grimaced. She hated caves. The whole bat thing just creeped her out. Using the rock wall as a guide, she stood and stretched over her head as far as possible. No low ceiling. If she was right and the gunmen had dumped her in a cave, she would be foolish to explore too far. Some cave systems extended back for miles with multiple turnoffs where people could get lost. She might never be found or she might pitch headfirst over a steep drop.

Torn between staying put and exploring further, Mercy opted to take a hundred steps to the left to see if she could find an opening. Any light would be preferable to the inky blackness and give her a better sense of the enclosure's size and shape. To keep herself oriented, she trailed one hand along the wall while she held the other out in front of her. Wouldn't want to slam into a wall and give herself a concussion. Her head already pounded. No need to add to her misery.

When Mercy reached the count of one hundred, she still hadn't run into another wall of this cave. The sound of flowing water was louder, making her long for a drink. She knew it wasn't safe because the water wasn't treated.

After retracing her steps, Mercy walked one hundred steps the other direction. This time, her hand touched a rough, wet rock wall. Nice. She didn't dare remove her hand from the wall she'd been using as a guide. She also didn't want to sit against a wet wall, either.

Returning to her original position at the center of the guide wall, Mercy sank to the ground, her strength gone for now. She'd rest and think of some way to get herself out of this predicament. If she could escape and find to a phone, she could call for help.

She didn't know how many minutes passed when she heard a scraping noise to her left. She analyzed the sound. Before Mercy could decide what it was, a bright light shone into the interior of the cavern.

Wincing, Mercy shielded her eyes from the glare, but took a quick look around the interior. A cave, the chamber a large one. On the left side was the small stream of water she heard.

"You're awake. Good." Hard hands grabbed Mercy and yanked her to her feet. "Come."

Like she had a choice in the matter. Still averting her eyes from the flashlight's glare, she stumbled from the cavern into the open air. The stars were out, the night clear and muggy, and the moon was high in the sky. She had been unconscious for several hours.

When she stumbled, the man cursed, grabbed her arm, and hurried her forward. Mercy considered shaking off the hard hand gripping her arm like a vise and discarded the idea. If she fell and twisted an ankle, her chances of escape dwindled to zero.

She skidded in several places as the kidnapper dragged her down a rocky hillside. What she wouldn't give for a pair of hiking boots about now. Doing this kind of walking in dress shoes and a dress wasn't optimal.

By the time the terrain flattened out, Mercy was panting as though she'd walked miles instead of down a hillside. The man at her side yanked her along, cursing at her for being slow.

In the distance, she saw a complex of buildings with lights blazing from the windows. Her captor propelled her across the remaining distance and up the stairs into a large one-story cinder-block building.

Blinking against the light, Mercy made a mental note of the doors and rooms they passed in the wide corridor. At the end of the hall, the kidnapper threw open a door and shoved Mercy inside a room. Only one door and the two windows were barred. She wasn't getting out of here through a window.

The room was empty aside from a camera atop a tripod and a chair in the center of the space. The sight of the chair sitting on a blue tarp made Mercy's gut clench. Surely these men weren't going to interrogate her. She didn't know anything. Even if she did, she wouldn't betray her country or her uncle and his family. She would never put Charlotte in danger.

"Sit." The thug stood near the door, his back to the wall. He was muscular and heavily armed, his attention focused on her.

Since Mercy's legs were shaking with remnants of the drug and flat out fear, she sat. She didn't wait long.

A man dressed in black except for his silver-tipped cowboy boots walked into the room, flanked by two other men in similar garb. The man in the middle, though, wore authority like a second skin. Everything about this man said he was in charge.

Mercy memorized his face. Perhaps he would tell her why she'd been taken.

The leader swaggered into the room, his gaze sweeping over her body, a lingering perusal that made revulsion surge inside Mercy. Although she wanted to demand answers and insist this man to release her, she kept her mouth shut and waited for him to speak.

He motioned to the thug on his right, a man with hairy arms like a gorilla. Gorilla lumbered to the camera and flipped a switch. After the red light came on, he nodded to his boss.

In heavily accented English, Boss moved closer. "Look at the camera and beg for your life."

Mercy raised her chin and glared at the man. Muscle, the man who had dragged her down the mountainside, glanced nervously at Boss, then at her. His gaze implored her to talk.

Not a chance. If she did as Boss demanded, she had no guarantee she wouldn't get a bullet in the head immediately afterward. Logic said compliance would get her killed faster than defiance.

Boss scowled and moved a few steps closer. "Beg for your life." He gestured to the camera. "You plead enough, I get what I want."

"What do you want?" she asked, her gaze steady and her voice quiet.

"The release of our leader, Jorge Morales."

"The US government doesn't negotiate with terrorists. Let me go. I'm not important, just a representative of the government expressing the condolences of our people to the Soldado family for their loss."

Boss's eyebrows rose and a wide smile curved his lips. "Ah, you should hope this is not true. If the president won't release Jorge, I have no reason to keep you alive."

Yeah, pretty much what she'd figured.

Boss checked that the camera was still on, then faced her once more and backhanded her. The sound of the slap echoed in the nearly empty room as shock and pain rocketed through Mercy. A warm trickle of liquid trailing from the side of her mouth told her Boss had split her lip.

He reached back with his other hand and slapped her on the other side of her face. This time, the pain exploded on her cheek.

The boss walked around behind her and, with this fist in her hair, yanked her head back against his chest. He forced her face toward the camera. "You see this pretty woman, President Martin? She won't be so pretty when my men and I are finished with her if you don't release Jorge Morales in the next 24 hours. Don't test me. If you do, the woman will beg me to end her life long before I agree to kill her."

He motioned for the camera man to turn off the camera. "Send it to the White House." Boss circled to the front of Mercy again. "I am most unhappy with you. No food for you." Boss tilted his chin at Muscle. "Take her back to the cave and post guards in case the Americans are stupid enough to send someone for her."

Muscle jerked Mercy to her feet and hauled her from the room. As he forced her down the hallway, Mercy saw a bathroom. "Wait." She gestured toward the room. "Please."

A scowl, then he shoved her inside. "Fast or I force you out."

Not wanting to antagonize Muscle, Mercy used the facilities, washed her hands in a hurry, and cleaned the blood from her face. The door opened just as she tossed the used paper towel into the trash. "Thank you."

"Out, now," he hissed. He grasped her arm again and hauled her outside the building.

Although Muscle hurried her from the compound, she noticed a large SUV slowing to stop at the entrance to the building she'd just left. The driver circled the hood to the back door. Seconds later, a distinguished-looking man with gray hair stepped out. When he reached for the knob of the front door, the man turned slightly under the light, glanced at her, then proceeded inside.

"You should not push Hector," Muscle said. "He can kill you in the most painful ways."

"He'll kill me anyway." She slid a sideways glance at him. "Why do you work for him? You'll die an early death if you don't free yourself from this life."

"I have no choice. He threatened my family."

"Take me to a safe place and I'll help you." Uncle William would work something out to reward this man for saving her life.

He growled. "I have no wish to die tonight." With that, he stopped talking and lengthened his stride, forcing Mercy to jog beside him to stay on her feet. At the entrance to the cave, Muscle shoved Mercy inside the cavern and locked her in.

CHAPTER FOUR

Nico checked his phone's screen. He read Zane's text. With a frown, he clicked on his email and tapped the link Zane sent to his inbox. His heart skipped a beat when he saw the beautiful woman on the screen.

He stared at her picture, memorizing the features of a woman he' d have enjoyed meeting under better circumstances. This must be Mercy Powers, President Martin's niece. Nico pulled out headphones from the overhead compartment and plugged them into his computer. Didn't make sense, but he wanted to view this video clip alone first, then he would show the footage to his teammates. He tapped the icon.

A man speaking with a heavy Mexican accent said, "Look at the camera, and beg for your life."

As Nico watched the five-minute clip, his admiration for Mercy grew. He saw the knowledge in her eyes. She'd worked out the truth that if she complied with the thug's demand, he wouldn't have a reason to keep her alive.

Fury boiled in his gut as he watched the thug hit her. When the clip finished, he replayed it over and over, looking for anything that might give him an idea where Mercy was being held. Chiapas Province covered a lot of territory. Unfortunately, he saw nothing to help. The room was made of plain cinder block painted a neutral color. The one window he saw in the clip was covered with black bars.

When he was satisfied he couldn't glean more from the footage, Nico grabbed his phone again and called Zane. "Tell me you have something to point us in the right direction," he said when the communications guru answered.

"The thug who hit Mercy is Hector Blanco, Jorge Morales's right-hand man. I just sent you the latest intel on the Scorpion operation in Chiapas Province and their known strongholds. I'm tracking the origin of the email, but it will take a while."

"I want to know as soon as you get anything." He didn't know how long ago the video had been sent to the president and the deadline from Hector was only 24 hours. Not a lot of time to track down a woman being held captive in an area covering thousands of square miles, including the stinking jungle.

After he ended the call with Zane, Nico moved to the conference area of the jet and signaled his team to join him. "The Scorpions sent this video clip to the White House."

He connected his laptop to the large television and hit play. Each of the men scowled when Hector hit Mercy. Sam flinched. "What did you notice?"

"Hector isn't afraid for people see his face," Joe said.

Trace scowled. "The Scorpions think they're untouchable."

"Worse, they're not worried about Mercy seeing their faces." Sam pointed to the shadows on the wall of the room where Mercy had been recorded. "Even though he doesn't step into camera range, this guy's face isn't covered by a mask."

"How can she defend herself? She's unarmed and untrained." Ben said. "They aren't worried that she'll escape. This group is made up of only men. Women are seen as sex objects and nothing more. She's not a threat to them."

"They're arrogant idiots," Nico said. "Mercy Powers is a smart, resourceful woman. She told Hector nothing, refused to comply with his demands, and bought herself and us time."

"She has to know the president will send someone for her," Trace pointed out.

"We don't negotiate with terrorists."

"That's the party line. Martin wouldn't abandon her."

"She knows that, but Hector and his cronies don't. Mercy was careful not to mention that she was the president's niece. Hector is trying to force Martin to act without realizing the value of the bargaining chip he has in his hands." Nico clicked on the latest intel from Zane. "The Scorpions have two strongholds, here and here." He pointed at the highlighted portions of the map Zane sent. "Chances are high Mercy is being held in or around these two villages."

"We need to narrow it down to one choice." Joe folded his arms across his chest. "These two villages are miles apart in rugged territory with a river between them. If we guess and infiltrate the wrong site, Mercy is dead."

Nico didn't need the reminder. The clock ticking down to Mercy's final breath ran in his head. "Zane's working on the intel, but with us on a short clock, I need to reach out to one of our contacts. Maybe he'll be able to point us in the right direction."

Trace folded his arms across his chest, eyes narrowing. "Julio?"

A shrug. "Who better?"

His teammates groaned.

"You can't trust him, Nico." Joe's intense gaze locked with his. "He's for sale to the highest bidder."

A fact of life in this business. "He owes me." Not wanting to waste more time that could be used to plan this mission, Nico grabbed his satellite phone and punched in the number for his informant.

A moment later, Julio said, "It's been a long time, my friend."

Nico's lips curved. "How have you been?" Although he wanted to push for the information he needed to save Mercy, he had to play the role he established working undercover in Mexico, that of a hired thug for sale with no moral character or capacity to care about anything but his own hide. He hated this side of his life.

"Not bad. How is your family, Esteban?"

He gave Julio tidbits of information about his fake family, then asked after the other man's wife and children, a subtle reminder to the informant that Nico knew a lot about them, enough to be dangerous to their health.

With the greetings completed at last, Julio said, "When will you be in Mexico?"

"Soon if you have information for me."

"What kind?" Caution rang in the man's voice.

"The kind worth $10,000 in American currency."

"For that amount of money, I'd sell my own mother to you."

Nico chuckled even as his skin crawled. "I have my own, thanks, and she has expensive tastes. Know anything about a special guest of the Scorpions?" Silence greeted his statement. "I see that you do. I want my hands on that package."

"These are not men to cross, my friend. They are very dangerous and enjoy hurting people before they grant the victim's wish to die."

His teammates scowled as they listened to the conversation on speaker. Julio was angling for more money. Nico sighed. "Julio, you wouldn't be trying to squeeze more money from me, would you?"

"These men, they are evil," he reminded Nico. "And the package is very beautiful. Or so I hear."

Yeah, she was. He didn't want to talk to Julio about Mercy as though she was a commodity to be traded on the flesh market. "I thought we were friends, Julio. Guess I'll have to take my money to another friend more willing to accommodate my interest."

"But I'm the best in the business. You are not the only one interested in the Scorpion's guest. Other information brokers, they take your money and give you nothing. Julio tells you true, yes?"

Nico pretended to think about the money for a moment. In truth, he'd been authorized to go a lot higher to get the information he needed for this operation. He didn't want to hand an informant that much money unless it was necessary. "I want the package, but not enough to pay more than $15,000. Last offer, Julio. Take it or leave it. My pool of friends is wide and deep."

"You wound me, Esteban. Very well. Because we are friends, I agree to your price."

"Information, Julio. Now."

The informant named one of the strongholds mentioned by Zane. "You're sure the package is there?"

"Rumors only, but solid ones. Heavier guard presence than usual."

Not what he wanted to hear, but unsurprising. Their hostage was more valuable than they realized. When he'd learned as much as possible from Julio and promised never to mention where he learned the information, Nico ended the call.

"Wish I felt better about his honesty," Ben muttered. "I don't want a bullet in the head because this clown gave us up and found someone willing to pay more for the information he gave you."

Nico glanced at his watch. "We have an hour before we land. Time to make a plan."

By the time the Fortress jet landed, Nico and his teammates had a plan in place. Like always, the plan was flexible and could be adjusted at a moment's notice, depending on the challenges they found at the site.

The SUV was waiting at the edge of the airstrip, keys under the driver's seat. His teammates piled into the vehicle, weapons within easy reach. Trace took the wheel while Nico claimed the shotgun seat. He called Zane. "Boots on the ground. Anything new?"

"A lot of chatter, nothing concrete. Maddox authorized payment to your informant. The money has been wired into his account. No information has surfaced yet about outside interest in Mercy."

"Won't last. If Julio knows people are sniffing around, someone is making careful inquiries about her. Let me know when the rumors surface. We're headed to the Scorpion compound outside Rio Azul. My informant says the Scorpions are keeping an important package at the compound. Heavy guard presence."

"I'll let Maddox know and put Adam Walker's team on alert. They're two hours away from that location."

Close, but not close enough to save Shadow if they ran into trouble. "Copy that. I don't know what kind of injuries Mercy may have at this point. Might be wise to alert Dr. Sorensen." The veterinarian, Ted Sorensen, used to be one of the finest trauma surgeons in the country and a Fortress operative himself before he'd burned out. Now he was the first stop for injured operatives when they returned to the US.

"He'll be ready."

After Nico ended the call, he grabbed his phone and checked the infrared images coming from one of four Fortress satellites. Frustrated when he couldn't find a figure that might have been Mercy, he slid the phone into his pocket.

One mile from Rio Azul, Trace parked under heavy tree cover. Shadow climbed from the vehicle and closed the doors with a soft snick. Nico signaled his team to turn on their comm systems. Time to get this party started. They had two hours to breach the compound, find Mercy, free her, and escape from Mexico. Piece of cake. If there wasn't an army of well-armed terrorists guarding the president's niece.

A half mile from the encampment, Nico held up his fist. His team froze in place as he moved a step closer to the wire stretched between two trees, glinting in the moonlight.

The mission clock in his head counted down the minutes. "Ben," Nico murmured.

Shadow's EOD man moved to Nico's side and crouched to study the wire.

"How long?"

His teammate held up his index finger and got to work. At one minute to the second, Ben glanced up and nodded.

Nico resumed the lead, moving toward their goal. Ben disarmed two more explosives, each stop testing Nico's patience. Six hundred yards from the edge of the compound, he and the rest of his team crouched in deep tree cover, watching the guards in rotation around the complex of buildings.

He gritted his teeth. Nico counted at least thirty terrorists in plain sight. No telling how many more in the buildings. He trusted his teammates. Shadow was the best he'd ever worked with. Still, with that many tangos, the sun would rise and Mercy's stay of execution would be over before Walker's team arrived to lend a hand. As much as he wanted to follow the president's orders, he may not be able to rescue Mercy without announcing their presence. Nico refused to let her die on his watch.

He scanned the area surrounding the compound, looking for guards. Nico frowned at the sight of ten men stationed around the side of the mountain. Two of them were stupid enough to be messing with their phones. The light from their screens pinpointed their locations.

He turned back to the compound. Not one of the buildings had an extra cordon of men surrounding it. The only thing that seemed off was the contingent of men on the hillside.

"Hillside," he whispered. Grabbing a pair of night-vision binoculars from his pack, Nico brought the mountain into focus and studied the terrain. The guards had ranged themselves around the top third of the hillside.

He checked the right quadrant, almost moved on to the left when he noticed a faint metallic gleam. Zooming in further, Nico spotted the wooden door with a metal lock.

Touching Trace's shoulder, he pointed toward the hillside and the door, and handed over his binoculars. The sniper stared through the lenses a moment, then nodded.

If Nico was a betting man, he'd lay odds on Mercy being inside a cave on that hillside. For Mercy's sake, he'd better be right. If they infiltrated the wrong defenses, she would be dead in seconds.

CHAPTER FIVE

Nico moved his teammates deeper into the cover of the trees. "We come at them from the top. The guards are focused on threats coming up the hillside. Take them down before they raise an alarm. We'll circle around on the right flank. Watch your step. Hector and his buddies probably have other booby traps laid in the area." He signaled his team to move out.

Chafing at the further delay, Nico pushed the pace as fast as he dared. He was right. Hector and friends had strung more trip wires. It was a miracle some of the villagers didn't stumble on one of these and blow themselves up.

Finally, they emerged from the tree line at the back of the hillside and began the climb to the top. Within minutes, they crested the peak, split their unit into groups of two and three operatives, and began a slow, careful descent on both sides of the hill.

In silence, Nico and his teammates stalked the first two of the ten men stationed around the cave. Nico targeted the closest tango and took him out with a knife to the kidney. He would have knocked the guy out with a sleeper hold, but Mercy's life depended on the utter silence of this operation. If one of the men raised a ruckus, Shadow would be caught in the open. Mercy needed his unit to stay alive if she had any chance to survive.

Trace clamped a hand over the mouth of the next target and drew his Ka-Bar across the man's throat.

One by one, his team rid the hillside of threats. When the last tango dropped to the ground, Nico hurried over the rocky terrain to the wooden door with the lock. He shoved his hand into his pocket and pulled out a set of lock picks. Within seconds, he dropped the flimsy lock to the ground, moved aside the latch, and yanked open the door. "Trace, Ben, Joe, keep watch. Sam, with me."

He walked inside the cave, his NVGs allowing him to pinpoint Mercy's location immediately. She sat up as soon as he walked inside her prison. Once Sam was inside, Nico pushed the door until it was almost closed. Sounds carried long distances at night. He didn't want to alert the circling guards at the compound to their presence.

"Who's there?" Mercy asked. "Miguel, is that you?"

Who was Miguel? More important, why did it bother Nico to hear another man's name on her lips? "My name is Nico. Your uncle sent my team to bring you home."

She got to her knees. "You're American."

"Yes. My team medic is in the cave with me. Her name is Sam."

"Do you have any injuries that need immediate treatment?" Sam asked.

"Nothing that can't wait. What happened to the guards?"

"They won't stop us from leaving," Nico said, not wanting to see disgust or fear on her face. "We have to move fast. I brought a change of clothes for you." He slid his pack off his shoulder. "Hurry, Mercy. The sun will rise soon and we need to be a long way from here before Hector discovers you're gone. I'll turn my back while Sam helps you change."

"How can you see? It's pitch black in this cave."

Nico handed the cargoes, t-shirt, and boots to Sam, and turned to face the door. "We're using night vision goggles. Makes it easier to navigate unfamiliar terrain." And spot trip wires at night.

"How did you know where to find me?"

"We ran facial recognition on Hector from the video he sent to your uncle. That gave us a general idea where to start. Then I called in a favor from an informant to help us pinpoint your location."

"I'm grateful to you for coming after me. How many people did you bring with you?"

"There are five of us."

"But there must be forty or fifty men with Hector."

His lips curved. "A good reason to hurry, Mercy. Our closest teammates are two hours away."

A few seconds later, Sam said, "She's ready."

Nico turned, took the clothes and shoes Sam handed him, and shoved them into his pack. "Did they give you water or food, Mercy?"

"No. Hector was angry that I wouldn't cooperate."

"As soon as we're in a safe place, we'll feed you." He reached into his pack again and grabbed a small bottle of water. "We have to move fast. Do everything I tell you to do without question. All our lives depend on it." Nico broke the seal on the lid and pressed the bottle into her hand. "Small sips. If you gulp, you'll barf."

"Thanks." After a few sips, she capped the bottle and slid it into a cargo pocket. "Ready."

"Hold out your hand." He was afraid to touch her without warning. He didn't know what happened to Mercy while she'd been in Hector's hands, didn't want to contemplate the possibilities too deeply. He needed his emotions in check. When she extended her hand toward him, Nico wrapped his hand around hers. "Don't let go. If you need to stop, tell me."

"But don't need to?" she asked with a smile.

"That would be best." He tugged her forward. "We're coming out," he told his teammates on the outside.

"All clear," Trace murmured.

Nico led Mercy outside and up the hill. To her credit, she didn't question his direction or look around, just did her best to keep up with his fast pace.

When she stumbled, Nico wrapped his arm around her waist to steady her and kept going. At the foot of the hillside, he motioned for Trace to take point and steered Mercy into the trees.

He eyed the sky. They were running out of time. Any minute, Hector would send guards to relieve the ten men on the hillside and discover Mercy gone. "Faster, Trace," he whispered. If Mercy couldn't keep up, Nico would carry her.

The sniper picked up his pace. They continued the silent trek until a shout sounded in the distance.

"Go," Nico ordered his team. He scooped Mercy into his arms and broke into a run as his team surrounded him, providing a wall of cover for their principal.

A quarter of a mile from the SUV, Trace signaled his unit and they scattered to deep cover. Nico carried Mercy behind a cluster of trees. He pressed his finger to her lips for an instant, then motioned for her to sit with her back against the trunk. He crouched beside her, Ka-Bar in his hand. If one of Hector's men stumbled upon them, he would take care of him as quietly as possible. The last thing he wanted was to bring down a pack of terrorists on their position.

Two minutes later, a stick snapped and muttered curses reached his ears. Nico motioned for Mercy to lay flat as he shifted his gaze to his left. There. A hundred yards away, one of Hector's men approached, the beam of his flashlight beam crisscrossing the dirt.

Nico removed his NVGs, handed them to Mercy, and waited. The thug moved past their location, his gaze glued to the ground. He crouched to study scuff marks. As Nico stood, the other man's hand shifted to the gun shoved into his waistband.

No choice but to handle the problem. For reasons he couldn't justify, Nico didn't want Mercy to view him in a bad light. How could she do otherwise with bloody proof that he was a trained killer? Resigned, he slipped out from the stand of trees while his target's attention focused on the shoe prints of Nico and his teammates.

He considered and discarded options as he stalked Hector's man, irritated with himself for even considering non-lethal choices because Mercy was close. The president sent him and his team for Mercy because they were lethal. If he wanted to get her and his teammates home in one piece, he couldn't change who and what he was now.

His target turned toward the trees where the president's niece hid. The man stood, pulling his weapon free. Nico moved in, clamped a hard hand over the man's mouth as he plunged the knife deep into his kidney.

He activated his mic. "Report," he whispered.

Ben, Sam, and Joe reported they were clear. A moment later, Trace answered Nico's order with two clicks. "Ben," Nico whispered.

"Copy."

If the odds were better, Nico would let Trace hunt the two men searching for Mercy. His friend was more than capable of taking on two opponents. Right now, Nico was more interested in getting Mercy and his teammates to the SUV without attracting attention.

Nico returned to Mercy and helped her to her feet. He slid his arm around her shoulder. "Look straight ahead," he murmured, and moved them forward to meet his teammates.

Finally, Trace murmured, "Clear."

As the sky lightened to twilight, his teammates rejoined him and Mercy. Nico scooped the president's niece into his arms again, and the operatives ran.

Mercy leaned close to Nico's ear. "I'm sorry you have to carry me."

"If you were well hydrated, you could run."

She gave a short, soft laugh. "Not even on my best days. I hate running."

He flicked a grin at her. The rest of the run through the woods was completed in silence. When they reached the SUV, Ben dropped to the ground and rolled under the vehicle as Joe walked around it, checking for trackers.

"What are they doing?" Mercy asked.

"Making sure Hector didn't leave us surprises."

Joe and Ben finished their perusal. "Clear," Ben said.

Nico opened the back door and lifted Mercy to the middle row of seats, then joined her. Joe and Sam slid into the back while Ben climbed into the shotgun seat with Trace behind the wheel. "Go."

As they sped down the road, Nico and his teammates stayed vigilant, expecting trouble to materialize at every bend in the road. Five miles from Rio Azul, Joe said, "Company coming up on our six, fast."

"How many vehicles?"

"Two."

"Get on the floor, Mercy. Sam, change places with me. Joe, take the vehicle on the left. I'll take the goons on the right. Ben, be alert in case there are more ahead."

Trace snorted. "We're heading into an ambush. There are only a handful of roads leading away from Rio Azul."

"This province is owned by the Scorpions," Ben added. "I hope we have enough ammunition."

"Here they come." Joe climbed over the seat into the cargo area, twisted, and kicked out the hatchback glass. Sam handed him his AR-15, grabbed her own, and clambered into the seat near Mercy.

Nico checked to be sure Mercy was still on the floor and shifted into the cargo area with his rifle. "Cover your ears, Mercy. No matter what you hear, don't get up until we tell you it's safe to move."

"Do what you need to," she said.

Amazing. Taking Mercy at her word, he settled down to do his job.

CHAPTER SIX

Mercy flinched as gunfire echoed inside the SUV. She pressed closer to the floor as she waited for her five rescuers to eliminate the threats to her life. When a hail of return fire sounded, Sam slid from the seat and sprawled over top of Mercy.

"Sorry," Sam murmured. "I'll get up as soon as we're clear."

"Please tell me you're wearing protective gear."

A pause, then, "We wear it on every mission."

Tension lessened in her muscles. "Good." She didn't want anyone injured or dead on her account, although the odds of escaping the conflict unscathed were slim.

A loud crash made Mercy jerk. What was that?

"One down," Joe said.

Another crash. "Two down," Nico peered over the seat. "Doing okay, Mercy?"

"Just peachy. Can't remember when I've had more fun."

He gave a short laugh as he peered through the front windshield. "Two incoming. I'll take the vehicle on the left."

"RPG?" Ben asked.

Mercy's eyes widened. Her rescuers had rocket-propelled grenades on them?

"No need for stealth. By now, Hector knows where we are. We'll take out of these vehicles and try to outrun the ones sure to follow." Nico scrambled over the seat and lowered the window. Grabbing his grenade launcher, he levered himself through the opening to sit on the window frame and hefted the weapon to his shoulder.

A moment later, the grenade deployed. Within seconds an explosion ripped through the early morning, followed quickly by a second.

Nico ducked back into the vehicle. "There's probably a roadblock ahead. Take us off the main road, Trace."

"Copy that." In less than a minute, the SUV veered to the right and accelerated.

"You can get up, Mercy." As soon as Sam rose and slid back into the cargo area with Joe, Nico helped Mercy into the seat. "Don't get comfortable. You'll be back on the floor if we run into more trouble. Any new injuries?"

She shook her head. "I'm fine." Aside from the tremors setting in. Ticked her off, too. Nico must have noticed because he thrust his hand into his bag and pulled out a lightweight silver blanket, shook it out, and wrapped the cover around her.

"The adrenaline's bleeding off," he murmured. "The shakes will pass soon."

Not soon enough. Nico and the rest of his team weren't having a problem with adrenaline. They're used to it, she reminded herself. Her world was boring and sedate compared to the one they worked in.

She wasn't cut out for that world. Not much danger in her line of work. Most of the time, she labored in seclusion, her greatest dangers paper cuts, dry skin, and ink stains.

As the sky lightened enough to see the landscape, Mercy realized her earlier plan to escape and find a phone to call for help would have been doomed. The area where she'd been held was remote and barren. Miguel had mentioned a village nearby. Maybe Nico's driver had zoomed past it while she'd been on the floor. Since this area was under the control of the Scorpions, chances were high the villagers would have been too afraid to aid in her escape.

"Activity ahead," Trace said.

Mercy stared through the windshield. Several vehicles were arranged across the road, blocking their passage.

Nico scowled. "Evade. I'd rather not engage again and confirm where we're headed for Hector."

Trace turned down a side street on the left and sped through residential neighborhoods where a few lights shone in windows. He took turn after turn until they emerged onto a main thoroughfare.

"Have you been here before, Trace?" Mercy asked the operative.

"No, ma'am. I have a knack with maps." He shrugged. "I've always loved them. When I study one, the map stays in my mind."

"I'm directionally challenged. Can't find my way out of a paper bag no matter how many maps you give me."

Nico pulled out his cell phone and made a call. "It's Nico. We're ten minutes out and coming in hot. Have the jet ready."

"Company," Joe said again, disgust in his tone. "They're inching up on us."

The SUV leaped forward.

"Straight to the airfield," Nico told Trace as he glanced out the back of the vehicle to check the position of their tail. "We'll make it, but it will be close."

Mercy gripped the edge of the seat. Why were the Scorpions determined to get their hands on her? She wasn't important. If the terrorist group wanted to pressure Uncle William, they'd do better to target Charlotte. Her breath caught. Charlotte and the children.

She twisted in her seat, her hand gripping Nico's forearm. "You have to warn Charlotte. She needs extra protection."

"They're safe, Mercy. She and her family are at Camp David under heavy guard."

Mercy sank back against the seat. "Oh, thank goodness. I couldn't bear it if anything happened to them."

Nico turned to glance out the back of the SUV again. "I'll slow down Hector's men."

"Don't miss," Trace said. "Too many houses on this section of road."

After readying the RPG, Nico balanced on the window frame, this time facing toward the back of the vehicle. "Hold it steady, Trace." He aimed and fired.

Mercy squinted at the flash of bright light followed by an explosion.

Nico growled as he returned to the SUV's cab. "Although I eliminated one, there are still two on our six."

"Four minutes to the airfield." Trace dodged around a slow-moving vehicle in their path and surged ahead.

"Get your gear ready," Nico told his teammates. "We'll have to bail and run to the jet." He turned to Mercy. "We'll park at the edge of the airfield. Will you be able to run to the plane?"

"Watch me."

He grinned at her, then divided his attention between keeping watch out the left side of the vehicle and the back.

Moments later, Trace said, "Airfield's ahead. Jet's powered up."

"Floor it," Nico said. "I want more than a thirty-second lead."

The tires squealed as the operative followed Nico's order.

Mercy expected a small airport. Instead, the airfield Trace had mentioned consisted of an airstrip and a small hut with a single light burning over the side door.

Trace guided the SUV onto the grass and parked at the safest point near the jet. The operatives threw open their doors, grabbed their bags, and bailed from the SUV. Nico wrapped his hand around Mercy's and grabbed his bag. "Go. I'll cover you."

She opened the door, slid to the ground, and sprinted for the plane. Mercy ignored the pain in her leg. Sam could take a look after they were airborne and her rescuers were safe.

The pursuing vehicles came to a stop with a squawk of tires. Mercy glanced over her shoulder to see four men from each race vehicle spill out with guns in their hands. Gunfire echoed in the night.

Nico's team dropped back to place themselves between Nico and Mercy and Hector's men. He wrapped his arm around her waist and forced her to run faster.

As Mercy climbed the first step, something hit her left shoulder, shoving her forward. She gritted her teeth as pain radiated through her body.

Nico grabbed her and hauled her up the stairs, ignoring her gasp of pain. He helped her to one of the seats, snatched his rifle, returned to the open entrance, and began to fire. Within two minutes, the shots ceased and Nico's team hurried into the plane with their bags in hand.

Once the door was secured, Nico pressed the intercom. "Go." He shoved his bag into the overhead compartment as the plane began to taxi down the strip. "Sam, Mercy's been shot."

CHAPTER SEVEN

Nico looked at Joe, a ball of ice forming in his stomach. "Help me take Mercy to the back. Trace, tell the pilot we're flying into Bayside instead of Nashville."

The sniper nodded and rose.

Between them, Nico and Joe maneuvered Mercy down the aisle and to the bedroom at the back of the plane. Sam trailed them with her mike bag.

"Joe, spread plastic over the bed." The medic hurried to the bathroom to wash up.

Nico's hold on Mercy tightened as her breathing became labored. "Hold on," he murmured. "Sam will fix you up."

"Guess I'll have a scar to show for my time in Mexico," she whispered.

"Badge of honor," he corrected gently. "You'll be fine. I promise."

"Bed's ready," Joe said.

Sam returned. "Help her to the bed, then leave. I'll have to remove her shirt. I doubt she'll be comfortable with you two in here."

Nico waited until Mercy was situated on the bed before he tipped his chin at Joe for his teammate to return to the main cabin. When the door closed behind him, Nico crouched beside the bed where Mercy lay on her back. He gripped her bloodstained hand with his own. "I want to stay. If I promise to keep my gaze averted, will you let me?"

A small smile formed and she gave a slight nod.

The ice melted. "Thank you for trusting me." He stood and turned to Sam. "I'll be back in a minute." He didn't know if Sam would need help or not, but he wanted to be clean enough to lend assistance if necessary.

By the time he returned from washing his hands and face, Sam had cut one sleeve and shoulder from Mercy's shirt, exposing the wound but leaving her modesty intact. Perfect.

"Bullet went through her shoulder. I'll clean it up, use a couple pressure bandages to control the bleeding, and start pumping her full of antibiotics and a pain killer. She'll hold until Sorensen sees her."

"What do you want me to do?"

"Prepare the IV. We'll start the fluids, antibiotic, and pain killer before I clean out the wound." Sam looked at Mercy. "Are you allergic to anything?"

"Sulfa, morphine, and ibuprofen."

The medic blinked. "Wow."

Her lips curved. "That's what my doctor says. I'm allergic to all the helpful drugs."

Sam told Nico what to pull from the jet's medicine supply as she examined Mercy's wound. She sighed. "I'll have to flush this out, Mercy. I won't lie. This will hurt. Can't be helped, though. The bullet dragged bits of cloth into your shoulder. Pain meds in the IV will help, but you'll feel this."

After Nico readied the IV, he handed everything to Sam and sat on the bed beside Mercy. He wrapped his hand around hers. While the medic located a vein and inserted the needle, then administered a local anesthetic to deaden the area around the wound, Nico said, "Start from the beginning and tell me what happened." He wanted to know who to hunt in Rio Azul. He'd make sure the people who hurt her never hurt anyone else again. He wanted her safe. The only way to do that was to rid the world of the thugs' presence. Permanently.

While Mercy talked, her muscles relaxed as the pain meds kicked in. Nico nodded at Sam. The meds had been in her system long enough to make Sam's ministration at least tolerable.

Mercy's face paled when the medic flushed the wound. "Stay with me," Nico said softly. "This will be over soon and you can sleep. Tell me more about your abduction. You said the clowns who grabbed you jabbed a needle in your neck. Did you wake up en route to Rio Azul?"

She shook her head. "I woke up in the cave where you found me. Miguel, one of the guards, dragged me out and down the hillside to see Hector."

"I saw the recording he sent to your uncle. Did he say anything or question you off camera?"

"No. He was furious when I wouldn't cooperate."

"You figured out he would kill you if he got what he wanted, didn't you?"

"My husband told me that terrorists have no reason to keep you alive if they learn what they want to know."

Nico froze. In a neutral voice, he said, "Husband?"

Sadness filled Mercy's eyes. "I'm a widow. Aiden died in combat two years ago. His Humvee rolled over an IED in Afghanistan. No one survived."

"I'm sorry. He was Army?"

A nod. "A Ranger." She hissed and arched away from the bed as Sam flushed more fluid into the wound.

"Sorry," Sam murmured. "I'm going to roll you toward Nico and place a bandage on the back of your shoulder."

"Let us do the work, Mercy." Nico worked with his medic to shift the president's niece to her side. He held

Mercy in place with a hand on her waist to steady her as Sam ripped open the package and applied the pressure bandage.

After cleaning blood from the plastic covering, they rolled Mercy to her back again and applied a pressure bandage to the exit wound.

Sam pulled off her rubber gloves and tossed them in the waste bin she'd positioned near the bed, then pitched the rest of the debris in as well. After flicking a glance at her team leader, she squeezed Mercy's hand briefly. "Do you feel like eating anything?"

A head shake. "Wouldn't be wise. My stomach is unsettled."

"I'll add nutrients and something for nausea to your IV. Do you have other injuries I need to treat?"

"Check my left calf. I think I cut it when Miguel shoved me into the cave after I talked to Hector."

Nico rolled Mercy to her side again and held her in place while Sam raised her pant leg and examined her calf.

"This is going to need stitches."

Mercy grimaced. "Hate needles."

"Yeah? What a coincidence. So does Nico." She grabbed another pair of gloves and tugged them on.

Mercy eyed him. "You don't look like you're afraid of anything."

He winked at her. "Maybe one day I'll tell you what I'm really afraid of."

Sam bent closer to her patient's leg. "Little stick," she murmured and administered a local anesthetic. "When this is numb, I'll clean the cut and stitch it. Shouldn't take more than four or five to close the wound." The medic turned away to get more supplies and add meds to the IV bag.

"Do you and your team work for the government?" Mercy asked Nico.

"Sometimes."

Her brow furrowed. "You're not military?"

41

"Most of us are former military and law enforcement. We work for a private security organization."

She thought about that a moment. "Why would Uncle William ask your organization to rescue me instead of a Special Forces teams in the military?"

"Hector claimed to have a source inside the Pentagon. If he was telling the truth, Martin couldn't send a military unit after you without the mole alerting the terrorists. Hector would have killed you before the team set foot in Mexico."

"Can you feel this?" Sam asked.

"Just pressure."

"Good. Keep talking to Nico while I take care of this."

"Who do you work for?" Mercy asked.

"Fortress Security." His gaze sharpened when her breath caught. Pain from Sam's work or something else? "What is it?"

"Aiden wanted to work for Brent Maddox. He'd planned to interview for a job after he mustered out. He was killed a month before his time in the military ended. He said applying for a job there was by invitation only, and he was proud of the fact he'd been asked to come for an interview."

Although she fell silent and closed her eyes, Mercy didn't let go of his hand. Pleased, Nico's thumb stroked the back of her hand in a soothing motion, reminding her he was there for her.

Unable to tear his gaze from her face for some reason, he gave into the madness and memorized her features. Long lashes feathered against her fair skin. Her bow-shaped lips were perfect for kissing. High cheek bones, cute button nose. Altogether, Mercy Powers was beautiful. Add that to her spine of steel, sharp brain, and never-quit attitude, the woman fascinated him and made other women he'd met pale in comparison.

He reminded himself that she was off limits to him. A job, nothing more. He frowned, not liking the lurch of his heart at that thought. No matter what he might want or wish, Mercy had a life of her own and when this job was done and she was safe, Nico would probably never see her again.

Sam straightened. "Finished." She removed her supplies, pitched the trash into the garbage along with her gloves. "Roll her to her back."

Mercy's eyes opened as they settled her flat on the bed again. "Thanks, Sam."

"If you need anything, tell Nico." She turned her gaze toward him. "Let me know if she develops a fever or something changes. I'll check on her in an hour." After she squeezed Mercy's hand, she left the bedroom.

"I should leave you to rest." He tightened his grip on her hand. "I'll go if you want me to, but I'd like to stay with you."

"Don't go," she whispered, her eyelids drooping.

Nico scooted closer until his thigh pressed against her shoulder and he could stroke her hair easily. "Sleep, Mercy. I'll watch over you."

"Tired. Afraid to sleep in Mexico."

"Understandable and smart." He wouldn't have slept, either. "Rest now. I'll be here."

She sighed and drifted to sleep while Nico's fingers threaded through her hair. The silken strands caught on his calluses, reminding him that they were from two different worlds.

Mercy was stable and asleep. He should leave. But everything in him rejected that logic. Nico had promised to keep an eye on her, and she was his responsibility. He'd see this through. He assured himself this didn't have anything to do with the fact that she was beautiful and vulnerable. He sighed. When had he started lying to himself?

An hour later, Sam tapped lightly on the bedroom door and stuck her head in. "How is she?"

"No change. She fell asleep right after you left. She was afraid to sleep while she was being held hostage."

"I don't blame her. I'll be back in an hour to check the IV."

Nico settled against the headboard and allowed himself to fall into a light sleep. Shadow had spent much of their flight time studying maps and satellite photos, and planning contingencies. A soft moan woke him sometime later. He looked down at Mercy, frowned. Her face was beaded with sweat.

He felt her forehead. Oh, man. She was burning up with fever. Nico eased away from her and opened the door. "Sam."

The medic appeared seconds later. "What's wrong?"

"Fever."

She checked Mercy. "I'll give her a stronger antibiotic and check her wounds. Take a break and tell the pilot to find a good tailwind."

Although reluctant to leave Mercy, he needed to visit the head and stretch his legs. "I'll be back soon."

"I'll stay with her until you return." Amusement lit her gaze.

Face hot, he left the bedroom. After visiting the facilities, he detoured to talk to the pilot. On his return trip from the cockpit, Nico snagged two bottles of water.

"How is your girl?" Joe asked.

His girl. Although inaccurate, he liked the sound of that. "Fever."

The spotter grimaced. "Sorry to hear that. Sam and Sorensen will pull her through."

With a nod, Nico continued down the aisle. Before he reached the bedroom, he called Zane.

"Yeah, Murphy."

"We rescued the package and we're en route to Bayside. Call Sorensen and tell him we're bringing him a customer."

"Who?"

"One of Hector's men nailed Mercy in the shoulder. Through-and-through."

"How bad?"

"Sam cleaned the wound and bandaged it. Says Mercy will hold until we reach the States. She's developed a fever, though."

"No one else hurt?"

"Negative. Hector lost twenty men tonight. He won't be happy."

"I'll update Maddox and Sorensen. The safe house is fully stocked with food plus clothes for Mercy. I talked to Charlotte and made sure the supplies included things that your principal likes and finds comforting."

"Thanks, Z." He ended the call and walked into the bedroom to see Sam bending over the bed trying to hold Mercy still. He set down the water and laid his hand on Mercy's cheek. She stilled.

Sam straightened with a bemused expression on her face. "You have the magic touch. I'll be back in a minute."

While she was gone, Nico returned to his original position on the bed with his thigh pressed to Mercy's shoulder. "You will be fine. Your body is fighting off an infection."

"Nico," she whispered.

"Right here. I left to get water and talk to the pilot."

Mercy sighed and settled back to sleep.

Nico's heart turned over. No one had ever accused him of being comforting. This woman, however, seemed to gravitate to him where others rejected him as being too harsh and jaded.

Sam returned with a plastic container and a washcloth in her hands. She disappeared into the bathroom. A moment later, Nico heard the water running. When Sam entered the bedroom again, she placed the container now filled with water on the nightstand by the bed and handed Nico the cloth. "Bathe her face and neck with cool water. We need to bring down the fever. I strung up a new IV with a stronger antibiotic. Do you want me to stay and help?"

Nico noted the pallor of his medic's face and the fatigue evident in her posture. "I've got this. Go sleep. I'll get you if Mercy grows worse."

A nod. "I'll check back in a couple hours."

After Sam left, Nico dunked the cloth in water and wrung it out. As soon as he began to smooth the damp fabric over her face, Mercy shivered. "I know it's cold," he murmured. "We have to reduce your fever so you'll be more comfortable."

He spent the rest of the flight alternately wiping her face and neck, and praying she'd survive long enough to reach Bayside.

CHAPTER EIGHT

By the time the plane landed in Texas, Nico's muscles were knotted with the need to do something, anything, to alleviate Mercy's suffering. She had spent several hours alternating between shivering in misery and sleeping fitfully. He'd bathed her face and neck with cool water, and tucked blankets around her during the times when she was freezing, none of it enough. Throughout the flight to Bayside, Nico's teammates had checked in every hour, insisting that he take short breaks to stretch his legs. Every time he left, Mercy was restless until he returned, laid his hand on her cheek, and reassured her that he was with her. Her trust in him sank hooks into his heart. Would she feel the same if she knew the real Nico Rivera?

As soon as the jet stopped and the door opened, two muscle-bound men boarded and came to the back bedroom. "Need a stretcher, Nico?" Bruce asked.

He shook his head. "I'll carry her." Sam had put Mercy's arm in a sling to immobilize her shoulder during transport to the vet clinic.

A nod from the former operative. "How many of your unit are staying with you?"

"All of them. Our principal is a high-value target."

Speculation lit Bruce's gaze. "We'll set up cots in the back. Dr. Sorensen has been in touch with Sam so he's aware of your patient's condition and is ready."

Some of the tension left Nico's body. "Good. I'll bring her out in a minute. Make sure we don't have company."

"Copy that." The two men left the plane.

Trace walked in. "I've got your Go bag. The others followed Bruce and Ken to the tarmac to provide security. Need help with her?"

"The IV." Nico looked down at Mercy to see her gaze locked on him. "Welcome back."

"What's going on?"

"We landed in Texas. We're transporting you to a doctor who's on retainer with Fortress. I'm going to carry you to the SUV."

She gave a slight nod and closed her eyes again.

Praying he didn't hurt her, Nico lifted Mercy into his arms, careful to avoid contact with her shoulder injury. He maneuvered her through the jet and down the stairs to the tarmac, trusting his teammates to do what was necessary to protect him and their vulnerable principal.

He climbed into the backseat of one of the waiting SUVs and laid Mercy on the seat, sitting on the floor beside her to keep her from rolling off or to cover her with his body if trouble developed.

Bruce parked behind the vet clinic at a private entrance and hurried to open the door for Nico.

Scooping Mercy into his arms once again, Nico eased from the SUV and carried her into the clinic.

"In here." Ted Sorensen indicated the room to his right. "Lay her on the bed and take a break."

He shook his head. "I'd rather stay."

The cantankerous doctor scowled. "Tough. I don't need an audience, and you need a shower and food. You won't be any good to her if you collapse from neglecting yourself."

Nico scowled. "I won't collapse." Sorensen should know better than that.

"Go, Nico. I'll send someone for you if she needs you."

As he laid her on the examination table, Mercy opened her eyes again and stared at him. "I'll be fine," she murmured. "Take care of yourself."

"See?" Sorensen pointed at the door. "Out before I have Bruce kick you out."

Nico stilled. "It will take more than Bruce to make me leave," he reminded the doctor softly.

"Yeah, yeah," he said, proving that he was not in the least bit intimidated by Nico. "I'm not the enemy here. This young woman's shoulder wound is. The sooner you get out, the faster I'll be able to patch her up. Send Sam in. I can use an extra pair of hands."

Nico looked down at Mercy who still watched him. "I'll be down the hall. If you need me, send Sam for me." He couldn't say why he did what he did next, but Nico couldn't stop himself. He leaned down and brushed her lips with his. A butterfly kiss, so light as to almost not qualify as a kiss. The light caress, though, sent a bolt of lightning through Nico's body.

When he straightened, Mercy's eyes were wide. "I'll be close," he reminded her and forced himself to leave the operating suite without looking back.

Sam was waiting in the hall.

"The doc asked for you."

She laid a hand on his shoulder. "I'll take care of her."

With a nod, he continued down the hall to the kitchen where the rest of his team was loading their plates with the sub sandwiches, fruit, and chips Sorensen had ready for them.

Trace glanced up. "Your bag's in the recovery room. Figured you'd want to stay with her."

"Thanks. I'm going to clean up. Leave me a few crumbs."

He found his bag and pulled out clean clothes. Depending on how long Mercy needed to stay in Bayside, he'd have to send one of his teammates to buy clothes for her. Probably Sam, he decided. The others wouldn't be comfortable buying personal items for Mercy.

He frowned as the hot water pounded his tired body. Now that he thought about it, he didn't want one of the other men on his team to buy anything personal for her.

Forcing the uncharacteristic possessiveness to the back of his mind, Nico focused on completing his shower as fast as possible. Clean and dressed, he returned to the kitchen to see a loaded plate waiting for him at the table along with Trace.

"What do you want to drink?" the sniper asked.

"Water."

Trace stood. "How's Mercy?"

"Lucid, at least. Sorensen's looking at her now. Sam's in there with him."

"We set aside food for Sam, too." Trace fell silent.

Nico chewed and swallowed a bite of the sub before he said, "What's on your mind?"

"If this mission drags on for a time, Maddox might pull us off for another job."

"I know." He wasn't happy about it, either.

"Will you be comfortable with someone else tasked with Mercy's safety?"

He slid his friend a look. "Why do you ask?"

"You have an attachment to the lady."

Nico froze. Had the sniper seen the kiss? "Is that a problem?"

A snort. "Not for me. Might be for you if you have to leave her while she's still a target of the Scorpions."

He took another bite before replying. "I'll handle it." Didn't mean he wanted to. He could, however, hand pick the team tasked with her safety. If Shadow deployed, he'd insist that Adam Walker's team take over Mercy's protection. They were well-trained and tough as nails. It also didn't escape his notice that his mind automatically turned to an excellent team where all the members of the unit were married. What was wrong with him? He was never territorial over women. Somehow, this one mattered. A lot. "Where are the others?"

"Joe's in the other shower. Ben fell face down on the bed."

"When Joe is finished, take a shower and rest."

"We'll spell you, Nico. You haven't slept in over 24 hours."

He shrugged. "I've gone longer without sleep. So have you and the others."

Trace inclined his head in acknowledgment of that fact. "If the Scorpions find us, you'll have to be sharp and ready."

"I'll rest, but I won't leave her side. You and the others can relieve me while I'm in the room."

"Understood."

Joe returned. "Shower's open," he said to Trace. "I'll take the first watch."

A nod from the sniper. "Wake me in four hours to take over."

Nico ate the rest of the sub and fruit, then polished off his water. "I need to check in with Maddox."

The spotter rose. "I'll be in the hall outside the operating room. No one will disturb the doc or get to Mercy."

He clapped his teammate on the shoulder and closed himself into the room Mercy would be using during her recovery. A moment later, his call was answered.

"Talk to me."

Nico updated Brent Maddox on everything that happened since Shadow stepped foot on the Fortress jet in

Nashville. When he learned about Mercy's fever for the last hours of the flight, Maddox growled. "Prognosis?"

"Unknown. Sorensen and Sam are working on her now. I'll let you know what the doc says. Sam did a good job with Mercy. I'm afraid the time in the cave with the open cut on her leg introduced an infection to her system. The bullet wound added to the problem."

"Do you need backup?"

"Not yet. Brent, if you have to send Shadow for another mission before Mercy is safe, I want Walker's team as her protection detail. No one else."

His boss was silent a moment. "Something you need to tell me, Nico?"

"No." He couldn't explain to himself what was going on inside much less his boss.

"If that changes, I need to know."

Anger simmered in Nico's blood. "I know how to handle myself, Brent."

"When emotions are tangled, our objectivity goes straight out the window."

"You ought to know."

A bark of laughter came over the phone's speaker. "Well said. Let me know how I can help. We'll take care of it. Keep me posted. I'll expect a sit rep as soon as you know anything about Mercy."

"Copy that." Nico slid his phone into his pocket as a light tap sounded on the door.

Joe stepped inside. "Sorensen needs you."

Heart in his throat, he hurried past his teammate and into the operating room. "What's wrong?" he asked the doctor.

"Mercy needs a pint of blood. Sam tells me you're the same blood type and would want to donate."

"Absolutely."

"Excellent." Sorensen patted the gurney he'd positioned beside the operating table. "Lay down, Nico. Can't have you passing out from donating a pint."

With a roll of his eyes, Nico climbed on the bed and stretched out. He turned his head to look at Mercy who slept. "How is she?"

"She'll be fine. The stronger antibiotics Sam administered started her on the road to recovery. Mercy had a couple bullet fragments in her shoulder that would have been impossible for your medic to remove without actually doing surgery on the plane. The bullet wound was a through-and-through, and I stitched the damage once I was sure the foreign particles were removed from the wound. That cave in Mexico didn't do your girl any favors. She had a number of scraps and cuts, though none needed stitches aside from the one on her leg. She should be fine as long as she rests and takes her meds. Have Sam keep an eye on her once you return to Nashville. Take her to one of the doctors Maddox trusts in Nashville to check Mercy if her symptoms worsen."

"I'll take care of her, Doc. Thanks."

Sorensen nodded, then looked at Sam. "Handle the transfusion. I have four-legged patients to see in the clinic."

As soon as the doctor left, Nico slid his hand over Mercy's and threaded his fingers with hers. Stupid, but he wanted her to know he was there. Maybe it was his imagination, but he thought her fingers tightened around his a fraction.

"Relax, Nico. This should take a few minutes. Catnap. I'll wake you when this is finished. I won't leave the room, and Joe's guarding the door. You and Mercy are safe."

With those reassurances, Nico fell into a light sleep.

CHAPTER NINE

Mercy woke in an unfamiliar room in the dim light of early morning. Utilitarian walls, but no bars on the windows. She was definitely not in Mexico with Hector and his buddies. Her shoulder hurt and she was thirsty. She also needed to visit the bathroom in the worst way.

She became aware of another person breathing in the room. She looked to her right. Nico slept on a cot beside the bed, his hand wrapped around hers. An invisible band squeezed around her heart at the sight. She didn't have to ask if he had been there the whole time. She knew he had.

More than two years since she'd awakened with someone else in the same room. Not since Aiden. Having Nico here, even under the guise of protecting her, felt strange.

Mercy's breath stalled. He'd kissed her. She didn't remember much about the past three days, but that memory was clear as glass. Nico Rivera had kissed her. Hadn't he? Maybe the pain and drugs tricked her mind into thinking the handsome operative kissed her.

As if sensing she was awake, Nico's eyes opened and focused on her. He sat up. "How do you feel?"

"Muzzy headed. My shoulder hurts."

"Not surprising. Sorensen operated on you. He cleaned out a couple bullet fragments and stitched the wound."

"I need to get up."

His lips twitched. "Ah. Hold on a minute." He strode to the door and spoke to someone in the hall. His teammate, Ben, followed him into the room.

"Looking good, beautiful," the other operative said. "Nice to see you're awake."

"If you'll handle her IV, I'll carry Mercy into the bathroom," Nico said.

Mercy's cheeks flamed. "I can walk."

"I doubt it. Your body went through trauma fighting off that infection. You're weaker than you realize. Plus, if you fall and rip out those stitches, Sorensen will tear a strip off my hide. I'd prefer to avoid that. Doc Sorensen is one scary dude when he's riled."

"Is he what you're afraid of?"

Nico smiled as he scooped her into his arms. Ben maneuvered the IV pole into the bathroom ahead of them. As soon as Nico set Mercy on her feet and steadied her, Ben left the room. "I'll be right outside the door."

Mercy staggered to the door two minutes later, dragging her IV pole behind her. Nico caught her up in his arms again. Between them, they managed to shuffle the IV to the bedside, and he returned her to the bed.

She drew in a deep breath. "Thanks. You were right. I can't believe how weak I feel."

"It will pass. You'll be stronger than ever soon."

"Where are the others?"

"Ben's on watch in the hall. Joe and Sam are buying clothes for you. The doc says you can't leave here until tomorrow at the earliest. Trace is sleeping."

He'd mentioned everyone but himself. "When do you go on guard duty?"

"I've never gone off."

She blinked. "You have to rest, Nico. Don't you trust your teammates with my safety?"

"Of course. I'm not leaving you."

Exasperating man. She knew his type. Nico reminded her of Aiden. He would knock himself out to protect her without regard for his own needs if he were still alive.

A quick knock sounded on the door. Between one heartbeat and the next, Nico's gun was in his hand and pointed at the door.

"It's Sorensen. I'm coming in soft."

When the doctor opened the door, Nico relaxed and holstered his weapon.

"You're awake, Mercy. Good. How do you feel?"

"Like someone shot me in the shoulder."

"Cranky, are we?"

"Sorry."

Sorensen waved her comment aside. "I want to check your shoulder and leg." He glanced at Nico. "Wait in the hall."

Nico wrapped his fingers around Mercy's. "I'll be right outside the door." With a pointed glance at the doctor, he left the room, shutting the door behind himself.

"What was the look for?" Mercy asked.

"Put me on notice that he was holding me personally responsible for your safety," came the doctor's wry reply. "If you so much as stub your toe while he's gone, I'll be hearing about it from your young man."

She opened her mouth to object to labeling Nico her young man, and decided it wasn't worth wasting her waning energy. Besides, it was nice to belong to someone for a few minutes, false relationship or not.

Sorensen checked her shoulder and leg and declared her in excellent shape. "If you keep progressing as you are, I'll release you to return to Nashville."

"I live in Kentucky."

"Until your pesky problem with the Scorpions is resolved, you'll be staying with the Shadow Unit."

Shadow Unit? "Nico and his friends?"

A nod.

"Why are they called the Shadow Unit?"

"That's a question to ask Nico." The doctor patted her foot. "Rest. You'll need every ounce of strength for the plane ride tomorrow." He left, had a low-voiced conversation with the men in the hallway, and hurried away.

Nico walked inside. "Doc Sorensen says you're doing great."

"Lucky me."

His eyebrows rose.

Mercy held up her hand. "I'm grumpy when I hurt. Ignore me."

Before he could reply, a light tap sounded. "It's Sam. I have Mercy's clothes." The medic walked into the room with two bags from a big box store. "Comfortable clothes. Button up shirts and jeans, socks, and tennis shoes. Underwear. We'll have more clothes for you at the safe house."

"Thanks, Sam."

"How do you feel?"

She forced a smile to her lips. "Not bad considering I was the hostage of some gang in Mexico yesterday."

"What did Sorensen say?" While she and Nico updated the medic, Sam replaced the empty IV bags with new ones. "Sounds good. The doc wouldn't turn you loose if you weren't ready. Tomorrow morning, we'll remove the IV and switch you to oral meds. We'll walk with you up and down the corridor a few times today. Other than that, you should rest. Tomorrow's going to be tough."

The rest of the day, Nico and Sam helped her walk every couple hours, insisted she drink plenty of fluids and eat. Thankfully, everything they brought her was easy on her stomach.

Late in the afternoon after another circuit of the hall, Mercy settled back on the pillow, frowning. "Why do I hear dogs barking? Does Dr. Sorensen have more than one?"

An amused smile curved Nico's lips. "Sorensen is a vet. You're hearing his patients."

She froze. "You brought me to a vet clinic for medical treatment?"

"He used to be a trauma surgeon, one of the best in the country. He joined Fortress as an operative for several years, then decided he'd had enough and became a vet. Fortress is lucky to have him on staff."

A vet. Amazing. After the vet clinic grew silent, Sorensen returned to check on Mercy. Following a thorough checkup, he straightened. "You may tell your contingent of bodyguards you're cleared to travel at their convenience." Although his expression morphed into a scowl, his eyes twinkled. "I need the bed space for real patients."

Mercy grinned. "Thanks for patching me up, Dr. Sorensen."

"Do me a favor. Keep yourself out of harm's way. I'd rather not redo my handiwork."

"I'll do my best."

A pat on her foot. "Listen to Nico and his team. They'll keep you safe." With that, he pivoted and left the room.

She wanted to do something in return for his kindness and excellent care. Maybe Sam wouldn't mind going to the store one more time for her. Bayside might not have an arts and crafts store, though. If not, Mercy would draw the portrait from memory unless Nico copied a picture of the doctor and his family for her to use.

Nico returned a minute later. "What did Sorensen say?"

"He needs the bed for real patients."

Satisfaction lit his features. "Excellent. We'll leave early tomorrow morning, then. I want to land in Nashville while it's still dark. Safer for you."

"Do you know if the doctor has a picture of himself with his family in his office?"

"Why?"

"I'd like to repay him for helping me."

"What does the picture have to do with that?"

"You don't know who I am?"

A pause. "Mercedes Powers, the president's niece."

"I'm also known as MJ Powers, the artist."

He sat down heavily on the side of the cot. "The pen and ink artist."

"You've heard of me?"

Nico dragged a hand down his face. "I have several of your sketches in my home. Those drawings were so powerful, I had to have them for myself, in my own space."

Charmed by his words, Mercy studied the operative with new eyes. "You like art."

He shook his head. "I'm not an art connoisseur. Your drawings gripped me and wouldn't let go." His cell phone signaled. Nico glanced at the screen, his expression going blank as he read.

Something was wrong. "Is Charlotte all right? Her family?"

He stood. "They're still at Camp David. We need to leave Texas. I'll send Sam in to help you dress while I contact the pilot."

"Nico, what happened?"

"The Scorpions know you're back in the States."

"That's not all." That knowledge would have been logical. Where else would she go but back to her home country?

He paused with his hand on the door knob and looked back. "Hector put a contract on you."

CHAPTER TEN

Nico met with his team in the kitchen of Sorensen's clinic. "Zane contacted me. The Scorpions know Mercy is in the US, and they placed a bounty on her head."

Trace whistled softly. "How much?"

"Two million, dead or alive."

Ben scowled. "Hector is that petty? Come on. Mercy isn't a threat to their operation. She's just the pawn who was rescued before Hector and his pals did any real damage to her. They should come after us."

"She's easier to target. We're an unknown variable in the equation. We'll have to figure out why she's so important to them after we have her in the safe house. Sam, help her dress. Ben, find Sorensen and warn him that trouble might be coming. He'll know what to do. Joe, Trace, grab our gear and take it to the SUV. Ken left the keys on the microwave in case we needed to leave in a hurry. I'd say this qualifies. I'll contact the pilot. We leave here in fifteen minutes."

After his teammates left, Nico alerted the pilot and told him to expect his team soon. Once that was done, he called his boss, regretting the necessity.

"Maddox."

"It's Nico. We're leaving in fifteen minutes."

"Problem?"

He summarized the information from Zane. "I don't want to put Sorensen or his family at risk. With the bounty on Mercy's head, she'll be a magnet for trouble."

A growl from the buzz-cut blond. "I'll assign the Texas team to watch over his family even though it will tick off Sorensen. He's too valuable a resource and friend to lose him through carelessness. What do you need?"

"Have an operative go to the safe house and make sure we don't have nasty surprises waiting for us. It's probably safe, but I don't want to take chances with her. Mercy's improving but she's still fragile." She would take umbrage at the characterization.

"Done. I'll send Jon and Eli. They'll stay until you arrive."

Some of the tension left Nico. Jon Smith and Eli Wolfe were Navy SEALs and as tough as they came. If someone had booby trapped the cabin, the operatives would recognize the signs and deal with it. Aside from his team, he knew of no one else he trusted more with Mercy's safety. "Thanks."

"You suspect a leak?"

Nico's grip on his phone tightened. "Yeah, I do. I doubt it's in our house."

"Can't discount that possibility. I'll start the process in house, then contact the president, and have him tighten security around Charlotte and her family."

"She'll hate that."

"She'll deal with it since the safety of her family is at stake. The safe house is ready for Mercy. Jon and Eli will give you the codes for the alarm system and the safe room. Need anything else?"

He started to say no. "I need a supply of drawing paper and a variety of pens."

"Okay."

The way Maddox drew out the word made Nico smile. "Ever heard of MJ Powers?"

"The artist? Sure. Rowan has a couple of Powers' drawings in our home. Powerful pieces. Why?"

"Mercy is MJ Powers."

A soft whistle sounded over the speaker. "I'll make sure the safe house is stocked with art supplies. Will she be able to work with the shoulder injury?"

"I think so. From what I've observed, she's right handed. The bullet went through her left shoulder."

"All right. What else?"

"Provide magazines and books for her. An e-reader would be better since we don't know what she likes to read. Aside from keeping her secluded because of the bounty, Mercy needs time to recover from her injuries." Whether he made her angry at him or not, he'd see to it she had what she needed.

"I'll take care of it. Let me know if you need anything else."

"Thank you, sir." Nico ended the call and went in search of the picture Mercy asked for. Although he would insist she not sign the portrait to protect Sorensen, he didn't see a problem with her giving a gift to the doctor. The work would keep her mind occupied. For a day or two, she would be fine. Most of their principals were. After that, Mercy might become restless with the enforced seclusion.

He walked into the doctor's office and found the picture he remembered seeing during Shadow's last visit to the clinic a month earlier. Nico removed the picture of Sorensen and his family from the frame and copied the photograph. He returned the photo and went to the recovery room door. "It's Nico."

Sam opened the door and stepped back. "We're ready."

Nico walked inside. Mercy sat on the side of the bed, face pale. "Need me to carry you to the SUV?" he asked, his voice soft.

She shook her head. "I can do it. I'm wobbly, though. Make sure I don't fall on my face."

"Deal. Come on. It's time to leave." He gripped her waist and lifted Mercy to her feet, then slid his arm around her for stability as she walked from the room. Sam followed behind them, carrying Mercy's clothes.

When they reached the back door, Nico glanced over his shoulder at Sam who moved past them and slipped outside. A moment later, she returned. "We're clear."

As soon as Mercy was safely inside the SUV, Nico climbed in beside her. "Go, Trace." The ride to the airport was uneventful. On the tarmac, Nico's team surrounded them, providing a barrier between Mercy and unseen threats as they crossed the open space to the waiting jet.

By the time Mercy stepped foot in the cabin, she was leaning heavily on him and her face was glowing with perspiration. "You should lay down, Mercy. We had to move you too soon, and this is a strain on your body."

Another head shake. "I've done nothing but lay in bed and walk the hall for the past day. I can handle sitting in a comfortable seat for a plane ride."

Skeptical, he opted for compromise. "I want your word that you'll tell me if you need to stretch out for a while. Your body is using every bit of your energy to heal. If you work with your body instead of fighting it, you'll heal faster."

She stared at him. "You are a clever man, Nico. I promise to tell you if I need to lay down."

With a nod, he escorted her to the back row of the jet so she would be close to the bedroom. As soon as they were airborne, Nico pulled a blanket from the overhead compartment along with a pillow for her to use. "Rest. I have work to do." Internet searches to run. Yeah, Zane would be doing them, but Nico needed more information now. Z would compile information and send it in bulk unless the information was critical.

He shook out the blanket and spread it over Mercy, then showed her how to recline the seat when she was ready. Nico grabbed his laptop and began a search on the Scorpions.

In under fifteen minutes, he became aware of a warm weight against his shoulder. He glanced down at Mercy, noting the contrast of her blond hair against the black sleeve of his t-shirt.

Nico reached toward her before he caught himself and drew back. His hand fisted. Mercy was sleeping. He didn't want to disturb her.

Forcing his attention back to the screen where it belonged, he ignored the sweet, warm weight of her head against him and continued digging into the Scorpion organization. He followed trails as far as he could without tripping an electronic sensor that might alert the terrorist organization that someone was looking at them.

By the time he finished, Nico was convinced the only way to protect Mercy was to dismantle the Scorpions. Otherwise, the members of the group would keep coming after the woman in Nico's care until they achieved their objective. He vowed they would never get their hands on Mercy while he drew breath.

At two in the morning, the Fortress jet landed at John C. Tune Airport and taxied to the area where the other company jets were located. While the others gathered their gear, Nico rubbed Mercy's arm to ease her to wakefulness. "Mercy," he murmured.

She stirred, winced. "Ouch."

"Pain meds have worn off." He glanced up to see Sam coming toward them with a small bottle of water and a small packet in her hands. His lips curved. Their team medic was on top of things, as usual. "Sam has pain medicine for you."

Mercy's eyes widened when she realized she was leaning on him. She straightened. "I'm sorry, Nico. You should have insisted I go lay down."

He lifted one shoulder in a shrug. "I didn't mind." In fact, he'd liked it. A lot.

"Take these, Mercy," Sam said. She laid two pills on Mercy's palm and handed her the opened bottle of water.

Once Mercy had swallowed the meds and most of the water, Nico helped her to her feet and steadied her when she swayed. "Easy."

"Thanks." She blew out a breath.

On the tarmac, Nico scanned the area for trouble, but at this time of morning the airport was quiet, part of the reason he'd wanted to leave Bayside so quickly. His only regret was forcing Mercy to leave the clinic before she was ready. The original plan discussed with and approved by Sorensen was to complete the flight tomorrow morning at this time. With the escalation by the Scorpions, Nico hadn't wanted to wait. A further delay could have put Sorensen and his family in the terrorists' crosshairs, might still have compromised the man who saved so many Fortress operatives. The Texas team may have their work cut out for them.

Nico tossed the keys to his SUV to Joe. Once Mercy was seated in the backseat, he signaled Sam to sit in the shotgun seat, stored his Go bag in the cargo area and climbed in beside Mercy.

As soon as Joe put the vehicle in gear, Nico called Eli Wolfe, the connection going through his Bluetooth system.

"Thought I'd hear from you sooner, Rivera," the SEAL greeted him. "I hear you have a friend with you."

"I knew you missed me, frog boy."

Eli's laughter filled the SUV's cabin. "Like a bad rash, jar head. How have you been?"

"Too busy."

"Yeah, you've been breaking my heart, ignoring all my phone calls and invitations to dinner."

Nico snorted. "Your memory's going, old man. You haven't called, and if your wife invited me to dinner, I'd be there in a heartbeat, with or without you present."

"Don't even think about trying to sweet talk Brenna into a dinner invite unless you bring your friend."

"Yeah, yeah." Like he'd make a move on the SEAL's wife. Eli would gut him in a New York minute if he tried. The operative adored Brenna. "Any problems?"

"Nope. It's clear. Security system is up and running. Jon and I came out as soon as the boss contacted us. We've rigged a few surprises for the troublemakers if they're stupid enough to show their faces around here. We left a passage for an escape route that we'll show you. We also brought along the extra supplies you asked for. Brenna called in a favor with her favorite bookstore owner."

"Excellent. We're ninety minutes out unless we attract attention and have to take a few detours."

"We'll be waiting. How is your friend?"

"Ask her yourself. Mercy, this is Eli, a friend of ours."

"Hello, Eli. Thank you for being part of my safety net."

"You're welcome, sugar. I hear you got up close and personal with a Sig."

"Unfortunately. I've had excellent medical care, though. I'm better."

Nico couldn't help but admire Mercy's careful conversation. She'd picked up on his and Eli's couched terms and copied their discretion. Mercy Powers was a sharp woman, another thing he found attractive about her. The list was growing longer by the minute.

"Glad to hear that," Eli said. "Nico, do you need backup? Jon or I can meet you en route."

"My unit is with me. If we run into trouble we can't handle, I'll call."

"Copy that." Eli ended the call.

"Where are we going?" Mercy asked Nico.

"Outside Murfreesboro, a town almost an hour from here. We have a safe house set up for you, one I think you'll like."

"Anything is fine, as long as you and the others are safe."

He twisted to stare at her. "What about you?"

"I don't want anyone hurt because of me."

His heart skipped a beat before surging ahead into a normal rhythm. He couldn't remember the last time anyone had been concerned for his welfare aside from the people he worked with. The experience was extraordinary. A man could get used to having someone care.

He gave her a short nod and turned away again to keep watch. When they left Davidson County, Nico said to Joe. "I don't see a tail."

"Me, either."

"Why am I uneasy?"

"Same reason I am. It's too easy."

"You were expecting trouble?" Mercy asked.

"Always. Keeps us alive," Joe said.

She was silent a moment. "Is that true for the military as well?"

"Yeah, it is. Why do you ask?"

"That explains a few things about my husband."

Silence fell like a heavy wool blanket in the SUV. He probably should have told them more about her background. "Mercy's husband was killed in Afghanistan by an IED."

Sam reached over the seat and laid a hand on Mercy's knee. "I'm sorry. How long has it been?"

"Two years. Seems longer."

"What branch of the military was your husband in?" Joe asked.

"Army Ranger. Absolutely loved his job. He died a month before he mustered out."

The rest of the trip passed in silence as Mercy stared out the window at the passing landscape. Nico didn't think she was seeing anything, not with the darkness and the sparse streetlights on their route.

He kept a close watch on their surroundings as did his teammates. The only vehicle following them was Ben and Trace in the second SUV. Joe still took a few detours to be sure, then headed to the safe house.

At the two-hour mark, Joe turned into the long drive leading to Rod Kelter's log cabin. As they parked at the front of the three-story home, Jon and Eli stepped out on the porch.

"Who is that?" Mercy asked.

"Our friends. You talked to Eli Wolfe already. He's on the left. The man with him is Jon Smith." Nico held up his hand when Mercy's lips twitched. "Yeah, I know, but that is his real name."

"He's touchy about it, too," Joe muttered. "Hates for people to give him grief over that."

"You ought to know." Sam opened the door. "You rag on him all the time about it. You're lucky to be breathing. Smith is one scary man."

Joe climbed out of the vehicle and rounded the hood to meet Sam on the way to the cabin.

"Should I be worried about Jon?" Mercy's eyes were large in her too-pale face.

"He's intense, not mean, unless you're a terrorist."

A small smile curved her lips. "Good to know."

Nico helped her from the SUV, tucking her against his side when she staggered. On the porch, he introduced her to the two SEALs, then ushered her inside the cabin.

He turned to Jon. "What's the safest room for Mercy?"

"Second floor, corner room on the right. There's a hidden passage from there leading to the escape route."

"Safe room?"

"First floor office. I'll show you after you get Ms. Powers settled."

"Mercy, please," she said.

He gave her a curt nod and shifted his attention back to Nico. "I'll take you to her room."

Nico walked with Mercy to her room. After Jon showed them the secret passage, he left.

"Will you be comfortable here?"

"How could I not be? This cabin is gorgeous. Do you know the owner?"

"Not personally, but several of the Fortress operatives do. He's a detective with the Otter Creek police. Our training facility is located there." He studied her face a moment, noting the pallor and fatigue. "Once Eli and Jon brief my team, at least one of us will be on watch at all times. I'll be close if you need me, Mercy. Can I get you anything before I leave you to rest?"

"I'm fine. Thanks for everything, Nico." She laid her hand over his heart briefly.

Though light as a feather, her touch burned Nico to the bone. He had to get out of this room before he crossed the line with a hurting, vulnerable woman. "Sleep well."

Out in the hall once more, Nico leaned against the wall and drew in a shaky breath. He needed to get his head on straight before he made a mistake that could be fatal to them both.

CHAPTER ELEVEN

Mercy walked into the kitchen as the sun peeked over the horizon. The aroma of strong coffee filled the air along with the scent of muffins, eggs, and sausage. The aroma combination made her feel slightly ill.

Nico turned and closed the space between them, frowning. "You okay?"

Ben, Sam, and Joe straightened from their places at the kitchen table.

"I thought I was until I walked in here." Mercy pressed a hand to her stomach. Oh, man. She didn't want to barf in front of the operatives, especially Nico.

"Take her outside," Sam said to Nico. "I'll bring her a cup of tea to settle her stomach."

"This way." Nico wrapped his hand around hers and escorted her out the back door to a large patio. He led her to a cushioned outdoor couch and crouched in front of her. "Are you sensitive to smells, Mercy?"

"Not usually. It might be the medication I'm taking."

"You also haven't eaten much in the past few days. Is it too cold out here for you?"

Mercy shook her head. "Truthfully, after being held captive in that cave, I'm enjoying the fresh air."

An odd look crossed Nico's face, and he swallowed hard. "I understand."

She opened her mouth to ask him what that look was about when Sam arrived with a mug in her hand.

"It's chamomile mint. I didn't sweeten it. If you need sugar, I'll bring you some."

"No, this is perfect. Thanks, Sam. Sorry you had to go to the trouble."

The medic grinned. "Compared to what I'm usually handling for my teammates, this is nothing. If the nausea continues, I have a patch that will alleviate the symptoms."

Nico chuckled.

Mercy sipped her tea and stared thoughtfully at Nico. "Why is that funny?"

"Sam keeps a stash on hand in case we have to be on a boat. Trace has problems with seasickness."

"Problems?" Sam laughed. "He turns green the moment he steps foot on a boat. Mercy, how is your shoulder this morning?"

"Sore," she admitted. "I wanted to leave off the pain pills today, but I'm not sure I'll be able to."

"Let's wait until tomorrow. The time you spent in the jet and SUV aggravated your shoulder. Keep the sling on today. Tomorrow, we'll see how you're doing and decide whether or not to try leaving off the pain meds. There's no harm in giving your body the chance to recover comfortably. You'll be taking over-the-counter meds soon."

When the medic returned to the cabin, Nico sat beside Mercy. He scanned the area, appearing totally relaxed. Mercy figured he'd explode into action if trouble erupted and even though she didn't see weapons, she'd bet he was heavily armed.

The silence between them was comfortable as she sipped the tea. Mercy kept her hands wrapped around the mug, savoring the warmth. When her mug was empty, Nico placed it on the table in front of them.

Would he answer a question? Mercy hesitated to ask, but her curiosity was aroused. "May I ask a question?"

The operative turned. "Ask. I'll answer if I can."

That made her pause. "There are things you can't discuss?"

"Some of our missions are for the government and classified. If you ask something I can't answer, I'll tell you."

Good enough, she supposed. Aiden hadn't been able to talk about his work with her, either. Most of the information he gave her was about day-to-day life and the quirks of his friends and teammates. "When I mentioned enjoying being out of that cave in Mexico, an odd look crossed your face."

Nico stilled. "Okay."

"Will you tell me why?"

Where the operative's body language had been open although alert, now his hands clenched into fists and his jaw was set. Mercy regretted asking the question. The last thing she wanted to do was make him uncomfortable. "I'm sorry, Nico. You don't have to answer. I shouldn't have asked." The sense that he didn't want to talk to her about it hurt.

He had a right to his privacy, she reminded herself. They were virtual strangers, no matter how much her heart suggested otherwise.

He said nothing for long minutes, long enough that Mercy was convinced what little friendship she hoped was developing between them might have been blown apart by her curiosity and made her regret the impulsive question even more.

"I was taken captive on a mission last year," he said, his low and rough voice breaking the silence. Nico stared into the distance, expression bleak and body tense.

At his words, pain stabbed Mercy's heart. Having seen firsthand what horrible people the operatives fought against, she knew he'd suffered. She almost begged him not to finish the story. She wanted to do something to alleviate the pain he must be feeling. She could only think of one thing to show her support but not interfere. She entwined their fingers and waited.

"We were targeting human traffickers in a cesspit. The mission went south. The traffickers had joined forces with another group larger and better armed than they were."

"You were outnumbered?"

He gave a bark of laughter. "You could say that. There were at least thirty tangos in that camp. We freed fifteen kids from the compound and were almost clear when one of the thugs decided to take a leak on our evac route. He fired a few shots before I took him down, alerting the others in the compound. I held them off long enough for the others to escape with the children."

Mercy's fingers tightened around his. "You sacrificed yourself to save the others?"

"I would have had it been necessary, but that wasn't the plan. Getting separated from my team was pure bad luck. A severe storm had blown in. Trees were falling because the wind was high and the ground a soggy mess from the rain. Anyway, a large tree fell between me and my teammates. One of the limbs knocked me out. When I woke up, I was in the hands of furious human traffickers."

"They left you?" Mercy's stomach twisted. "Your current teammates went off and left you in the hands of traffickers?"

"They were outnumbered three-to-one and had fifteen children to save. If they had stopped to rescue me, they would have been captured or killed, and the kids would have been either sold or killed within 24 hours. My teammates made the only choice they could under the circumstances. They rushed the children to safety and returned for me. Obviously, they got me out."

"How long were you a prisoner?"

"Seventy-two of the longest hours of my life. They alternated between keeping me locked in a dark cave and making me pay for costing them so much money." He fell silent again.

"Tell me."

He shook his head. "You don't want to know the details, Mercy. It's enough for you to know that I spent a month in Sorensen's recovery room."

"Oh, Nico. You fully recovered?"

"I'm fine." He squeezed her fingers. "More important, the children have been reunited with their families and are receiving the help they need to put that ordeal behind them."

"I'm sorry I asked but thank you for telling me." She thought he would free his hand. He didn't. Maybe he needed the comfort of her touch as much as she needed his to convince herself he was alive and well. Stupid. She'd only known Nico two days and most of that time she'd been asleep. How could he come to mean something to her this fast?

They sat in silence together, watching the sun rise higher in the sky, warming the air and reminding Mercy that she was free and safe. At least for the moment. How long would that last? "The Scorpions aren't going to stop, are they?"

"Not until we make them stop."

"How? You can't stop them if you're babysitting me."

He looked at her. "You don't want me watching over you?"

Mercy frowned. "That's not what I meant. I'm glad you're protecting me. I trust you with my life. However, you can't be in two places at once. You will have to go after them."

"I don't think that's going to be an issue."

"Why not?"

"The Scorpions have placed a bounty on your head."

She stared at him, stunned by the news. "How much am I worth to them?"

"They're offering two million."

Two million dollars. "What a waste of their money. I don't have any power or influence, and I don't know anything important. I do my best to stay out of the political arena. No one would pay that much to free me from the Scorpions."

"I don't think your uncle would agree with that assessment of your value to him. He's the one who called us in."

"Fortress?"

"The president requested Shadow unit specifically."

"Why?"

"We spend a great deal of time in Mexico and have developed many contacts throughout the country."

"Will you go after the Scorpions, Nico?"

"If they don't come to us." He lifted his free hand and trailed the backs of his fingers down her cheek in a light caress that stole her breath. "One way or another, I will take care of this, Mercy. No one is going to hurt you again while I still draw breath."

CHAPTER TWELVE

After Nico coaxed Mercy into eating a plain toasted bagel, he took her into the office on the first floor. "I asked Maddox for a few things I thought you would like. Jon and Eli left them in here."

Her eyes lit when she saw the drawing pad and the broad assortment of pens along with the copied photo of Sorensen and his family. "Thanks, Nico. My fingers have been itching to draw. You found a photo of Dr. Sorensen for me."

"You'll be in seclusion for a while. Depends on how quickly we resolve your problem with the Scorpions. Since I didn't know what you liked to read, we opted for several magazines and an e-reader. Download as many books you want." He didn't intend to tell her the e-books would be charged to his account. Covering the cost for her books wouldn't be a hardship.

"That's perfect. I love to read."

Pleased he'd guessed right, he said, "I hope this helps make you more comfortable while we dismantle the Scorpions."

"I'm a low-maintenance woman with simple tastes, and I spend a lot of time by myself. As long as I can draw and spend some time outside, I'll be fine no matter how long you and your team take."

Nico's heart lurched. Mercy didn't have a boyfriend? "You have friends, right?"

"A handful. They have full-time jobs and families to care for. I drifted away from friends I made when I was married to Aiden. They don't know what to say to me now that he's gone. I think they're afraid to talk about military family life for fear of upsetting me. When we talk, the conversations are stilted. In a world of couples, I don't fit anymore."

Sympathy bloomed inside him. "I'm sorry. You not only lost your husband, you lost your friend group as well."

"Yes, exactly." Mercy leaned back against the desk. "You do understand."

Now was the perfect opportunity to find out if she had someone special in her life. "What about a boyfriend?"

She let out a short laugh. "No one's expressed interest."

Nico blinked. "The men in Kentucky must be idiots."

Surprise crossed Mercy's features. Before she could comment, Nico's phone signaled an incoming call. He checked his screen and frowned. "You're on speaker with Mercy," he told Zane when he answered.

"Good morning, Mercy. How's the shoulder?"

"Sore, but I'm improving. Nico and Sam are taking good care of me."

"Glad to hear it."

"What's up, Z?" Nico asked.

"Fed problems."

"What kind?"

"The worst. The alphabet agencies and Secret Service want to talk to your girl."

Nico expected Mercy to object to the moniker and was surprised when she didn't. "Do they know about the bounty on Mercy?"

"Oh, yeah. They don't care. They insist on talking to her anyway, taking a swipe at us in their demand."

"Let me guess. If Fortress can't protect her, the feds will?"

"Smart man."

"How long can you delay? She's not ready for an interrogation." If Nico had his way, she wouldn't talk to them at all. He knew that wasn't likely. "Tell them she's injured and still recovering."

"Tried that. Didn't fly. According to them, if she's healthy enough to travel from Mexico to the US, she can talk to law enforcement agencies who need answers. They're playing the national security card."

Of course they were. "It's too soon." He didn't want her enduring an interrogation. Mercy thought she was ready. She wasn't. The questions would continue for hours, and Nico didn't believe her strong enough for the grueling ordeal.

"Nico." Mercy laid a hand on his arm. "I'll be fine."

He covered her hand with his. "This isn't a good idea. Besides the feds grilling you, we'll have to meet them somewhere. That means finding a place secure enough to protect you."

"Why won't you bring them here?"

"Compromises the safe house," Zane said. "Trust me, someone will notice if a bunch of obvious fedmobiles drive to and from the cabin, and report the unusual occurrence online."

"He's right," Nico said. "Zane, book us a suite at the Garden Hotel in Murfreesboro, the honeymoon suite if it's available so Mercy can rest if she's tired. The feds can keep themselves occupied until she's ready to answer more questions."

"When?"

"Tomorrow at noon." Not enough time for her body to recuperate, but hopefully she would rest better tonight than she had this morning. "No matter how much they push, I won't bring her out of hiding until then. My priority is her safety and wellbeing."

Zane chuckled. "Maddox will take great pleasure in passing along the message. Mercy, rest as much as you can today. Tomorrow will be long and hard. I'll be in touch, Nico." He ended the call.

Nico slid his phone into a pocket and turned to Mercy. "Are you sure you want to do this?"

"You don't think I can handle it?"

He needed to tread carefully. Wouldn't do to tick off the lady if it wasn't necessary. "You're not at full strength and haven't talked to anyone about your kidnapping and cave imprisonment."

She flashed him a smile. "I talked to you."

"I'm not a counselor."

Her smile faded. "Did you talk to someone after your experience?"

Nico snorted. "I didn't have a choice. Maddox insisted."

"Did it help?"

He nodded. "I still have flashbacks, but they're not as frequent." Why had he admitted the truth to a woman he'd known two days? Would Mercy view him as a head case?

"I'm glad," she murmured.

"Would you be willing to talk to a Fortress counselor?"

"Do you think I should?"

"You'll handle the interrogations better tomorrow if a counselor helps you work through the details before you tell your story to the feds."

"Interrogations? Plural?"

"Oh, yeah. Each agency will take you through the story multiple times, asking different questions each time."

"Can't they interview me at the same time?"

"That's not how it works. Each agency has their own agenda, and with feds, they don't believe the other agency's interrogator will get the answers everybody needs."

"Do you have a counselor in mind?"

"He's a good friend and counsels many of the units my teammates and I work with. He lives in Otter Creek and is friends with the man who owns this cabin. The counselor I talked to retired a few months ago. This man used to be military. He understands PTSD better than a civilian counselor would."

Mercy sighed. "I wanted to draw today."

"You'll have time for that, too. Will you let me call and set up a video chat with him?"

"All right."

Relief swept through him. Nico called Marcus Lang, the pastor of Cornerstone Church in Otter Creek. When his friend answered the phone, Nico said, "It's Nico. You're on speaker with a friend. Her name is Mercy."

"Hi, Mercy. I'm Marcus Lang. What do you need, Nico?"

"Counseling session for my friend. She was kidnapped and tossed in a cave by terrorists."

A soft whistle from the pastor. "Rough. Are you in town or will this be by video chat?"

"Video. We're holed up in a safe house at the moment."

"Ah. Give me ten minutes to drive home, then contact me."

"Thanks, Marcus." He turned to Mercy. "I'll get you a bottle of water." He inclined his head to the chair behind the desk at the computer. "Make yourself comfortable. I'll return in a minute."

He grabbed two bottles of water from the refrigerator and a box of tissues. Although she was a strong woman, the decompression process could include a round or two of tears. She hadn't had a chance to deal with the trauma yet.

Nico stopped Joe in the hallway. "Tell the others to stay away from the office. Mercy will be talking to Marcus in a few minutes."

Concern filled his friend's eyes. "She okay?"

"She hasn't had a chance to process what happened to her in Mexico, and now the feds insist on interrogating her."

"Where are we meeting?"

"Garden Hotel in Murfreesboro. I asked Z to book the Honeymoon suite in case Mercy needs a break."

"Smart. I'll find the schematics for the hotel, and Trace and I will look at the security situation while you're with Mercy."

Nico nodded. "Thanks." When he returned to the office, Mercy was seated in the big leather chair behind the desk, head tipped back and eyes closed, fatigue evident on her face.

He stepped inside the room and closed the door. After setting the water and tissues on the desk, Nico crouched beside the chair. Despite the bruises, Mercy Powers was a beautiful woman, one he'd love to know better.

He hated to wake her, but Marcus should be home by now. "Mercy."

Heavy eyelids raised. "Sorry. I only meant to close my eyes for a minute. Is it time?"

"No need to apologize." Nico wiggled the mouse and entered the information necessary to connect with Marcus. A moment later, his friend's face appeared on the screen.

"Good to see you, Nico." Marcus's gaze shifted to Mercy. "I'm Marcus. Three things you should know before we begin, Mercy. Anything you tell me will not leave my office. No one will know we talked unless you tell them. Second, if you need to stop and regroup, tell me. We'll take a short break. Third, knowing Nico, I assume he'll want to stay in the room to provide protection. If you don't want him to overhear what you're saying, he can slip on his headphones and listen to music or an audiobook. If you allow him to listen, he'll keep your confidence as well. Tell him what you want him to do."

Her gaze locked on Nico's. "You don't need headphones. I've already told you most of what happened anyway."

Most? She'd been holding something back. He looked at the computer screen. "The feds want to interrogate Mercy tomorrow."

"Ah. Mercy, start at the beginning. Tell me where you were and why."

As Mercy related her story to Marcus, Nico moved one of the chairs around behind the desk. He sat out of camera range but was close enough to press a handful of tissues into Mercy's hand when tears began to roll down her cheeks.

Hearing what she'd gone through gutted him and brought back memories of his own experience. Once Mercy was safe, he might call Marcus to silence his own nightmares again.

By the time Mercy's session with Marcus ended, she was swaying from fatigue. With the counselor still on screen, she said to Nico, "I'm going to rest for a while. Talk to Marcus." She cupped his cheek for a second, then left the room.

He slid into the seat Mercy had vacated. "Thanks, Marcus."

"No problem. Tell me what's going on with you."

"I'm fine."

Marcus smiled. "Mercy doesn't seem to agree. Why does she think you need to talk to me?"

Nico dragged a hand down his face, wondering how she'd figured out her story had triggered deep-seated emotions in him. "I was taken captive last year by human traffickers. When they weren't torturing me, they locked me in a cave."

"Hearing Mercy talk about her experience in Mexico must have brought up some bad memories."

"Yeah, it did. I was going to call you about it after she was safe."

"Did you get counseling?"

"Maddox had one of our counselors in Bayside before the jet carrying Shadow landed. He stayed with me the full month I was in Sorensen's recovery room."

"Tell me what happened, Nico."

An hour later, he ended the video chat with Marcus after promising to call him if he or Mercy needed to talk. Nico polished off the rest of his water and pushed away from the desk. He walked into the kitchen and pulled up short when he saw Mercy sitting at the breakfast bar. "I thought you were resting."

She slid off the stool and crossed the expanse of the kitchen to stand in front of him. "Are you angry with me?"

"Why would I be?"

Mercy dropped her gaze to his chest. "I shouldn't have insisted that you talk to Marcus. I'm sorry for overstepping my boundaries."

"Hey." Nico cupped her chin with the palm of his hand and lifted her head so he could look her in the eyes. "You were trying to help, and you were right."

Her eyes widened. "I was?"

"Hearing what you went through triggered memories of my own. Talking to Marcus helped. Thank you." He brushed his thumb lightly over her bottom lip. "You didn't tell me Hector threatened to rape you, then sell you to the highest bidder."

"Because it didn't happen. You had enough on your shoulders without me adding a threat that didn't materialize."

"Mercy, if it concerns you, I want to know about it. I don't care if it's big or small."

"Why?"

"You matter to me."

CHAPTER THIRTEEN

Mercy's heart skipped a beat at Nico's words. How could she matter to him? Did he mean she mattered because she was a job? She couldn't deny the possibility disappointed her. "Because you're protecting me."

His dark eyes stared down into hers as his hand left her chin and curled around her nape. "Is that what you think? That you're just a job to me?"

"I don't know what to think."

"Yeah, Mercy, you do. You don't know if you're ready or willing to explore the attraction." Nico moved a step closer and slowly lowered his head until his lips touched hers. "I hope I can change your mind."

Heart slamming against her ribcage, she stood still and waited to see if he would deepen the kiss or leave her with a tantalizing taste of him on her lips. It had been three years since her last kiss, Mercy realized. Aiden had been deployed for a year when he died.

Nico changed the angle of his head by infinite degrees until he found the perfect fit. Mercy's blood heated, anticipating the deeper caress she suddenly craved. When he kept the kiss light, teasing her lips with the tip of his tongue and igniting a wildfire inside her, Mercy increased the pressure herself and initiated the kiss she wanted more than her next breath.

His thumb brushed against the side of her neck, and he let Mercy control the kiss. She edged closer still with a soft moan as her pulse soared. It had been a long time since she'd been held like this. Sometime during the kiss, Nico's other arm had wrapped around her waist and held her tight against him.

When he broke the kiss, Mercy whispered, "No. Not yet."

"Easy, kitten," he murmured. "Company."

As the rush of emotion eased, she became aware of voices drawing closer. Nico's teammates. She should move away from him, but Mercy didn't think her legs would hold her weight. Now that she was more cognizant, she realized she was leaning heavily against Nico and he was taking the brunt of her weight. "Kitten?"

"Your hair reminds me of the color of my childhood pet and it feels as soft as a kitten's fur. Do you mind if I call you that?"

She shook her head, grateful he didn't call her Sweetie like Aiden had.

The back door opened and the male voices she'd been hearing petered off into silence.

Face burning, Mercy started to move away from Nico, but he tightened his grip around her waist to hold her in place and continued to stroke her neck with his thumb. Instead of fighting against of his hold, she relaxed into his embrace and rested her cheek against his heart.

"Do you have a security plan worked out?" Nico asked his teammates.

"We do. When you have a chance, we'll go over it with you. You can evaluate the plan for weaknesses," Trace said.

"You already know there are several weaknesses. We can't secure all the rooms on the floor with such short notice, and we can't lock down the hotel."

"Not to mention the feds coming and going," Joe commented. "They're not inconspicuous. We thought it would be better to leave Sam in the suite with you and Mercy. Trace, Ben, and I will cover security at the door, the stairs, and the elevator."

"We have the schematics on Joe's computer," Trace said. "Ben offered suggestions between security rounds."

"I need to take over the watch," Joe said and left the kitchen.

"I'll meet you outside," Trace said. A moment later, a door closed, and the kitchen was silent again.

Nico cupped her cheek. "Do you want to see the hotel's schematics and know the security plan? Might help you feel more secure."

"I'll pass." After the kiss she'd shared with Nico, Mercy wouldn't be able to concentrate long enough to make sense of the plan.

He bent down and brushed his lips over hers in a brief caress and eased away from her. "Stay inside the house. If there's trouble, wake Sam. She'll know what to do. I'll be on the patio."

When he closed the door behind him, Mercy leaned against the closest wall, hissing when her injured shoulder pressed too hard against the flat surface. Good grief. Nico Rivera's kiss almost melted her into a puddle on the floor.

Sam walked into the kitchen a moment later, her eyebrows rising when she saw Mercy against the wall. "Are you okay?"

"Sure."

A frown. "I'm not convinced. What's wrong? Is it your shoulder or leg?"

"They're fine."

"Well, something is up. Talk to me, Mercy."

She hesitated a moment. Should she tell her what happened a moment ago? Two of Sam's teammates already knew or suspected. Mercy had a feeling Nico's team was close knit. Wouldn't take long for Trace and Joe to pass the word to Sam and Ben that something was going on between Mercy and Nico. "It's Nico."

"Is he okay?"

"More than."

Sam stared, then a smile curved her mouth. "Oh. This sounds like a story. I need coffee, then tell me all the details." She swept past Mercy, filled her mug, and glanced around. "Too much potential for male traffic through here. There's a suite with a sitting room on the second floor. Let's sit in there. Joe won't do a security sweep in the suite."

"You have the watch schedule memorized?"

The medic's face reddened. "Not really."

Hmm. "Sounds like you have a story to share, too. Come on. Show me the suite. Why won't Joe do a sweep through there?"

"It's where he and the others put me. The suite is large enough to serve as an infirmary if we need one."

If Shadow needed an infirmary, it would mean the Scorpions had found them and one of the unit was injured. Mercy prayed that would never happen. She didn't want to be responsible for an injury to one of these brave men or Sam.

As soon as they were behind the closed door of the suite and settled on the couch, Mercy said, "You go first. Is something going on between you and Joe?"

"I don't know." Sam looked frustrated. "He's hard to read."

"He hasn't made a move?"

The other woman shook head. "He has had opportunities. Shadow unit usually works in pairs except for Nico. He's comfortable working alone if the rest of us are paired off. Anyway, if Joe isn't working with Trace, he's with me. I've given him chances, but he must not be interested enough to follow through."

"I don't know about that. I've seen the way he looks at you when your back is turned. Perhaps he's afraid of ruining your working relationship by changing the dynamics."

"Other units have married couples working together. I don't see why we can't do the same if we're dating."

"If you try a relationship and it doesn't work out, what will that do to the group's cohesiveness?"

"We're adults. We'll figure it out."

"Maybe you need to convince Joe a relationship is worth the risk."

Sam sighed. "I'll think about it. Enough about me. I brought you up here to talk about you. Dish, Mercy. Why were you holding up the wall in the kitchen?"

Should she tell Sam what happened? The others might suspect, but they wouldn't know for sure unless Nico confirmed their suspicions.

"Don't even think about holding back." Sam narrowed her eyes. "I already spilled my deepest secret. Your turn."

Maybe the medic would have some insight. Right now, Mercy's thoughts were running in circles and getting her nowhere. "Nico kissed me."

"Yes! I thought he was attracted to you. He's never treated our principals the way he treats you or looked at them the same way. I never dreamed he'd act on his attraction while we were here. I figured he'd wait until we took down the Scorpions." She stopped abruptly. "Wait. Are you interested in him?"

"I'm attracted to him." Boy, was she. Her pulse was still elevated. "More important, I like him and I like spending time with him."

"But?"

"But I never thought I'd be interested in anyone again after I lost Aiden. Whatever is going on between me and Nico seems to be developing at warp speed. I don't know what to do with that."

"Happens a lot in our business." Sam set aside her mug. "Our work is intense and dangerous. Because of that, we realize life is unpredictable. If we wait, we might miss the chance of a lifetime."

Mercy knew that from her own life with Aiden. She'd lost him much too soon, but if they hadn't grabbed their chance at a life together, she and Aiden wouldn't have shared four wonderful years as husband and wife despite him being deployed for more than half of those years. She wouldn't have traded one minute of their time together even knowing the pain that awaited her. The time she spent with him had changed her for the better, and she believed the same was true for him.

"Don't be afraid to take a chance, Mercy. Nico is worth the risk."

She already knew that much. Was she willing to suffer heartbreak again? His job was more dangerous than Aiden's. What if she agreed to see where the attraction went, fell in love with Nico, and then lost him? Could she handle the pain of losing another mate?

Enough. She couldn't make a snap decision. Besides, Nico had only kissed her, not vowed undying love and begged for her hand in marriage. Time to change the subject. "How long have you and Joe worked together?"

"Five years."

She laughed. "That's not an example of a fast-moving relationship, Sam."

The medic grimaced. "I know. Some men are stubborn. Joe happens to be one of them."

"Does he know you're attracted to him?"

"Of course." She stopped, frowned. "I think."

"Sounds like you should show him."

"If he gives me the chance."

"Create an opportunity." She grinned. "I dare you. I'd love to see a relationship work out between you and Joe."

A knock on the sitting room door brought their conversation to a halt. Joe stepped inside. "Everything okay?"

"Yes. Why?" Sam asked.

"Nico was concerned when he couldn't find Mercy."

Mercy straightened. "Does he need me for something?"

"He has information. Says it's important."

Both women rose and followed the operative to the patio. When Nico came toward them, Sam reached over and squeezed Mercy's hand, then crossed the patio to sit beside Trace and study the schematics on the computer.

Nico stopped in front of Mercy, his body blocking her from the view of his teammates. "You're all right?" he asked softly.

She nodded. "Sam and I were talking in her sitting room."

He studied her face. "Did I scare you?"

Amusement bubbled inside her. "It takes more than a kiss to scare me off, Nico."

Satisfaction filled his gaze. "Good to know because I want to kiss you again. Will you let me?"

Whew. Talk about moving at warp speed. Fine. She could be honest and see what he did with the information. "Yes, because I want to kiss you again, too."

His eyes darkened. "Tell me that again when we're alone," he murmured. Nico lifted her hand to plant a kiss on her palm then drew her toward the outdoor couch they'd sat on earlier. "Zane sent photos you need to see."

Nico tapped the screen of his phone and showed her a snapshot.

Her eyes widened. "That's my living room. Someone broke into my house." And trashed everything she owned from the looks of the photo.

"Zane activated a bot to keep track of any mention of your name. He caught this from a police activity report. Your neighbor called when he saw someone leaving your house in the middle of the night and knew you were still gone."

"Mr. Stonebridge," she said. "He's retired and keeps watch over the neighborhood at night. Are there more photos?"

Nico scrolled through the pictures. Each photo shot an arrow straight to Mercy's heart. Items that she and Aiden chose for their home had been destroyed. By the time Nico showed her the last picture, Mercy couldn't see the images.

Tears spilled down her cheeks. Handiwork of the Scorpions. What purpose would the destruction of her home serve? Nothing in there would indicate where she was hiding. This had been petty and mean, a way of reminding her that they intended to find her and punish her. But for what? She wasn't of value to them.

"I'm sorry, Mercy." Nico wrapped his arm around her shoulders and tugged her gently into his embrace. "We'll make sure everything is replaced."

She let him hide her face from his teammates. Her belongings could be replaced, but seeing the physical representation of her and Aiden's hopes and dreams destroyed devastated her. It was almost as though she lost the last part of Aiden. She had memories and photos, items that were more valuable to her than the furniture, dishes, and her framed drawings. Still, seeing the destruction gutted her.

As though from a great distance, she heard Nico say something to one of his teammates. When Mercy lifted her head, Nico pressed a handful of tissues into her hand. "Thanks," she choked out. After drying her face and blowing her nose, she glanced around the patio and found it empty except for the two of them. "Guess I chased away your teammates with the waterworks."

"They thought you would be more comfortable without an audience." Nico cupped her face between his rough palms. "Please, don't cry anymore. I can't take your tears."

She gave a watery laugh. "Big tough guy like you can handle a few tears."

"Not yours." He pressed his lips to hers. "Spare my heart, kitten." Nico's gentle kiss was a balm to Mercy's aching heart. When he lifted his head, he threaded his fingers into her hair. "Fortress will help you rebuild your life."

Fortress Security might help reconstruct her life, but Mercy didn't know if she would ever feel safe again.

CHAPTER FOURTEEN

Nico kept a close watch on Mercy the rest of the day and evening. She had taken the destruction of her home hard. He didn't blame her. He'd be livid if anyone did that to his safe haven, and he didn't have the same emotional connection to his home as Mercy.

The devastation was more deeply rooted than the loss of property. Although she didn't say, Nico suspected Mercy felt as though she had lost her husband all over again, resurrecting the pain of Aiden's death. Thankfully, Mercy's tears remained absent.

What he appreciated the most was instead of brooding, Mercy organized the meal. With her limited mobility, she drafted help with things that required two hands. Before long, two large pots of beef stew simmered on the stove and biscuits baked in the oven, filling the cabin with the homey scent of home cooking.

"Thank goodness you can cook," Sam said from her perch on a barstool. "I was afraid we'd starve on this op."

"None of you cook?" Mercy filled her glass with water and sat beside the medic.

"The closest thing we come to it is microwaving frozen dinners and that is iffy."

"She's right," Nico said from where he was leaned against the counter. "We've been known to burn food despite simple microwave instructions."

"That is a sad state of affairs." Mercy turned to Sam. "Would you like to learn how to cook?"

The medic looked doubtful. "You would need a boatload of patience."

"I'm patient and it looks like I'll have plenty of time. We'll start with simple things to boost your confidence before we try something more complicated."

"I don't know." Sam scowled at the interest of the rest of her team. "I don't want to be stuck in the kitchen every time we're secluded with a principal."

"No problem." Mercy smiled. "I'm teaching them, too."

Nico chuckled as his male teammates groaned and protested Mercy's plan.

Joe glared at him. "Why don't you stop laughing and tell the lady that we're all thumbs around knives?"

Mercy rolled her eyes.

Nico didn't blame her. He shook his head at his teammate. "That's not going to fly, Joe. No one will believe operatives skilled with a Ka-Bar can't handle a kitchen knife or read directions."

Trace looked blank. "Directions?"

"You didn't notice the cookbooks on the counter?"

"What cookbooks?"

With a sigh, Nico grabbed a volume and placed it in front of the sniper who could drop a man from 1,000 yards away but claimed not to see a book ten feet in front of him.

Trace eased back as though the book would bite his hand. "I don't cook."

"Yet." Sam gave him a pointed look. "I'm not going into this venture alone. I say Mercy chooses a different meal for each of us to learn. Once we learn those, she can choose something else. Maybe we won't starve on missions anymore."

"This is a dumb idea," Ben muttered.

"Suck it up, cupcake," Nico said, his tone mild. "It's a good skill to learn." He followed up his words with a hand signal for his EOD man to shut his mouth. Ben's face reddened, but his protests subsided.

"Tonight's dinner is already underway," Sam said. "Who wants to volunteer for breakfast duty?"

When no one piped up, Nico said, "I'll take the first lesson. I doubt we'll be back here in time for lunch. Maybe not dinner, either. Besides, after the fed grilling session, I don't think Mercy will feel up to cooking herself much less teaching an unenthusiastic student."

"We'll pick up something for dinner if we're not stuck in the hotel," Joe said.

Once dinner was over, Nico sat with Mercy on the couch in the living room. She looked tired and uncomfortable. "Your shoulder is hurting?"

She nodded. "I'm overdue for pain meds. I wanted to leave them off. They make me feel loopy."

He rose. "I'll find you something over-the-counter." Nico returned with two bottles of pain reliever.

Mercy tapped the red and white bottle. "I'm allergic to the other one."

Huh. He'd never heard of anyone having problems with the painkiller he preferred. He shook a couple capsules into her palm and passed her the water he'd brought to wash them down with.

"Thanks," she murmured.

Nico settled beside her again and picked up the remote. "What's your favorite type of program to watch when you relax?"

"Cozy mystery or police procedural."

"Movie or television series?"

"Series. I don't watch many movies. Most of the time, I'd rather read a book."

"Right now, indulge me, okay? I want to help you relax before you try to sleep tonight."

Mercy stared. "How did you know I didn't sleep well last night?"

He didn't want to admit he'd listened at her door several times during his watch and heard her tossing and turning. "With the kind of trauma you suffered, it's natural to have a hard time at night."

"Do you?"

"Sometimes."

"How do you cope?"

Oh, man. She would have to ask that question. Nico glanced around to be sure his teammates were out of earshot. "When I can't sleep, I quilt," he muttered.

Mercy's head whipped his direction. "Seriously?"

He stiffened. "Yeah. Is that a problem?"

"I think that's amazing. I'm all thumbs when it comes to needles. I end up sticking myself so much I bleed all over the fabric."

"You quilt?"

"My grandmother tried to teach me. I was hopeless. I wasn't bad at knitting, though. Do your teammates know about your skill?"

He flinched. "No, and I'd appreciate it if you didn't rat me out."

Mercy grinned. "I'll keep your secret. What do you do with the quilts? Do you keep them for yourself?"

Nico shook his head. "I give them to a children's home in east Tennessee." Narrowing his eyes, he studied her face a moment. "I think you should even the playing field."

"How?"

"Tell me a secret of yours."

"Something you can hold over my head?" She shook her head. "I don't think so."

"It's only fair, Mercy." He tapped the tip of her nose. "Come on. Spill."

"Are you familiar with the Boston Bear comic books?"

"Who isn't? The story lines are cute and the illustrations amazing." He stilled. "Wait. Are you saying you're the illustrator?"

She nodded.

A broad smile curved Nico's lips. "Why don't you want anyone to know?"

"My reputation in the art community would take a hit if they knew I moonlighted with children's comic books."

"You took over the illustrations five years ago, didn't you?"

She stared. "How did you know?"

"The graphics side of Boston Bear moved up several levels at that point. I've always loved reading those." He felt his face start to burn. "I started collecting them when you took over the illustrations instead of passing them on to my neighbors' kids. I didn't want to disappoint the kids so I always bought two copies. One to keep, one to share."

"Do you still collect them?"

"Never miss an edition." He pointed his index finger at her. "And, yes, my teammates do know about that habit of mine. That's not blackmail material."

She grinned. "I'll keep your secret if you keep mine."

"Deal." Nico picked up the remote and scrolled through the listings until he found an old television series that Mercy liked. "Rest your head against my shoulder and relax."

"I might go to sleep if I do that."

He shrugged. "If it helps you sleep, I'll offer my shoulder anytime." Nico draped his arm across her shoulders, careful not to put pressure on her injury. By the thirty-minute mark, Mercy was sound asleep.

Excellent. He sat with her for another hour, then slid one arm behind Mercy's back, the other under her knees, and carried her to the bedroom. She stirred when he laid her on the bed. "Shh. You're safe," he murmured. "Go back to sleep, kitten."

Nico waited until Mercy was out again, then left the room. Trace glanced up when Nico walked into the security room. "Anything?"

His friend shook his head. "Nothing except a few deer and a raccoon or a fat cat."

"Hope it stays that way. Mercy doesn't need an interrupted night's sleep on top of facing hours of interrogation tomorrow."

"Agreed. You on watch?"

"At midnight."

A nod. "I'll wake you in a couple hours."

He clapped the sniper on the shoulder and climbed the stairs to his room. He sprawled across the cover and was out in seconds.

When the knock from Trace came two hours later, Nico sat up immediately, weapon in his hand.

"It's Trace," his friend murmured. "Time for your shift."

Nico dragged a hand down his face. "Give me five minutes." He swung his legs over the side of the bed and made his way into the bathroom. After a quick shower, most of the sluggishness was gone. A mug of coffee would chase away the rest.

He listened at Mercy's door for a few seconds and heard nothing. Good. She'd need every ounce of strength to weather interrogations by the fed agencies.

Nico walked into the kitchen, filled a large mug with coffee, then went to the security room. "I've got the watch. Get some rest."

Trace pushed back from the console. "Wake me in three hours."

"Copy that." He settled down behind the computer screens and scrolled from one camera angle to another.

From what he could see, nothing had been disturbed since the last time he sat at this desk.

A few minutes later, Sam wandered in. "Anything happening?" She handed him a bottle of water.

Nico had to smile. The medic was always on Shadow's case about drinking more water to balance the vats of coffee they consumed. "Nothing new."

"How was Mercy?"

"Sleeping as far as I could tell when I came down."

"Will you encourage her to see a counselor about what happened in Mexico?"

"She talked to Marcus yesterday morning. They're scheduled for another session tomorrow."

Sam remained silent a moment, her expression troubled.

"What's on your mind, Sam?"

"She's been horribly battered by life."

"I know."

"Do you know what you're doing?"

"Be specific, Sam."

"You can't toy with her emotions, Nico. If you're not serious about her, you need to lay off."

Where was this coming from? Had Mercy expressed concern to Sam? "I believe I've made my intentions plain. I don't plan to hurt Mercy. I care about her."

An emotion Nico couldn't identify came and went in his medic's eyes. "After only a few days?"

"I can't explain it. You know as well as I do relationships can develop fast."

"And sometimes they never develop," she murmured, her shoulders slumping.

"Want to talk about it?" Nico patted the chair next to his. "I can't leave the console, but I can watch screens and listen at the same time."

"I shouldn't." She sat.

"Joe?"

Her head snapped his direction. "You knew?"

He glanced at her before returning his attention to the screens. "I'm responsible for the wellbeing of my team. Conflict between teammates will affect us all."

Sam stiffened. "Nothing is going on between us."

"But you wish it was otherwise."

"Would that be a problem?"

"Not for me. I don't want to lose either of you. If you two decide to change your relationship, be adult enough to find a way to work together if the relationship doesn't gel."

She gave a huff of laughter. "I'm not the one with the problem." The medic turned her attention to the screens. The rest of their shift passed without incident. At four, Joe and Ben took over.

Nico returned to his room to sleep for another two hours. When he opened his door a second time, he noticed that Mercy's door was open.

Peeking inside, he found her sitting on the side of the bed, scowling at the floor. "Good morning."

She glanced at him over her shoulder. "It would be if I could use both hands."

He walked inside. "What do you need?"

"To tie my tennis shoes."

Nico knelt in front of Mercy and tied her shoes, then leaned up and brushed her lips with his. "Sleep well?"

"Better." Her eyes sparkled. "You put me to sleep."

"Ouch. I prefer you to say I helped you relax." He stood and lifted Mercy to her feet. "Teach me to make something edible."

By the time breakfast was over, Nico felt confident he could handle a redo of the pancakes Mercy taught him to make. While the others cleaned the kitchen, he clasped Mercy's hand and walked outside with her. She would be cooped up all day and probably into the night. He wanted her to have a chance to breathe fresh air.

Partway through the walk, he said, "Are you sure you want to do this today?"

"What if I don't?"

"I'll have Maddox pass the word to the feds that you aren't ready. They'll wait. They won't have a choice."

"I'm tempted," Mercy admitted. "I won't do it, though. If I can tell them anything that will help, I want to. My security detail's friends, families, and co-workers need information and closure. It's the least I can do."

Unsurprised by her decision, Nico squeezed her hand. "When you talk to them, remember a few things. Don't volunteer information. Answer questions they ask, nothing more. Any time you need a break, take one. The feds will cooperate."

"What if they don't?"

"I'll make them. Take opportunities to stretch your legs and clear your head between agencies. They will all insist time is of the essence, that every minute counts. They're correct, but nothing is worth hurting yourself over. If you sit too long, you risk muscles spasms and blood clots. Whether or not you think you need a break, I'll cut in every two hours and see that you take one anyway. If you become too tired, we'll stop the questions and retreat to one of the bedrooms where you can rest for a few minutes."

"That's why you insisted on the suite."

"Interrogations are difficult at the best of times. You aren't at your best physically. I'm trying to accommodate your desire to help and the feds' need for information."

He turned them around and started back toward the cabin. "I'm staying in the room with you at all times as is Sam."

"Surely that's not necessary. They are federal agents, after all."

"Doesn't matter. I don't trust anyone with your safety but my team. All the feds are unknowns, and we suspect there's a leak on the fed side. I won't risk your safety by leaving you alone with them."

CHAPTER FIFTEEN

Nico placed his hand on Mercy's arm. "Wait here." He opened the door along with Trace and stepped out of the SUV to scan the parking garage. Joe, Sam, and Ben parked a few slots away and spilled from their vehicle to search for threats to Mercy.

When he was satisfied she was at minimal risk for the moment, Nico opened her door and assisted her from the vehicle. He slid his arm around her waist and got her moving toward the stairs. "We're taking the stairs to the Honeymoon suite which is on the third floor. We'll go up while Ben gets the key card to the suite."

"Why take the stairs?"

"We can maneuver better on the stairs if a problem develops. In an elevator, we'd be easy prey." There was nowhere to go trapped inside a metal box.

Mercy blew out a breath. "I never would have thought of that. I won't look at an elevator the same way from now on."

"We're trained to think of the worst-case scenarios and plan for contingencies." He rushed her inside the staircase and stopped her by the door while his team swept the stairs for threats.

Two minutes later, Trace said, "Clear."

"Let's go." When they reached the third-floor landing, Joe and Sam checked the corridor. A minute later, Ben arrived with the key cards. The three of them swept the suite and declared it clear of unwanted occupants.

Once Nico had Mercy inside the hotel suite, he pressed his finger to her lips and pulled the signal tracker from his pocket and searched the rooms for bugs and other electronic devices. Ten minutes later, he was convinced no one had accessed the suite and left a surprise. For now, at least, Mercy was secure.

He returned to Mercy's side. "No bugs or cameras. We can talk freely."

She motioned toward his hand. "That's what the gadget is for?"

Nico nodded as he led her toward the living room couch. "It alerts us of electronic signatures. We have over an hour before the feds are scheduled to arrive. Are you hungry?"

Mercy grimaced. "I'm not sure I could handle anything."

"You need to try," Sam said. "Once the questions start, you won't have a chance to eat for hours and you're still rebuilding your strength."

Nico grabbed the room service menu and scanned the hotel's offerings. "What about a chicken salad sandwich, Mercy?"

"That's fine. Thanks." She turned to Sam to ask how soon she could lose the sling.

He placed orders for Shadow and Mercy. The feds could fend for themselves. Nico had no intention of giving them a reason to stay longer in the suite with Mercy than necessary. With the added incentive of a large tip if the order was delivered quickly, the bellman brought up their order within thirty minutes.

Mercy's gaze locked on the carafe full of hot water. "What's that? Coffee?"

"Hot water." He reached into his pocket and brought out four packets of chamomile mint tea. "I thought you might like this."

She gave him a one-armed hug. "You are one of a kind, Nico. Thank you for thinking of me."

The knot in his stomach loosened. He'd guessed right. Nico led Mercy to the table and set the plate with her chicken salad sandwich in front of her. "I'll fix your tea." While the tea steeped, Nico distributed the rest of the food to the others.

As he swallowed his last bite, Ben unlocked the suite door and stepped inside.

"The first group of feds is here."

Nico turned to Mercy. "You ready?"

She breathed deep and nodded. "Let's get this over with. Maybe they have answers."

Doubtful. That's why the feds were coming to her, hoping for answers themselves. He tipped his chin at Ben. A moment later, three men walked into the suite, each one dressed in black suits with dark ties, white shirts, and black shoes. His eyes narrowed when he saw the last man to enter the suite. Interesting. "Let me guess. FBI."

A scowl from the agent in charge, a man who acted as though he owned the place. "Clear the room. We'll take it from here."

"Not a chance." Nico shifted his weight, prepared to make his point physically if he had to. "Ms. Powers is under my protection. If I leave, so does she, and you'll lose your chance to learn information to aid your investigation."

"Who are you?"

"My name is Nico. I'm with Fortress Security."

The agent's face darkened with fury. "I should have known. Maddox and his cronies can't keep their noses out of my business."

His boss would be happy to know he ticked off the feds. "IDs." Nico held out his hand, already knowing Ben had scanned their identifications and cleared them. He wasn't above antagonizing the arrogant agent in charge. After a moment's hesitation, the agent handed over his cred wallet and motioned for the others to do the same.

The special agent in charge was Craig Jordan. Nico's eyes narrowed. He'd heard of this man from several sources, and none of them were complimentary about the agent. Made him doubly glad he'd insisted on seeing the IDs.

He scanned the other two, focusing briefly on the third man's ID. The last time he'd seen Rafe Torres had been on an operation in Afghanistan. Never would have figured Rafe for a fed.

He exchanged nods with the former Navy SEAL as he handed back the wallet. Turning to Jordan, Nico said, "This is Mercy Powers."

Jordan, Rafe, and Agent Wilson Reed introduced themselves to Mercy.

Nico laid his hand on Mercy's shoulder. "Here are the ground rules. You may ask your questions, but every hour, Mercy will need a break. She's still recovering from a gunshot wound. I won't allow you to exhaust her. If she grows too tired, you will have to wait while she rests a few minutes. Am I clear?"

"I could have you charged with obstruction," Jordan snapped. "You aren't in charge of this investigation. I am."

"Mercy's health and safety are my priority. If you want to talk to her at all, you will follow the rules I've laid out. Mercy is not a criminal. She's a victim."

When she stirred at his characterization of her as a victim, Nico squeezed her shoulder in warning.

"You don't have authority," the agent spat out.

Nico's lips curved. The agent wanted to play the power card? Fine. He was going to lose the contest. Nico grabbed his cell phone, made a call, and placed it on speaker.

After four rings, a distinctive male voice answered. "Nico, everything all right with Mercy?"

The woman in question jerked in surprise. Another squeeze of her shoulder kept her silent for the moment.

"Yes, sir. The FBI is insisting on questioning your niece. The agent in charge is protesting the ground rules I've laid out for Mercy's benefit. Do I have your permission to do whatever is necessary to safeguard Mercy?"

"You and your team have the authority to protect her and do anything necessary to safeguard her health. Who's the agent in charge?"

Nico glanced up, gratified to see Craig Jordan's face lose every ounce of color. "Craig Jordan."

A sigh. "Of course. Special Agent Jordan, I trust you're satisfied that Nico and his team have the right to make and enforce decisions regarding my niece's safety?"

"Yes, Mr. President."

"Good. Whatever rules Nico and his team have established for the interview, you will abide by them or I will have you removed from this investigation."

Between gritted teeth, Jordan said, "Yes, sir."

"Mercy."

"Hello, Uncle William."

"How do you feel, sweetheart?"

"I'm improving. Nico and the others are taking great care of me." Her voice choked off.

Heart in his throat, Nico moved his hand to cup her cheek.

"Thank you for sending Fortress to rescue me," Mercy finally managed. "I don't think I would be alive if you hadn't."

"How could I do otherwise? Charlotte would never forgive me if anything happened to her favorite cousin." His voice was filled with affection. "Trust Nico and his teammates, Mercy. Do whatever they tell you to do. Nico, need anything else from me? I left a meeting to answer your call."

"No, sir. Thanks for taking time for me." When the president ended the call, Nico slid his phone back into his pocket. "Satisfied, Jordan?"

"Let's get on with this," the special agent growled. "I've wasted enough time already pampering the princess."

Fists clenched, Nico took a step forward before he felt the small hand on his arm. He glanced at Mercy who shook her head. Reigning in his temper, Nico faced the fed again. "Mercy is no princess, but you will treat her like one or I'll escort you from the suite and leave the questioning to your colleagues."

He led her to the couch and sat beside her. Rafe leaned against the far wall behind his superior, a grin curving his lips. He gave Nico a subtle nod of approval. Jordan dropped into the armchair closest to Mercy, leaving Reed to grab a chair from the table. Sam took the second remaining chair and sat with her back against the outside wall.

"What happened in Mexico, Ms. Powers?" Jordan dragged a small notepad and pen from his jacket pocket.

Nico laced his fingers with Mercy's and listened as she told of her abduction, interrogation by Hector, and her imprisonment in the cave. At various parts throughout the story, her grip on his hand grew painful despite no change in her facial expression or voice.

When she finished, Jordan took her through the events again, this time stopping her to ask questions. "You didn't try to help your security detail?"

"I didn't know they'd been hurt. I heard a strange coughing noise, thought maybe one of the team was sick. I was walking toward the door when it burst open and the three goons rushed in."

"Did you recognize them?"

Mercy shook her head. "I had never seen them before. I told them I was on a diplomatic mission and of no value as a hostage."

"What did they say?"

"I don't know. They didn't speak in English and I can't speak Spanish. One of them pulled out a syringe and shoved the needle into my neck. The next thing I remember is waking up in utter darkness." She dragged in a ragged breath.

Sam was on her feet an instant later. "Mercy."

"Open the patio door," Nico said as he picked Mercy up in his arms. He carried her past a startled Jordan onto the balcony. Placing her in the chair, he knelt in front of her and cupped her face between his palms. "Mercy, look at me."

"Nico, I don't understand what happened. My lungs felt tight. I've been fine until now."

Sam walked out with a bottle of water in her hand. "It's not unexpected after all you've been through. Talking about the cave brought your emotions back in a rush and tricked your mind into believing there wasn't enough air to breathe."

"Caves are claustrophobic for many people," Nico said, stroking her cheeks with his thumbs. "I wouldn't suggest going spelunking anytime soon." He smiled.

"Fat chance of that. I never want to see the inside of a cave again."

"Can't say I do, either." He leaned up and brushed his lips across hers in a light caress. "You okay now?"

"I think so."

Sam pressed the bottle of water into her hand. "Drink this and relax for a few minutes. Take the time you need.

The FBI will wait until you're ready to talk." With that, she left the balcony, closing the door behind her.

"We shouldn't keep them waiting long." Mercy guzzled part of her water. "Agent Jordan doesn't strike me as the patient type."

He grinned. "I don't know. Might be fun to see how long we can make him suffer."

She chuckled. "You have a mean streak."

"Only with those who deserve it." When she finished the water, he took the empty bottle from her hands. "Are you ready or do you need a longer break?"

"Let's go." She stood. "Hopefully, I won't repeat that episode. That was scary stuff."

"I know. I've had a few myself."

"Stemming from your captivity?"

"Didn't have any before then."

Mercy's shoulders dropped. "Nice to know I'm not alone. You don't have many?"

"I had quite a few while I was in Sorensen's clinic. The counselor figured it out and made sure I knew I was free and able to walk away from the room at any time. I spent hours pacing the hall and the treatment room until the vet patients and owners cleared out at the end of the day. Once they were gone and the doors between where I was and the vet clinic were opened, the episodes stopped. I've only had a couple since."

With a nod, she squared her shoulders. "I'm ready."

The questions resumed. Near the end of the interview, Jordan pulled several photographs from his pocket. "Look at these men. Do you recognize any of them?"

Nico scanned the photographs as Mercy thumbed through them. "Who are they?"

"Known associates of Hector and his boss."

Mercy shook her head and handed back the photos. "I'm sorry, Agent Jordan. I don't recognize any of them."

Jordan stood. "I may have more questions later. Give me your contact number."

Nico snorted. "Not a chance. If you need to talk to Mercy, contact Maddox. We'll arrange something." If he had his way, she wouldn't be in the same room with Jordan again.

While Jordan and Reed stalked from the room, Rafe lingered. "Good to see you again, Rivera. How are Commander Maddox and his family?"

"Fantastic. Alexa is one amazing little girl and she has her dad wrapped around her finger."

The SEAL chuckled. "I'd pay money to see that for myself." He sobered and turned to Mercy. "You didn't recognize any of the men in the photos Jordan showed you. Did you recognize anyone in the compound while you were in Mexico?"

"No. Why?"

"Theory I'm working on. Did you notice anyone out of place?" He smiled. "Besides you."

A frown. "There was one man. I saw him the night I was taken from the church. He was an older man, distinguished looking. I don't know who he was, but he must have been someone important. The others treated him as though he was royalty."

Nico exchanged glances with Rafe. She saw the man. The question was, did he see her? If this man was as important as Mercy thought, he could be the reason she had a price on her head.

CHAPTER SIXTEEN

After the FBI agents left the suite, Secret Service agents arrived to question Mercy. Two hours later, Nico called a halt to the questions. "You've gone over the timeline four times. She doesn't know anything else that might help."

"We lost four agents in Mexico. Ms. Powers is our only witness to what happened and why." Agent Spinoza's eyes reflected his fury and grief at losing colleagues.

"I understand. You won't get more answers by badgering Mercy when she's exhausted. You might learn more when she has a chance to regroup." He stood. "The ATF also wants a crack at Mercy. They're not going to talk to her right now, either. If you have more questions, contact Maddox at Fortress. We'll arrange for you to talk to her."

Reluctantly, the three Secret Service agents followed him to the door. Spinoza handed Nico his business card.

"If she remembers anything else, even something minor, contact me."

"Count on it." He understood what it meant to lose a comrade in arms. Any information could be the difference between solving a case and having it go cold. The families of the dead agents deserved justice for their loved ones. He had to place Mercy's welfare above the families of the agents.

Nico brought his teammates into the suite, secured the door, and called Maddox. "Mercy needs a break. Tell the ATF to delay the interview by two hours."

"She holding up all right?"

"Barely," he murmured. "She looks ready to fall over."

"I'll take care of it. Do what's best for her."

"Copy that." Nico slid his phone into his pocket and studied Mercy a moment. "Sam, I think Mercy could use some OTC pain meds."

A nod from the medic. She handed Mercy a packet of two capsules from her mike bag. "Take these and stretch out for a while. Your muscles need a chance to relax."

Mercy looked at Nico, her expression troubled. "What about the ATF? Aren't they due to arrive soon?"

"Maddox will delay the team by two hours." He helped her stand. "Come on. You'll be more comfortable if you lay on the bed instead of the couch."

He led her to the bedroom and closed the door behind them. He'd leave soon, but he needed to hold her. Watching her handle question after question had been grueling on him, too. He couldn't imagine how exhausted she must feel.

Nico turned her gently to face him, wrapped his arms around her waist, and held her close. "You're amazing, Mercy." He pressed a kiss to her temple. "I know you're tired. I want to hold you for a minute, then I'll leave you to rest."

She relaxed into his embrace. "Now I know why you were concerned about me fielding so many questions. I can't believe how tired I am."

"It's not only a physical strain, but an emotional drain as well. Sometimes the emotional drain is worse." He rubbed her back, careful to avoid her injured shoulder.

Mercy groaned. "That feels good."

With a smile, he continued the massage for another couple minutes. "I should go." Nico released her and stepped back. "I'll come for you in ninety minutes."

He returned to the living room.

"How is she?" Joe asked.

"Wiped out, but Mercy has a spine of steel."

"Did you learn anything from the feds?" Trace asked.

Nico drank half a bottle of water before replying. "Mercy saw a man she described as distinguished in Hector's compound the night she was taken hostage."

"Did she recognize him?" Ben asked.

"No. If she got a good enough look, Mercy may be able to draw his face."

Sam sat beside Joe on the couch. "She draws?"

Nico grinned. "You could say that. You've heard of MJ Powers?"

Trace's eyebrows winged up. "That artist you're obsessed with? Sure. Why?"

"Mercy is MJ Powers."

A soft whistle from Joe. "Nice. Maybe we'll figure out who this guy is and whether he's a threat before something else happens to Mercy."

Exactly what he intended. "I'll talk to her about the drawing tonight. Are you hungry?"

After getting the response he expected, Nico wrote down their orders and called it in. Even though he'd requested a two-hour reprieve from the questioning, he was positive the ATF wouldn't wait the full time and he needed his team on the entrances and exits before the feds showed up.

When the food arrived, Ben, Trace, and Joe polished off their meals and returned to their positions in the corridor. Nico and Sam finished their meals in time for him to wake Mercy.

He knocked on the bedroom door and poked his head inside the room. "Mercy."

"It's time?"

Her drowsy voice made his heart turn over in his chest. What would it be like to hear that voice every morning the rest of his life? He wanted to laugh at himself. Right. Mercy would never allow him to be a permanent fixture in her world. "You have thirty minutes, maybe less, before the ATF arrives. I had room service send up a snack for you."

"I'll be out in a minute."

Nico shut the door and set the plate with her food on the table. He hoped she liked what he'd chosen for her. He was afraid anything heavy might make her sick.

The suite door opened. Ben walked in, frowning. "Did you order more hot water for Mercy?"

Nico straightened. "No." He followed his teammate into the hallway. A man with dark hair and eyes and a scar through one eyebrow stood with a serving cart draped with a white cloth. On top was a carafe and a mug and saucer.

The man dressed in an ill-fitting bellhop's uniform eased back a step as Nico approached. Ben shifted to cut off the man's escape should he try to run.

Nico grabbed one end of the cloth and twisted the cap off the carafe. Not hot water, but coffee. A drink he hadn't ordered for Mercy. "Who sent you?" he demanded.

"The kitchen. Look, I just work here. I do what I'm told." His eyes kept shifting to the carafe. "I got to deliver this to the lady or I'll lose my job."

"You're out of luck, pal, because this isn't going anywhere near my woman."

Ben's eyes widened a fraction at his declaration.

Yeah, surprised Nico, too, especially after his mental reminders that Mercy wasn't for him. "I want to see your ID."

Another step back and the bellhop bumped into Ben. When he tried to turn toward the elevator muttering under his breath about getting the manager, Nico grabbed the man, spun him toward the wall, and shoved him against the flat surface.

"What did you put in the coffee?"

"Nothing. I don't know what you're talking about."

He wrenched Scar's arm up behind his back. "Try again."

The man cursed. "Let me go or I'll call the cops."

The elevator doors slid open. Nico glanced at the occupants. A pity they were right on time. He would have preferred them to be ten minutes late. Now, Nico wouldn't obtain the answers he needed. "Don't bother. They're already here."

Two men strode from the car, badges displayed prominently on their belt along with their sidearms. "What's going on?" the blond agent asked.

"This guy brought up an order of coffee we didn't ask for."

"Is this related to our witness?" the dark-haired agent asked.

"Probably. I've never known a hotel to deliver room service not requested." Nico wrenched Scar's arm higher causing him to bellow in pain. "You want to search him, or should I?"

Blondie motioned for him to proceed.

Nico glanced at Ben who took over the hold, then he searched the man for weapons. A moment later, a pile of weapons and a small empty plastic tube littered the hallway. No ID on him. Scar, now facing Nico, glared at him. "What did you put in the coffee?"

The man remained mute.

"Wasting your time," the dark-haired agent said. "He's just a flunky. No way he's smart enough to call the shots."

Blondie pulled out his handcuffs. "Call the Murfreesboro PD, Mike. We'll let them take this guy off our hands."

Nico stepped aside after the bellhop was cuffed. "I'm taking a sample of the coffee," he told the ATF agents. Turning toward Joe, he said, "Get a clean, empty container from Sam. I'll arrange for a pick up to have the coffee analyzed."

"Copy that." He caught the key card Ben tossed him and disappeared into the suite. When he returned, he had a small capped test tube in his hand and a pair of rubber gloves. "She said to pour the coffee into the mug and let it cool before we dump it into the tube."

Nico tugged on the gloves and poured some of the steaming liquid into the mug. By the time the local police arrived, the coffee had cooled enough to pour into the tube. That done, he capped the tube and slid it into his pocket.

While the police talked to his teammates, Nico returned to the suite. Mercy hurried toward him, her face pale.

"What happened?"

"A man claiming to be a bellhop brought coffee we didn't order. He acted squirrelly, insisting he'd be fired if he didn't deliver the coffee to you. He didn't have an ID, but he had a pile of weapons on him along with an empty plastic vial."

"How did the Scorpions find me?"

Nico cupped her biceps. "Three government agencies knew we were here." The president had suspected a leak. Looked like his suspicions had been confirmed. With three government agencies involved, narrowing down the source of the leak would be almost impossible, even for Fortress.

Worse, if the tangos knew Mercy was in the Garden Hotel, they would be waiting for another chance to grab her when they realized the attempt to poison her failed.

CHAPTER SEVENTEEN

Mercy shivered at Nico's words. He didn't blame her. Not only had the enemy managed to find her despite Shadow's protection, they had cobbled together a plan to harm her, maybe even kill her.

"The Scorpions want to kill me now?"

Nico's hands tightened on her arms. "We don't know if the Scorpions are behind this. We also don't know what the bellhop poured into the coffee. It might be something as benign as sleeping pills. Even if you didn't drink the coffee, your security team might have. If he'd managed to take us out, you would have been vulnerable to attack again."

"Why do they want me?" She dragged a hand through her hair. "This doesn't make any sense."

"We'll figure it out and stop them."

"How? We don't know who to go after."

"With two million dollars at stake, someone will talk. We'll follow the money to see where the trail leads."

"And if the trail leads back to the Scorpions?"

Nico brushed his thumb over the line of her jaw. "I'll have a reason to dismantle the organization sooner."

Mercy's eyes widened at his solemn statement as she realized Nico had planned to destroy the Scorpions anyway. Had she honestly thought he would allow a threat to her safety?

"Nico, you can't take them on."

"They hurt you, Mercy, and are still a threat to your safety," he said, his voice gentle. "I can't let them continue to operate or you will never be safe."

"Your team was outnumbered in Mexico." She laid her hand over his heart. "I don't want anything to happen to you because of me."

"This is not on you. They drew the lines of battle. I won't walk away from the fight. The price is too high." Higher than she realized and that he was willing to admit.

Before she could form a strong argument for him to stay away from the Scorpions, a sharp knock sounded on the door. Ben stepped inside the room. "Local cops need to talk to you, and the ATF is ready to talk to Mercy."

Nico glanced at Sam, who nodded. He turned, brushed his lips over Mercy's, and returned to the hallway followed by his EOD man. The ATF agents nodded at him as they walked into the suite.

He spent several minutes fielding questions from the Murfreesboro police who were frustrated at the large gaps in his knowledge. They weren't the only ones. Nico would continue to tug at the strings of this knot. When he tugged on the right one, the whole thing would unravel and he would know who was at the center of this threat to Mercy. That person would pay.

"Did you know the bellhop?" Detective Whiddon asked.

"No."

A frown from the officer. "Why did you assume something was wrong?"

"Have you ever known of room service sending up anything without a guest requesting it?"

"Can't say that I have."

"Add to that Mercy is a protected witness, and you can see why I'm suspicious."

"I'll have the coffee tested. If there's nothing but coffee, I'll have to let the bellhop go."

"Understood." Releasing the bellhop would give Nico a chance to get the information he wanted. Unlike the police, he didn't have to follow the rule of law, and he was very good at getting answers.

After answering two more questions, the detective left and Nico returned to the suite.

"I didn't hear anything about weapons or a pipeline into the US," Mercy told Blondie. "Hector kept me in the cave except when he had the guards bring me into his compound."

"How many times did that happen?" Black Hair asked.

"Three. I don't know how long it was between grilling sessions."

"What did Hector want to know?"

"If the government would send someone to rescue me, how soon, and who. Hector wanted to know how to prepare for an attack." Her hand fisted. "He became more and more angry each time he questioned me. I didn't have the answers he wanted."

"When you couldn't answer the questions, what did Hector do?" Blondie leaned close to Mercy and laid his hand over hers. His gaze was intent, the expression on his face sympathetic.

Nico frowned at his gesture and crossed the room to sit beside Mercy on the couch. He laid his arm across her shoulders, settling her against his side. He stared at Blondie as he spoke to Mercy. "How do you feel, kitten?"

Blondie jerked his hand away. Smart man.

"I'm fine. Agents Jackson and Robard have been kind." Amusement filled her voice.

Nico broke eye contact with the agent and turned to Mercy. He winked at her.

"We have a few more questions," Black Hair said.

"Ask them now." Nico could already see fatigue setting in again on Mercy. "We need to take Mercy back to the safe house. Obviously, our location here has been compromised."

"We can arrange a safe house that will be more secure," Blondie said, his eyes glittering. "We'll assign agents who can protect her."

Nico's eyes narrowed at the insinuation that he and his team couldn't protect her. "Not a chance. You have ten minutes. Make them count."

With a glare Nico's direction, Blondie asked, "Mercy, when you couldn't answer Hector's questions, what did he do?"

Mercy shuddered.

Nico cupped her nape in a silent reminder that she was safe. Although he knew the questions were necessary, he hated allowing the agents to put Mercy through painful memories again.

"He told me if I didn't have answers the next time he questioned me, he would rape me, then pass me around to his men to see if that would loosen my tongue."

Sam scowled when she heard Hector's threats.

Black Hair flinched. "Did he give you any indication if he had an end game other than freeing his boss?"

Mercy shook her head. "That seemed to be his sole purpose."

They reviewed her story again, clarifying a minor point here and there.

At the ten-minute mark, Nico said, "Time's up. If you have more questions, contact Fortress Security. They'll get me a message and we will make arrangements for Mercy to talk to you."

"We need to bring her into the office for more questions," Blondie said.

"You know that's not going to happen."

"You can't deny us access to her."

"I'm trying to keep Mercy alive."

Black Hair stood, signaling to his partner. "We appreciate your help, Ms. Powers."

"I wish I could have done more."

"What you gave us is more than we had four days ago. Your information confirmed a few things."

"I don't see how, but I'm glad to be of some help."

Black Hair put a hand underneath his jacket.

Immediately, Nico and Sam were on their feet. Nico stepped in front of Mercy, weapon up and aimed at the agent. Sam had Blondie in her sights, her Sig aimed center mass.

Black Hair froze. "I'm getting a business card."

"Slow." Nico watched every move as the agent removed a small case, extracted a white business card, and handed it to him. He glanced at the name. "I'll have Fortress contact you if Mercy thinks of anything new, Jackson."

"Do you have a business card?" Blondie asked.

Nico's lip curled. "Unlike you, I don't pass them out like candy. If you need to contact me, call Fortress and leave a message for Nico. They'll make sure I get it."

With a sneer, Blondie stalked from the room without waiting for his partner. Jackson's gaze lingered on Mercy a moment before he refocused on Nico. "You didn't hear this from me, but there are rumors floating that there's a leak in Washington."

"Do they know where?"

Jackson grimaced. "Our house."

Nico stilled. "Have you heard a name?"

A head shake.

"Why do you think you have a leak in-house?"

"We've planned raids on known weapons warehouses frequented by the Scorpions. The intel's good, our sources solid. But in more than half of them, we came up empty. The stash is gone by the time we arrive. Three times, we were ambushed and lost agents. One of our own is selling us out. I don't know how many layers deep this goes, so watch your back. Don't trust anyone from the ATF."

"Including you?"

"Especially me or Robard. We were assigned to Mercy's case and instructed to offer her sanctuary and protection. In fact, our boss was quite insistent that we take her into protective custody. He's getting pressure from a bigwig in D.C. to get her under our control."

Nico snorted.

A wry smile curved Jackson's lips. "Yeah, that's what I told him when I found out a Fortress team was providing security."

Mercy moved to stand beside Nico. "Why does your boss want me in a safe house you control?"

"Someone thinks you know too much, Ms. Powers, and in our business, knowledge can be deadly." Jackson shifted his gaze to Nico. "I'll tell you the official line to keep me up to date on any further developments and information you come across. Do yourself and Mercy a favor. Don't. I don't want her to fall into the Scorpions' hands." With a nod, he followed his partner from the suite.

A moment later, Nico's teammates returned. He motioned for them to sit and summarized the information Agent Jackson shared.

Trace whistled. "Bet it hurt to admit they have a traitor in their midst."

"At least now I have a direction to aim Zane." He frowned. "I have a friend who works in ATF. I might contact him."

Mercy laid her hand on Nico's arm. "Agent Jackson said not to trust anyone from his agency."

"I'd trust Harry with my life and have on many occasions. He was my battle buddy. We watched each other's backs during several tours through the Sand Box."

"You would be trusting him with Mercy's life," Joe said.

He turned to Mercy, heart in his throat. "I know," he murmured. "Do you trust me?"

"You must know I do."

"We have to start somewhere. If it turns out I trusted the wrong man, we'll handle the fallout and dig up the information we need another way."

"But this is the fastest."

He inclined his head.

"Do it. The sooner we end this, the sooner you and the rest of Shadow will be safe."

Again, she'd put concern for his team ahead of concern for her own safety. Shadow had protected many principals in the past five years. None concerned themselves with anything beyond their personal safety. Mercy Powers was unique.

Nico turned to his team. "Sam, Joe, scout around. See if our bellhop has friends loitering in the area in case the coffee didn't work."

Sam hoisted her medical bag to her shoulder and followed Joe from the suite.

"Ben, settle the bill." Nico tossed him a key card. "Rendezvous with Joe and Sam. Make sure our rides haven't been tampered with."

"Copy that."

Nico turned to Trace. "Stay with Mercy while I talk to Zane." He walked onto the balcony and shut the French doors.

Mercy gathered the plates, cutlery, and glassware with Trace's help and laid everything on the serving cart. Once that was done, Trace wheeled the cart into the hall while Mercy collected the trash and tossed it into the waste can.

She glanced around to be sure she hadn't missed anything in the cleaning process. "Has your team used this hotel before?"

"Twice." His gaze darkened. "We haven't had problems with a security breach until today."

"Lucky me." When the operative didn't reply, Mercy turned to find him watching her. "What is it?"

"Nico is a good man."

"I know." She hadn't doubted that from the moment she first saw Nico in the Mexican cave.

"Do you? He can take a hit and still function. He'll act like the hit didn't faze him when he's bleeding inside. As tough as he is, someone could still hurt him."

"You mean I could hurt him." Mercy sat on the couch. "I have no intention of doing that to him or myself. I'm just as vulnerable emotionally right now as he is."

"Don't toy with his heart. If you can't see a relationship between you, stop it now before he slides any deeper. He's already had his heart ripped out and stomped on once."

Her stomach knotted. "What happened?"

Nico's friend shook his head. "It's his story to tell. If he shares the information, it's a sign he's invested in your relationship."

Before she replied, Nico returned from the balcony. He pulled up short, his gaze shifting from Mercy to Trace and back. "Problem?"

Trace turned his head to stare at Mercy, one eyebrow raised, leaving it up to her whether or not she told Nico about their conversation.

Right. "Everything is fine. We spruced up while you spoke to Zane. What did he say?"

Although he didn't look convinced, Nico said, "Zane's bots will continue scouring the Net for mention of our names, but he'll concentrate his own search on the ATF. Sam sent me a text. A team of two men are watching the entrance to the hotel. The back alley's clear for now. We need to move. Zane said the Net chatter about Mercy picked up a few minutes ago. He's afraid a second team is nearby waiting for a crack at Mercy."

Mercy pressed a hand to her stomach. Whoever these people were, they were persistent.

Trace frowned. "Won't do us any favors to give them time to set up an ambush."

"They've already had almost an hour." Nico pulled out his phone and made a call. "Joe, drive around to the back of the hotel. I'm sending Trace down to move the second SUV. Be ready. Got a feeling our bellhop didn't come to the party alone."

Trace gave Nico some kind of hand signal and left the suite. When Nico ended his call, he crossed the room to her side. He trailed the backs of his fingers over Mercy's bruised cheek, his touch so light she barely felt the contact. "Ready?"

She nodded despite ice water running through her veins. The sooner Shadow was out of here, the quicker they would be safe.

"Remember to do exactly what I tell you. You'll be safe, Mercy. You have my word."

He'd make sure of it, she realized. Even if he had to sacrifice his own life to ensure her safety. That's when she realized Nico Rivera was becoming more than a friend. "I want you safe, too, Nico. You and your teammates."

His eyes lit as he bent his head to kiss her lightly. "We're well trained, kitten, but thank you for caring." He clasped her hand and led her to the door. After checking to be sure the hallway was clear, Nico headed toward the stairs.

Instead of continuing to the parking garage, he wrapped his left arm around Mercy's waist and exited the stairwell into the hotel lobby. "To the left," he whispered, nuzzling the side of her head as though absorbed with her and unaware of his surroundings. The tenseness of his body told Mercy a different story.

Nico guided her toward the hallway to the left. Before they reached the entrance, he nudged her against the wall and captured her mouth in a deep kiss.

As fabulous as his kisses were, how could he think about kissing her at a time like this? Before she could pull away and ask him, footsteps approached from the hallway.

Nico moved closer, angling his body to prevent anyone from seeing her face, not changing his apparent focus on her.

The footsteps drew closer, paused at the entrance to hall, then continued on after a beat.

Nico had recognized the danger and reacted.

When the footsteps faded away, he raised his head. "This way." Once again, he clasped her hand. The hall was long with hotel rooms on either side. When faced with a choice between going right or left, Nico made sure the corridor was clear, then veered to the right and kept going.

"How do you know where to go?" As direction challenged as she was, Mercy didn't have a clue where they were in relation to the street.

"I memorized the hotel layout last night while I was on watch."

Her head whipped his direction. "Seriously?"

He spared her a glance. "We all did. It's the best way to protect you in case we need an alternate escape route." When they reached a door with an exit sign hung overhead, Nico held up his hand, signaling Mercy to wait.

She nodded and stood to the side with her back pressed against the wall. The operative gave her an approving smile, then slipped from the corridor into an alley. A moment later, he returned. "The SUV is ten feet away.

Back door is open for us." Nico wrapped his arm around her and held Mercy tight against his side.

In the alley, the two Fortress SUVs idled, lights off. Nico rushed Mercy from the hotel toward the first SUV. They had almost reached the vehicle when something moved from behind the Dumpster.

Nico shoved Mercy toward the vehicle and turned to face the threat.

CHAPTER EIGHTEEN

Nico hurried toward the man who had separated from the deep shadows behind the Dumpster, scowled when he spotted the second one. "Trace, go." A second later, the SUV carrying Mercy raced from the alley.

Ben scrambled from the second SUV. "Got dibs on the second clown," he muttered.

Suited Nico. The first man looked as though he had been a boxer. Big, beefy, and muscle bound, his face twisted in a snarl of frustration as his prize escaped from the trap he and his buddy set. Moonlight glinted off the knife in his right hand. From his stance and the way he held the knife, Boxer had training.

Anticipation firing in his blood, Nico moved into the shadows and balanced on the balls of his feet. Boxer pivoted and attacked. His size belied the man's speed. Nico blocked the knife strike and delivered a short punch to his ribs.

Boxer grunted, swept Nico's legs out from under him, and leaped on him with his bulky weight. Yeah, this guy had to weigh a good 270 pounds, all of it muscle.

He blocked another knife strike, wrapped his leg around his opponent's, and flipped them. Boxer managed to catch him on the jaw with an elbow. He saw stars for an instant. When his vision cleared, Nico twisted to avoid the blade and knew he was a second too slow. He ignored the sting of the steel slicing into his side.

He jabbed his finger into Boxer's right eye. When the thug howled and reflexively raised his hands to fend off another blow to the eyes, Nico slammed his fist into the other man's diaphragm, temporarily cutting off his oxygen. Three more roundhouse punches to the face and Boxer was out.

Breathing hard, Nico searched the man for ID and found zip. He did, however, find a Sig and a garrote. The latter made him growl in fury.

He glanced over his shoulder. Ben was also searching his target. "Anything?"

"Nothing except a knife and a sweet Sig."

"Same. Take his picture and prints and send them to Fortress." He did the same with Boxer. When he finished, Nico climbed to his feet, hissing at the pain in his side. Yep, Boxer had gotten him with the blade.

He clamped a hand to his side to staunch the blood streaming from the wound.

"What do we do with these clowns?" Ben stood, wiping sweat from his forehead with his sleeve.

"Leave them. I'm more interested in making sure Mercy is safe than questioning a couple thugs who are trying to cash in on the bounty."

"They wanted to hurt or kill your woman. How can you let that slide?" Ben demanded.

He paused before climbing into the back of the SUV and stared at his teammate. "If the cops show before they wake up, they won't have anything to hold them on except maybe illegal weapons possession. We have their prints. We can find them later."

Ben held up his hand, climbed into the shotgun seat, and slammed the door.

What was bugging him? Nico shook his head and got into the vehicle. As soon as he was in, Joe raced after Trace.

"You guys okay?" Sam asked.

"I'm fine," Ben snapped. "Nico isn't."

The medic scanned him. "Where?"

"Right side. I'll live. You can patch me up when we're back at the safe house. Any word from Trace?"

"No problems. They're in the parking lot of a diner off Interstate 65, waiting to rendezvous with us." Joe activated the Bluetooth.

"Go," Trace said in greeting.

"We're clear. We'll be approaching your exit in ten minutes."

"Copy that."

"No one followed you?" Nico asked.

"Negative. The tangos might not have realized there were five of us guarding Mercy. Sam, you need to check Mercy's shoulder when we reach the safe house."

Nico straightened. "What happened, Mercy?"

"I'm okay, Nico. My shoulder hit the door frame when I dove into the backseat."

"Sam will check it anyway. You might have popped stitches. Trace, stay alert."

"Yes, sir."

Forty-five minutes later, the two SUVs parked in the driveway of the safe house. Anxious to see for himself that Mercy was okay, Nico flung open the door as soon as the vehicle stopped.

He hurried to Trace's SUV. Mercy scrambled from the vehicle and threw herself into Nico's arms. "Are you sure you're okay?" he whispered in her ear.

She nodded.

The last of the tension left his body. "Come on. Let's get you inside." Nico turned and hustled her inside the cabin.

As soon as the cabin was cleared and the doors secured, Sam hoisted her mike bag to her shoulder. "My sitting room, Nico."

Mercy's face paled. "Nico. You're hurt?"

"Just a scratch." Although the pain escalating by the minute hinted at more than a scratch.

She wrapped her hand around his and tugged. "Upstairs. I want to see for myself."

He followed her, bemused at her worry over his injury. Besides, he could have Sam check Mercy's shoulder after she finished patching him up.

Inside the suite, Mercy pulled at his shirt. "Off. I want to see."

Lips curving at her insistence, Nico reached behind his head and yanked off his shirt. He grimaced at the intensified pain.

Mercy dragged in a breath. "Oh, Nico." Her soft hand trailed along his side.

He glanced down at himself, winced. Oh, man. No wonder he hurt. Boxer got him with the tip of the blade. The knife sliced a five-inch gash in his side.

Sam whistled. "Just a scratch, huh?" She opened her mike bag. "After I clean your cut, we'll see how many stitches you need."

"How can I help?" Mercy asked Sam.

"Go into my bathroom for a washcloth and towel. There's a metal bowl in there, too. Fill it with warm water and bring everything to me."

As she hurried away, Nico eyed Sam. "Are you giving her tasks to keep her busy?"

The medic shrugged. "I can take care of you without those things. It will be easier with them. Keeping her mind occupied is an added bonus. She'll crash soon. Mercy needs you taken care of before the adrenaline dump hits. She cares about you, Nico. I don't think she realizes how much." A pointed look from his teammate. "Don't hurt her."

When Mercy returned a minute later, she had the items Sam requested. Her teeth were chattering. Sam caught his eye and inclined her head toward Mercy.

"Sit with me, kitten." Nico brought her to the couch with him and wrapped his arm around her shoulders. "Remember when my teammates told you I don't like needles?"

She nodded.

"They weren't lying. I hate needles. You should hold me so I won't be afraid while Sam pokes and prods me." He twisted toward Mercy, leaving his injured side accessible for Sam, and urged the woman in his arms to lay her head against his shoulder.

He rubbed Mercy's back as her body processed the adrenaline coursing through her system from the alley attack and the race to safety.

When the body shakes and chattering teeth stilled, she sighed and buried her face against his neck. "I don't know how you and your teammates handle this all the time. Every time something like this happens, I fall apart."

He pressed a soft kiss to her temple as Sam cleaned his wound. His grip on Mercy's hair tightened as the antiseptic seeped into the injury and burned like fire. "Having the shakes is not falling apart. It's normal. My teammates and I react in different ways. You also have to remember we deal with the adrenaline rush every time we go on a mission."

"You're incredible," she whispered.

"Are you flirting with me, Ms. Powers?" he teased.

"I'm stating facts. I didn't see much because Trace left so fast, but I saw enough to know you are trained several cuts above a regular soldier." He felt her smile against his neck. "And at least two or three cuts above Aiden. I don't know what you were in the military, Nico, but I think Fortress sharpened and honed those skills to a level I never knew existed."

He nuzzled the side of her head, pleased with her assessment.

"Little stick," Sam murmured.

Mercy lifted her head and tried to moved away, but Nico held her still. "Stay, please."

She settled again.

"How is your shoulder?" he asked as Sam injected meds to numb his side.

"Aches. I'll take something for pain after I'm sure you're all right."

Nico glanced at Sam. "Check Mercy's shoulder while we wait for the meds to kick in."

"Good idea. Close your eyes, Nico. Mercy, let me look at the stitches."

Although he kept his eyes closed, Nico moved his hands to Mercy's waist. Sam would need to unbutton the shirt and tug it aside enough to check Mercy's shoulder.

After a moment, the medic said, "Looks good. I don't see evidence of a popped stitch. Here, take this pain reliever. If you're not too sore, we'll try leaving off the sling for a while tomorrow."

"Thank goodness. I hate this thing." Clothing rustled, then Mercy settled against Nico again. "You can open your eyes now."

He looked at Sam again, his eyebrow raised in silent question. The medic gave him a short nod. Good. At least he didn't have to worry that he'd hurt Mercy when he shoved her toward the SUV.

Sam examined Nico's side again. "Tell me if you can feel this." She pinched his side.

"Pressure. No pain."

"Hold onto your girl, Nico. She looks like she could fall asleep." A grin. "Maybe she thinks you're boring."

Mercy laughed. "Bite your tongue, Sam. I'm not in the market for more excitement at the moment."

"Spoilsport," Nico murmured. "I'd planned to take you skydiving tomorrow. Liven up your life."

"Never in this lifetime, Nico Rivera. There is no reason to jump out of a perfectly good airplane."

"What do you like to do on dates?"

Mercy's body jerked. "Dates?"

"Yeah, dinner, movies. Dates."

"I don't know. I haven't dated in six years."

"More proof the men in Kentucky are idiots not to have asked you out. Think about what you'd like to do on our first date."

She raised her head. "You're asking me out?"

He traced her the outline of her lips with his fingertip. "Are you going to reject me in front of Sam? She's ruthless when she has blackmail material."

Sam snorted and kept working.

"We live in two different states."

"Not at the moment."

"What about when the danger is over and I return to Kentucky?"

"There's this amazing thing called the interstate system that connects Tennessee to Kentucky. You live four hours from Nashville."

"How do you know that?"

"I checked when you were asleep. I can drive to Sherwood when we're not deployed or on rotation." Not as often as he'd like, but he'd make the most of his time with Mercy if she would give him a chance.

"Long distance relationships are hard."

"You made one work for years. Shadow isn't deployed for a year at a time, unlike the military. Plus, we're due for a break. Once you're safe, I want to spend time with you."

She sighed. "I have baggage."

"Who doesn't? Unpack yours. I'll unpack mine, and we'll put away the suitcases."

Sam sat back and ripped off her gloves. "Finished." She dug into the mike bag, pulled out two packets, and pressed them into Nico's hand. "You know the drill. Take the antibiotics until they're gone. Two a day. Mild pain killers as you need them. I'm going to the kitchen for coffee." She left the suite without a backward glance.

Nico shoved the pills into his pocket and cupped Mercy's nape. "What do you say? Will you take a chance on me?"

CHAPTER NINETEEN

Mercy stared into Nico's dark eyes, astonished at his words. He wanted to date her? She felt guilty for even contemplating agreeing to his request. But her husband had been gone for two years, and Aiden would tell her to go for it if Nico was a good man. He hadn't wanted her to mourn him and be alone the rest of her life if he lost his life in combat.

She and her husband had talked about her possible future without him before they married. Aiden's job had been dangerous, and he was deployed in hotspots around the world. The possibility of Aiden dying was one Mercy had faced before their wedding day. He returned from deployment with a bullet wound to his side the day before the ceremony. Rather than waste time regretting his loss following his death, Mercy had given thanks for every day they'd shared. Her only regret was not having started a family with him before he was killed. Another phase in their lives she and Aiden had looked forward to before he'd been taken from her too soon.

And now Nico was asking her to risk her heart again with someone whose job was more dangerous than Aiden's. If she agreed, the relationship wouldn't be friends going on a date now and again for fun. Mercy wasn't built that way. "I don't do casual dating, Nico," she warned him. "For me, dating has a deeper purpose."

Tenderness filled his gaze. He pressed a soft kiss to her lips. "I feel the same. Take a chance on us. I know this is fast. I don't know what's happening between us, but I want the opportunity to find out."

Did she dare? She wanted to fling aside caution and leap into the void. Although her brain screamed to choose caution over courage, Mercy's heart reminded her of the joy she'd shared with Aiden, a joy that made all the sorrow worthwhile. If she chose to walk away from Nico, she might lose an unexpected gift.

"I'm not ashamed to beg, Mercy. I need you in my life to balance out the darkness."

At his words, her heart melted. Mercy wrapped her arm around his neck and captured his lips with hers. She let the heat take them under. When she managed to ease away from him, Mercy knew what she needed to do. "Yes."

Relief flooded his face as he wrapped his arms around her. "Thank God. You won't regret trusting me, kitten. I swear it."

"Long-distance relationships are a lot of work. You may regret this."

"Never. You are worth the effort." The operative grinned at her, happiness gleaming in his eyes. "I'm going to enjoy romancing you, Mercy Powers."

After another lingering kiss, Nico released her and stood. "I'll grab a clean shirt and we'll join the others in the kitchen." He helped Mercy to her feet and led her to his room.

Along the way, Mercy had a good view of his back. A maze of scars marred the broad surface. An accident? She studied the lines across his beautiful skin as they walked toward his room.

No, not an accident. The lines were too symmetrical. A knife had caused the injuries and from the look of the scars, the damage had been done in the recent past.

A year ago? Mercy's heart ached at what Nico had suffered to protect those children.

Nico turned on the light in his room and walked to his bag with her hand still clasped in his. He let go to grab another black t-shirt. When he started to shrug on the shirt, Mercy laid her hand on his back.

Nico froze, then slowly lowered his hands and stood still while she trailed her fingertips over the scars. "I'm sorry," he said, his voice thick. "I forgot."

"Shh." Mercy replaced her hand with her lips and brushed kisses along the raised ridges. By the time she finished the task, Nico's muscles twitched at every touch. "From your cave experience?"

He nodded.

"Those children are alive because of what you endured." She pressed another kiss to the middle of his back and circled to stand in front of him. She took the shirt from his hands and reached up to kiss him.

Nico tugged her against his chest, his grip tight, and gave her a fevered kiss. When he broke the kiss, he eased back to stare into her eyes. "Do the scars bother you?"

"Knowing you suffered bothers me." She shrugged one shoulder. "I suppose I'll have a scar from the bullet. You called my wounds a sign of bravery. I see yours the same way."

Nico closed his eyes briefly, then stepped back and yanked on his shirt. "We have to get out of this room. My self-control is almost gone, and you deserve honor and respect from me."

She followed him to the kitchen in silence. The buzz of conversation dropped off as they walked into the room, and Shadow turned as one to eye them.

"Well?" Sam asked Nico.

"Well what?" He frowned.

"You know what." Trace scowled. "Don't keep us in suspense."

Joe shook his head. "Open your eyes. The answer is all over his face."

Nico rolled his eyes, then turned to Mercy. "You aren't allowed to change your mind because of my nosy teammates."

"Wouldn't dream of it."

He raised her hand to his lips and kissed her palm before facing his teammates. "She said yes."

A cheer went up from the men of Shadow. Sam leaped up from her seat and embraced Mercy. "Congratulations," she whispered. "I'm happy for you and Nico."

Over her shoulder, Mercy caught the longing on Joe's face as he watched Sam before he noticed her watching him and blanked his expression. Oh, yes, that operative was nuts about the pretty medic.

"I'll make the coffee," Ben said. "Who has first watch?"

"I do," Nico said. When his teammates just stared at him, he said, "I'm too revved to sleep, not to mention the million stitches Sam put in my side ache like a bad tooth."

"Fifteen," the medic corrected as she returned to her seat beside Joe. "I gave you pain killers to dull the ache. Quit whining and take them."

"Brat." His voice held no heat.

"I'll take the first watch with Nico." Trace stood and stretched. "Give me a few minutes to shower and the rest of you can scatter." He left the room.

"Anyone hungry?" Ben measured the coffee grounds. "I found the makings for sandwiches in the refrigerator. That will do for a quick meal tonight."

"I could eat." Joe rose and opened the refrigerator door. He peered inside, then grabbed several items and dumped them on the counter. He made a return trip, this time for soft drinks and water.

Mercy found bags of chips and carried them to the breakfast bar. "Sam, the plates are in the cabinet beside the stove. Nico, there are condiments in the refrigerator. Let's put everything on the breakfast bar and we can serve ourselves."

"Are you going to eat?" Nico asked.

"Not a chance. I'll make myself a cup of tea for now." When he looked concerned, Mercy laid a hand over his heart. "You said each of us processes adrenaline differently. I'm not a stress eater. I'll eat when I'm ready. Besides, you fed me very well at the hotel. I'll be fine even if I can't eat until tomorrow morning."

Once Shadow finished their meals, all of them scattered except Trace. He and Nico helped Mercy put away the sandwich material.

When the kitchen was cleaned, Trace turned to Nico. "You want the security room or the rounds?"

"Rounds for the first half, then the security room after Sam's meds kick in."

Nico's friend grinned. "Copy that." He headed for the security room.

Nico tucked a strand of Mercy's hair behind her ear. "Are you ready to turn in?"

"Not yet. I can go to my room if I'll distract you."

He chuckled. "You will always be a distraction I enjoy." His smile faded. "You said you saw a distinguished looking man in Hector's compound. Did you get a good enough look to draw his face?"

"Maybe."

"You mentioned wanting to draw again. Would you try to draw this man? I don't know if he's important, but it gives us another strand to tug and might lead to the answers we need to protect you."

Finally, something she could do to help end this nightmare. "I'll do my best."

"Excellent." He dropped a quick kiss on her lips. "I need to check outside. Where will you be able to sketch best?"

"Living room. I'm always more productive when I'm comfortable and relaxed."

A nod. "I'll see you in a few minutes."

Mercy went to the office and grabbed the pad of paper and a handful of pens. In the living room, she chose the couch. The cushioned back was comfortable for her shoulder and the lighting was good.

Before she started, Mercy closed her eyes and went back in her mind to the night of her kidnapping. Ignoring all the ugly things Hector had threatened, she concentrated on bringing the mysterious man's face into focus.

With the details in her mind, Mercy opened her eyes, selected a black pen, and began to draw.

CHAPTER TWENTY

Nico walked a circuit around the house and grounds, looking for signs of intrusion. When he was satisfied nothing had been tampered with and no one was waiting to launch an attack, he returned to the cabin and stood in the doorway to the living room, watching Mercy.

His heart turned over in his chest to see the beautiful woman working on the picture Nico asked her to draw. He couldn't quite get a grip on the fact Mercy had agreed to see where their attraction went. He was half afraid she would wise up and kick him to the curb.

Of all people, he knew exactly what a bad risk he was for a woman. His job was secure and he made a good living. Maddox saw to that for all his operatives. However, job security and money didn't make up for the fact his job was hazardous. Every mission could end with his death.

Mercy thought he was some kind of hero. Nico grimaced. He was a finely-honed weapon Fortress aimed at the enemy. No, the true hero in this situation was Mercy. She was the one putting her heart on the line with a man engaged in a risky career. If he died on a mission, Mercy would lose everything. Again.

Mercy was the one with a lion's courage, not Nico. He didn't know if he would have had the strength to take a chance on loving someone again after a devastating loss.

Nico backed away in silence and left her to work while he checked in with Zane and Trace. Shadow's sniper turned when Nico entered the security room. "Did Mercy go to bed?"

He dropped into a chair beside his friend. "She's working on a sketch of the man she saw in Hector's compound." He inclined his head toward the screens. "See anything out of the ordinary?"

Trace shook his head. "Makes me uneasy."

Nico scanned the screens. "Maybe we got away clean."

"Maybe."

If they didn't, why were the people after Mercy holding back? Perhaps they thought a delay would encourage Shadow to relax their guard. Unfortunately for her attackers, Nico had a personal stake in Mercy's safety, and that made him more dangerous than ever. Mercy was his to protect. To him, no price was too high to keep her out of Scorpion's hands.

A frown. If the gunrunners were the ones still pursuing Mercy. His teammates were right. The Scorpions should have moved on to the next easiest target to free their boss. Yeah, she was an HVT, but she wouldn't command much leverage unless the gang of criminals knew how close she was to President Martin and his family.

The handiwork of the ATF traitor? The law enforcement community had access to information about Mercy. Nico still wasn't satisfied with that conclusion. He shared his musings with Trace.

"She's important to Martin, but Mercy also brings a ton of trouble. She has a team of elite bodyguards protecting her with more a phone call away. Looking at it from that standpoint, she's too much trouble for them to continue the pursuit unless there is another, more compelling reason to target her."

Nico pulled out his phone and called Zane before he glanced at the time. He winced.

"Yeah, Murphy."

"It's Nico. Sorry, man. I didn't look at the time."

"No problem. How is Mercy?"

Didn't figure the tech guru wanted to know Nico believed Mercy Powers was the most beautiful woman on the planet. "Safe for the moment. We had some trouble at the hotel."

"I gathered that from the number of ID requests I received from your team. What happened?"

He gave Zane the short version of events. "Any hits on their prints?"

"I just sent the results of my search to your email. The men are associated with the Scorpions. I'm sure you won't be surprised to learn their last known location was in Mexico. No record of them having crossed the border into US territory."

Nico scowled. "The Scorpions are too persistent."

"Yeah, Maddox thought the same. He's expecting your call."

"As soon as our conversation is finished."

"Any injuries?"

"One of the clowns got in a lucky swipe with his knife."

"How bad?"

"Fifteen stitches in my side." He figured he might as well tell Zane the truth because his friend would ask who was injured. "I need a favor."

"Name it."

"Send an operative to the safe house to pick up a sample of the coffee the bellhop delivered for Mercy. Call the lab and expedite the analysis. I need to know if the contents contained anything besides coffee. If it did, I want to know if the cops held him or if he's been released from their custody. I also need a location on the two clowns who attacked us in the alley behind the hotel."

"Copy that."

"One more thing, Z. Mercy is working on a sketch of a man she saw in the Scorpion compound. This guy wasn't one of Hector's flunkies. If she's able to complete the sketch, I'll send a copy to run against facial recognition."

"I'll see what I can find out and send the results to your email. Let me know if you need anything else."

Trace got to his feet. "I need to walk for a bit. I'll run the next round of security sweeps while you watch the screens."

Once Trace returned, Nico would check the email from Zane and see who Shadow had dealt with at the hotel. He scanned the monitors, paused when he noticed a shadow moving in the fourth quadrant. He relaxed again when the shadow morphed into a deer foraging for food in the woods surrounding the cabin. Good thing Joe wasn't awake or he'd be plotting the demise of the 12-point buck.

A moment later, he received a text from Zane. Jon Smith was on his way to pick up the vial of coffee and would deliver it to the 24-hour lab Fortress used for analyzing substances.

When Trace returned to the security room, he brought two mugs full of coffee with him. "Thought you could use this. Have you taken the pain meds yet?"

Nico just stared at his friend who smirked.

"Didn't think so. Suck it up, Patch. You'll be more maneuverable if you aren't hurting as bad."

"I can handle it," he griped despite a slight curve of his lips from Trace's use of Nico's military nickname.

"You'll handle the pain better with help." His friend sent him a pointed look. "You're grumpy when you're hurt, man. We don't deserve your attitude and neither does your woman."

That last statement made Nico pause. "Yeah, all right." He didn't want Mercy to regret taking a leap into the unknown with him. Digging the pills out of his pocket, he popped an antibiotic and a pain pill after confirming by sight that the pain killer was mild. He didn't want to be sluggish in case a problem developed on his watch.

After two more security sweeps, Mercy walked in with her sketch pad.

Nico rose and went to her. "How did you do?"

"Take a look." She turned her pad around.

He and Trace examined the man she'd drawn.

"Nice," Trace said. "If this guy's face is anywhere on the Net, Z will get an ID on him from your drawing. I'm amazed you did this from a glimpse of a man you saw for maybe two or three seconds on a night you were afraid for your life."

"I remember faces. I guess it's part of my artistic nature."

"Lucky for us." Nico took the sketch pad to the office, scanned the drawing, and sent it to Zane's email, then sent his friend a text so he could start the process of running the man's likeness through the Fortress facial recognition program.

That done, he glanced at the clock and turned to the woman who had followed him into the office. "It's late. Let me walk you to your room. You need to rest."

"What about you?"

"I'll go to sleep in a couple hours." He didn't know how long he would sleep. Nico laced his fingers with Mercy's and escorted her to her bedroom.

He stepped just inside the door, circled her waist with his arms, and drew her close for a series of deep, drugging kisses. When Nico lifted his head, Mercy drew in a ragged breath.

"Wow."

Wow, indeed. His heart raced as though he'd just finished a ten-mile run. "Sleep well. I won't be far if you need me." He brushed the pad of his thumb over her lips and forced himself to release Mercy and walk from the room.

On the first floor, he took a moment to refocus his mind on protection rather than the woman who was fast worming her way into his heart. He returned to the security room and Trace. "I need to report to Maddox."

His friend rose. "I'll take the next circuit outside."

Nico dropped into the chair at the computer console and grabbed his phone. A moment later a gruff voice answered.

"Maddox."

"It's Nico."

"Sit rep."

He brought his boss up to date, ending with the news about the detailed sketch Mercy had put together of the stranger she'd seen in the compound.

"Excellent. I'll touch base with Zane in a few hours to see what progress he's made. Has Jon arrived yet?"

A black SUV slowly drove up the drive to the cabin at that moment. A few keystrokes brought the driver into focus as he exited the vehicle along with his companion. "He just pulled up with Eli."

"Keep me posted." Maddox ended the call.

Nico went to open the door for the two operatives. He waved them inside. "Didn't expect both of you to serve as courier."

Jon and Eli followed him into the kitchen and accepted the mugs of coffee he poured for them.

"Got to keep Jon in line," Eli said with a smile.

"How are Brenna and Dana?"

Jon's lips curved. "More beautiful than ever."

Nico stared at the legendary sniper. "I don't think I've seen you smile. Ever."

A snort from Eli. "All you have to do is mention Dana and he loses that sniper ice. He's nuts about his wife."

A cool look from his teammate. "You think anyone would believe you aren't as crazy about Brenna?"

Eli grinned and held up his hands in surrender.

Having made his point, Jon turned back to Nico. "Where's the package?"

He handed over the vial of brown liquid. "Coffee with a possible additive. The man who brought it to the room was antsy and insisted on delivering the coffee to Mercy."

"Was he armed?" Eli asked.

Nico frowned. "Sig, knife, and a garrote."

"Get information from him?"

"ATF showed up too soon and called the Murfreesboro PD."

"Too bad," Jon murmured.

Trace walked into the kitchen. "Jon, Eli." He poured the last of the coffee into a mug and found the supplies to make another pot. "Hungry?"

Eli shook his head. "We had a late dinner with Brenna and Dana. Need a hand tonight?"

Nico studied the SEAL. "You know something I don't?"

"You haven't had a chance to check your email yet, have you?"

"I was getting ready to do that when you arrived. Give me the quick version."

"The three men you encountered at the hotel are associated with Scorpion, and the bounty on Mercy has doubled."

CHAPTER TWENTY-ONE

A ball of ice formed in Nico's stomach. "What does she know worth $4 million?" He looked at Trace. "I left the sketch in the office. Maybe Jon and Eli know the man Mercy saw at the compound."

Jon frowned as the other sniper left the room. "Mercy drew this guy's face?"

"She's an artist. Ever heard of MJ Powers?"

Eli's eyes widened. "Who hasn't? Mercy is MJ, huh? Brenna loves her art."

"Dana, too." Jon set his empty mug on the counter.

Trace returned and handed the sketch to Eli. He and his teammate studied the paper a moment.

"Is that who I think it is?" Eli looked at Jon.

"Sure looks like it."

"Care to enlighten us?" Nico stared at the two operatives, his pulse racing at the prospect of a new direction to focus his search.

"Dwayne Jeffries." Eli handed the sketch to Nico.

He stared at the drawing. "Should I know him?"

"Only if you follow politics."

"He's the father of Senator Sean Jeffries."

Nico's head snapped upward. "Doesn't he head the Intelligence Committee?"

"That's the one." Jon leaned against the counter, arms folded across his chest. "The senator has a lot of power on Capitol Hill. He's one of those men who have a captive audience every time he speaks."

A power broker with influence. Was this man or his father the one offering the bounty on Mercy? "They come from money?"

"Dwayne founded Jeffries Industries. The company's net worth tops thirty billion. An import/export company with ties to almost every country on the planet."

"What do they specialize in?" Trace asked.

"Sporting equipment, including weapons for hunting." Eli set aside his mug.

"Guess the Jeffries wouldn't have a problem offering $4 million for Mercy."

"Chump change for them." Jon slid the vial of coffee into a pocket of his cargoes and glanced at Eli. "You staying?"

"I'll give them a hand." He grinned at his friend. "Tell Dana I said hello."

Jon's cheeks turned red as he pivoted and left the cabin.

"You're sure he's going to Dana?" Trace asked.

"He's breathing, isn't he? He'll detour by my house to check on the girls on the way back here. Nico, do you want me to take over your shift?"

Nico turned to Trace, noted his friend's fatigue. "Trace, go sleep."

A scowl from the sniper. "You're the one with new stitches in his side."

"Stitches?" Eli asked.

"Courtesy of thugs in the alley behind the hotel. Go, Trace. I won't be sleeping for a while anyway. I need to review the files Zane sent." And now he had more research to do on the senator and his father.

Trace clapped Eli on the shoulder and left.

"Time for another security sweep." Nico dumped his coffee mug into the dishwasher and grabbed a bottle of water. "You want the sweep or the monitors?"

"I'll take the tour outside. How bad is your injury?"

"Surface. Tip of the knife caught me."

"I'll be back."

Nico returned to the security room and studied the monitors. No change from the view fifteen minutes earlier and the motion sensors hadn't gone off. When Eli walked into the room to take over surveillance, Nico booted up his laptop and checked his email.

He brought up the file Zane sent. Nico finished reading the file by the time he needed to complete another security sweep. As he searched for signs of intruders, he processed the information he'd learned. All three men were losers. Multiple convictions and jail sentences here and in Mexico. The men were part of a gang while they were growing up in San Antonio, Texas, in and out of juvie with offenses ranging from drug and weapons possession to pimping kids and teens younger than themselves.

Nico's lip curled in disgust. Real princes, these guys. With their track record, he was surprised they survived to adulthood. Plenty of their friends didn't. The Scorpions swept into their area of Texas about the time these bozos got out of prison and tried to hook up with their gang. Turned out their territory had been taken over by the Scorpions.

They switched their allegiance to the new group and worked their way through the ranks. They were still bottom feeders except for Boxer who was a mid-level thug named Holden Tate.

So why had Holden allowed Bellhop to go after Mercy when he was obviously ill-suited to the task? His nervousness would have made Nico and his teammates suspicious even without the knowledge they hadn't asked for more room service.

He thought again of the poorly fitting bellhop uniform. Maybe Holden and the other alley thug couldn't fit into the uniform. When he returned to the cabin, Jon sat in the security room with Eli.

The SEALs turned. "We've got the watch if you want to sleep," Jon said. "Tell the rest of Shadow they're off duty until six. Sleep while you have the chance, Nico."

"If something happens, wake me."

"Count on it," Eli said.

Nico collected his laptop and water, and trudged upstairs to his room. Much as he hated to admit it, he was tired. Two hours of sleep the night before on top of short nights while Mercy was in Bayside and no sleep the night of the rescue plus months of unrelenting missions dealing with the dregs of society weighed on him. After Mercy was safe, Nico would insist Shadow be off mission rotation for at least a month. Otherwise, he and his team would skate too close to burnout.

He paused outside Mercy's room. She'd left the door open a crack. The compulsion to peek in and be sure she was resting well was too strong to resist. He nudged the door open a few more inches and looked in on her.

Mercy slept on her side, covers tossed aside and rumpled as though she had trouble sleeping. She was also fully dressed except for the shoes. Smart lady. Hopefully, that precaution would be unnecessary.

Satisfied she was safe and resting, he entered his room and dropped off his laptop and water before informing his teammates they were off duty. When he finally laid down to sleep, he dropped off in seconds.

His cell phone rang three hours later. Nico glanced at the screen and sat up. Only one person called him from a blocked number. The news couldn't be good or the information would wait until a normal hour. "Mr. President."

"I apologize for calling so early," William Martin said, his voice a deep rumble. "How is my niece?"

"She's recovering well. She's losing the sling today, something that makes her happy."

The president chuckled. "I can imagine."

"What's wrong, sir?"

"Am I that transparent, Nico?"

"Doesn't take transparency to know something is wrong when you call at three in the morning. Are Charlotte and her family safe?"

"They're fine. I'm afraid this problem concerns Mercy."

When the president fell silent, Nico swung his legs over the side of the bed and stood. "Talk to me, sir."

"The Senate Intelligence Committee wants Mercy to testify about her experience in Mexico."

Every muscle in Nico's body bunched, readying for a fight. "With respect, sir, I'm not taking Mercy to Washington, D.C. She's still a target for the Scorpions."

"Care to explain that?"

Nico summarized what happened at the hotel. He didn't want to give too many specifics, just enough to convince the most powerful man on earth that his niece would be in greater jeopardy if she was brought out into the open to testify before a senate committee.

"No injuries?"

"A minor one to an operative. Mercy sustained no new injuries. Mr. President, there's another reason I don't want to bring Mercy before that particular committee. Your niece saw a man in the Scorpion compound and was able to draw a picture of him. Sir, we think the man is Dwayne Jeffries."

Martin was silent a moment. "Are you sure?"

"Near one hundred percent. Senator Jeffries being the head of the Intelligence Committee raises red flags for me."

"I understand. I can't set wheels in motion until I have a positive link between the Scorpions and Senator Jeffries. I can have law enforcement keep an eye on Dwayne."

"No offense, sir, but there's a leak in the law enforcement community, and D.C. leaks information like a sieve. I'd rather task Fortress with surveillance."

"Very well. Look, Nico, I'll see what I can do to divert attention from Mercy and delay them as long as possible, but I have to tell you I think we'll only delay the inevitable. You and your team need to prepare for a trip to Washington. Do whatever you have to do to keep my niece safe."

Nico dropped his phone on the bed and scrubbed his face. He'd wait until after six to call his boss. Maybe Maddox could call in a favor and kill this committee appearance or at least delay it until the danger to Mercy ended. Doubtful, but it was worth a try.

Knowing he wouldn't be able to sleep now, Nico rose and readied himself for the day. Fifteen minutes later, he entered the security room.

Jon frowned at him. "Do we need to knock you over the head, Rivera? You're off duty for another three hours."

"Wasn't my idea to wake this early. The president called me."

Eli turned. "What's up?"

"Senate Intelligence Committee wants to talk to Mercy."

The SEALs groaned. "No such thing as coincidence in our business." Jon rose and stretched. "What are you going to do?"

"I asked Martin to delay or derail it. While he's exploring that possibility, I'll talk to Maddox, see if he'll call in a favor. I don't want to take Mercy into the lion's den."

The sniper watched him for a moment. "Your stance is about more than protecting your principal."

Yeah, Jon Smith was one observant man. "She's mine."

Eli lounged back in this chair, arms folded across his chest. "Does she know that?"

"She agreed to give us a chance." And he would do his best to see she didn't regret her choice.

A slow nod from Jon. "What can we do to help safeguard your woman?"

"Get me the schematics for Capitol Hill and the surrounding area." If he had to take Mercy to Washington, he wanted as much information as possible, and Jon was the perfect man for the job. In addition to being a top-notch sniper, he also rivaled Zane in computer skills. "I also need a safe place for Mercy to stay."

"I'll take care of it." He glanced at Eli in a wordless communication. When his teammate nodded, Jon turned back to Nico. "You'll need more than Shadow to provide protection in D.C. We're in."

"Shadow can handle it."

"You'll handle it easier with two more operatives at your disposal." Eli sipped his coffee. "Might as well give in, Nico."

He couldn't deny a sense of relief at knowing the two SEALs would be available. Aside from his own team, these two men were among the first operatives he would call upon for backup on any mission. "Thanks."

He just hoped the extra precaution was unnecessary.

CHAPTER TWENTY-TWO

Mercy walked down the hall, frowning when she noticed the rooms occupied by Shadow were empty. Something must have happened overnight, but Nico didn't wake her.

Anxious to find out what was going on, she descended the stairs in a hurry and followed the rumble of voices to the kitchen. When she walked into the room, the operatives fell silent. Nico turned from the coffee pot.

Her heart skipped a beat at the sight of him. He was armed with a handgun and Ka-Bar. And probably more weapons she couldn't see. The other members of his team as well as the two SEALs were also in full gear. The only thing missing was body armor.

Mercy faced Nico. "What happened?"

He grabbed a to-go cup and held out his hand. "Come with me."

Oh, boy. Whatever happened must have been bad. She clasped his hand and allowed him to lead her outside to the patio where he had already placed a blanket.

"Sit with me for a few minutes." He urged her toward the outdoor couch, pressed the to-go cup into Mercy's hand, and draped the blanket over her lap. "I thought you might like a hot drink this morning."

With her stomach in a knot, she couldn't keep coffee down. "I'm not sure I can handle coffee."

He smiled. "Guess it's a good thing I made you green tea with mint. Drink a little, then we'll talk."

They sat in silence as the sun started to make an appearance in the sky. When Mercy finished the tea and set the cup aside, she turned to face Nico. "Are you and the others okay?"

He captured her lips in a soft, lingering caress. "We're fine. We didn't have unwanted visitors last night."

"But something did happen. You're all armed to the teeth."

Nico eased back. "Do the weapons bother you?"

"Of course not. Aiden always carried a weapon as do my brothers and father. Tell me what's going on, Nico. I don't want secrets between us unless it's necessary because of national security or job secrecy. In this case, you and your teammates are my protection detail. I want to know everything."

"Fair enough. I showed your sketch to Jon and Eli last night after you went to bed. They identified the man you saw in Hector's compound as Dwayne Jeffries. Does that name sound familiar?"

Puzzled, she frowned. "He's Sean Jeffries' father. What was he doing in Mexico?"

"We don't know yet. Do you know the Jeffries?"

"I know Sean, but I never met his father."

"How well do you know the senator?"

"He took me to dinner a couple times."

Nico narrowed his eyes.

"Don't give me that look. Sean likes my art, nothing more. He commissioned me to draw a series of portraits depicting the evolution of the Jeffries estate. It's been in their family for more than one hundred years, and he thought his father would appreciate the pictures. He commissioned them for his father's birthday."

"And you never saw the senior Jeffries?"

She shook her head. "If his father met me, he would have known something was up. He has several of my drawings in his office at Jeffries Industries and I'm not in their social circle. Sean wants the drawings to be a surprise."

His expression darkened with her use of Sean's first name. Amused at his territorial attitude, she threaded her fingers through his. "Sean's a friend. I'm not interested in him, Nico. He's not a buff, tough-as-nails black ops warrior who makes my heart race."

Nico's eyes lit. "Glad to hear that. Did you hear Hector or his buddies mention Jeffries' name?"

"No. They were more interested in intimidating me and tossing me back in the cave to wait for the next interrogation session. I don't understand what Sean's father was doing in Hector's compound."

"That's a very interesting question and may be the key to why you're so valuable to the Scorpions."

She studied him a moment. Her heart sank when she realized there was more. "What else do you have to tell me?"

"You're sure I have more information?"

Mercy cupped his cheek. "Nico, I can handle it." She would rather know the truth than be kept in the dark.

He pressed a kiss on her palm. "The Senate Intelligence Committee wants you to testify at a hearing."

"In Washington, D.C." No wonder he and his team looked grim. "You don't want me to go?" Even thinking about telling a room full of strangers plus the rest of her protection detail about Hector and his threats made Mercy feel sick. Talking about her ordeal with Marcus Lang and Nico had been traumatic enough.

"Not in a million years. First, the Scorpions are burning up the Internet, looking for any clue to where you're hiding. Zane said his bots have picked up more than one hundred inquiries about your location. Second, protecting you will be much harder in D.C. The media is bound to find out you're in town and why. The hearing itself will probably be closed, but that doesn't keep the newsies from splashing your face all over the evening news. I'd rather keep you here where we have total control of the situation."

"If the news media exposes the fact I'm in town, the Scorpions will know where to find me. That makes your job harder."

"They'll have a specific city to search instead of the middle Tennessee area. I don't like this scenario."

"Can I refuse to testify?"

Nico shook his head. "They'll issue a subpoena. Your buddy Sean Jeffries is the head of the Intelligence Committee."

Oh, boy. Even more reason to avoid the hearing as long as possible. "That could be a coincidence." Mercy could tell from his expression that Nico wasn't buying her explanation. "How long before we have to go?"

"Not sure. Your uncle will try to buy us some time and Maddox is calling in favors. The intervention won't be enough to deter the committee."

If she had her cell phone, Mercy could call Sean and try to delay the inevitable further. Maybe Zane could help. "Would Zane talk to me?"

"Sure. What do you need?"

"A phone number."

Nico made a call and placed the phone on speaker.

"Yeah, Murphy."

"It's Nico. You're on speaker with Mercy. She needs a favor."

"What do you need, Mercy?"

"A phone number."

"Sounds easy enough. Who do you want to talk to?"

"Senator Sean Jeffries."

Silence greeted her statement.

"I have his personal number in my cell phone, but I don't have any idea where my purse ended up in Mexico. I want to talk to him about delaying the hearing."

"Hold." The sound of keys clicking drifted through the speaker. "Nico, I'll text the number to your phone. Anything else I can do for you?"

"Alert Maddox that Jon and Eli volunteered to join Mercy's protection detail when we go to D.C."

"Copy that. Will you be in Nashville today or should I have an operative deliver a cell phone for Mercy to the safe house?"

He looked at Mercy, his eyebrow raised. "Your choice, kitten."

"Is it safe if we leave the cabin?"

"We'll make sure you are. You're not a prisoner. I don't want you in a crowded space that we can't control like a restaurant. You'll be safe at Fortress headquarters."

"I need a few more clothes, especially if I have to appear before the committee soon."

With a nod, he said, "We'll be at Fortress by ten o'clock, Z."

"I'll have the phone and a few other things ready for Mercy." Zane ended the call.

"How long will I be able to borrow the phone?"

"It's yours to keep as long as we're in a relationship. The phone is encrypted so we can communicate without fear of someone hacking into the system." He draped his arm across her shoulders. "That also means I'll be able to text or talk to you while I'm deployed."

Mercy couldn't deny the relief she felt at having the ability to connect with Nico while he was gone. She would have enjoyed that convenience with Aiden. "Your boss won't mind me having the phone?"

"Immediate families of operatives have these cell phones. Maddox knows if the operatives aren't worried about what's happening at home, they're more likely to complete the mission and come home safe."

"I wish the military did something like that for troops."

"My mother would have enjoyed being able to talk to me more often. You mentioned needing more clothes. How many stores are we talking about?"

"One if you choose a department store. Should take me less than an hour. I'm easy to please."

He turned. "In clothes or everything?"

She thought about that for a moment. "Everything. I'm not high maintenance and simple things make me happy. What about you?"

"Same. I prefer to stay at home rather than go out. Too many people make me uncomfortable."

Mercy smiled. "I'm not a fan of crowds, either. I'm a homebody."

"Were you a homebody when you and Aiden were married?"

The sweet memories of their backyard barbeques and holiday parties with two or three of their friends flooded her. Her husband hadn't like being in crowds. "Aiden had PTSD. When he was home from deployment, home was his safe place. He spent as much time as he could at home. He told me he was storing up the memories for when he was overseas."

Nico nodded. "I do the same thing when I go home to see my family." He stood and held out his hand. "Come on. You need to eat. After that, I'll make plans with my team for the trip to headquarters and one of the local malls."

They walked into the kitchen to find Eli had taken over kitchen duty. He glanced over his shoulder. "Hope you like omelets because that's what we're eating."

"Love them," Nico said. "I thought you and Jon needed to leave first thing this morning."

"The girls are going out for breakfast. After we finish here, we'll head home to sleep."

Nico's cell phone signaled an incoming text. He looked at the screen. "Zane came through, Mercy. You can call Senator Jeffries after you eat."

All the operatives turned to stare at Nico and Mercy. "He commissioned her to do an art job a few weeks ago. Mercy is going to ask for a delay on the hearing."

"Good luck with that," Jon murmured. "I hear he doesn't accommodate anyone but himself."

She sat on a barstool since she didn't need to oversee breakfast preparations. "You're right. I'm hoping he'll make an exception."

"Why would he do that for you?" Sam asked.

"He owes me a favor."

Silence greeted her statement.

Nico climbed onto the stool beside Mercy's and explained the connection between her and the senator and his father.

Trace frowned. "You never saw Dwayne?"

Mercy shook her head. "He travels extensively for the company."

"Who was at the estate when you were there?"

"Several people. Sean doesn't go anywhere without an entourage."

"Did you recognize any of them?" Joe asked.

"To be honest, I didn't pay attention. I was more concerned about taking photographs of the house and grounds."

Jon set down his coffee mug with a thud. "You have photographs?"

"That's how I work. I take many pictures and form a composite shot in my head that I draw."

"What are you thinking, Jon?" Eli asked.

"Might be a worth taking a look at the pictures. Mercy, where are they?"

She already knew where this was going and didn't like it one bit. "The memory card is in a fireproof safe at my house in Kentucky."

Nico rubbed his jaw, looking resigned. "Guess we're going on a road trip."

CHAPTER TWENTY-THREE

"A trip to Sherwood might be a total waste of time." Mercy twisted in the front seat of the SUV to stare at Nico. They were parked in the underground garage at Fortress headquarters. The rest of Shadow had gone into the building. "There must be some other avenue to explore that would be more productive."

"It's worth the four-hour drive to find out." He wrapped his hand around hers and squeezed. "We won't know for sure until we look at your shots of the Jeffries estate."

"I don't want to go home, Nico." Couldn't he see how dangerous this was? What if one of Shadow was hurt? What if Nico was hurt again?

"We have to track down every lead, even ones that seem improbable, to find the person responsible for the bounty on your head and end the danger to you."

"I'm afraid the price is too high." She stared out the windshield, troubled and afraid.

"Mercy, look at me." When she did, Nico lifted her hand to his mouth and kissed her fingers. "This is what we do, and we're good at it. If the two of us have any chance to make this relationship work, you must trust me."

"I have since the moment I laid eyes on you in Mexico." That didn't alleviate the horrible fear something terrible would happen to Nico and the others because of her.

"Then know this. I won't take unnecessary chances with my own life or my teammates' lives." He leaned over the console and captured her mouth in a blazing display of passion and possessiveness. "I'm not Aiden, kitten, and I have an excellent reason to stay alive. You." Without giving her a chance to reply, he opened the driver's door and came around to help her from the vehicle.

She remained silent during the walk through the cavernous garage and the elevator ride to the third floor. Was Nico right? Could her near panicked state at the prospect of him facing danger be connected to her losing Aiden?

Mercy blew out a breath, frustrated with herself. She'd warned Nico she had baggage. Looked like she should have reminded herself of that fact. Even if she walked away from the relationship before giving it a chance, Mercy couldn't protect Nico from harm. He would never abandon her now. He wasn't built that way and neither were his friends. Might as well face up to the truth that she had no control over this situation.

Worse, if she didn't want to lose a chance at a special relationship with an amazing man, she had to find a way to accept who and what he was. And that's when she realized she wanted a deeper relationship with Nico Rivera. As improbable as it seemed, she was utterly fascinated by him and the prospect of walking away from him now left her feeling hollow inside.

Nico threaded his fingers through hers as they left the elevator and walked to a communications center. A broad-shouldered dark-haired man in a wheelchair turned at their entrance to the room.

"Nico, good to see you. Who's the pretty lady?"

"Zane, meet Mercy Powers. Mercy, our tech wizard and communications genius, Zane Murphy."

Nico's friend smiled and held out his hand to shake hers. "How's the shoulder?"

"Better today. Thanks for taking care of the phone for me."

"Happy to do it." He wheeled across the room to a file cabinet and pulled out a black phone with a handful of cases. "Nico said you prefer simple things. I thought you might like this case." He handed her one with a beautiful cover of gradually deepening blue.

Her breath caught as she trailed her fingers over the waterfall of color. "It's gorgeous. This is perfect. Why is the cover so thick?"

"A protective barrier in the lining to prevent someone from scanning your phone and stealing information."

"Nico said the phone was encrypted."

"It is." He shrugged. "Technology is evolving all the time. Better to be safe than risk you or Nico. I've already programmed Nico's number in there as well as the rest of Shadow's numbers, mine, and Maddox's. If you need help, one of us will be available."

On impulse, she leaned down and kissed his cheek. "Thank you, Zane."

His cheeks flushed a deep red. "You're welcome." Zane looked at Nico. "Brent's waiting for you in the conference room. President Martin is due to call any time." He zoomed back to his console, grabbed a small box, and handed it to Nico. "In case you think Mercy needs these."

Nico propped open the lid, nodded once. "Thanks." He slid the box into his cargo pocket and turned to Mercy. "Come on. It's not wise to keep your uncle waiting."

He laid his hand on her lower back and guided Mercy to the opposite end of the hall to the conference room. Inside, a buzz-cut blond waited along with the rest of Nico's teammates.

Zane rolled in behind them and moved to the computer console.

"Just in time," Sam said. She indicated the coffee. "Want a cup?"

"I do." Nico seated Mercy before taking the coffee Sam poured for him. He dropped into the seat beside her. "Brent, this is Mercy Powers. Mercy, my boss, Brent Maddox."

Brent shook her hand. "Good to meet you, Ms. Powers."

"It's Mercy. Thank you for sending Nico and the others to rescue me."

"I'm glad I had a team available."

"Call coming in," Zane said.

"On screen." Maddox sat down and faced the wall.

The screen flickered and a moment later, Mercy's uncle appeared.

Although he looked tired, he smiled. "Mercy, you look good, sweetheart."

"Can't say the same for you. Another late night?"

He chuckled. "An early morning. I see your protection detail is present. My thanks to all of you for a job well done. I'm happy to say the Scorpions are rattled by the mysterious team who stole their valuable hostage in the middle of the night."

"They're searching for Mercy," Nico said. "Have you made any progress delaying the hearing with the Intelligence Committee?"

"I'm afraid not. They're insisting that Mercy's testimony is critical to national security."

Under cover of the table, Mercy gripped Nico's hand. "There's nothing you can do, Uncle William?"

"I contacted Senator Jeffries personally. He's not budging, honey. You and your security detail can stay at the White House. You'll be close to the Hill and behind protective barriers. You'll be safe."

Nico shook his head. "With respect, sir, I don't want Mercy to draw that much attention. I'd prefer to make arrangements for lodging myself."

"The Secret Service agents are well trained."

"We're better. More important, we don't have a security leak."

Her uncle straightened. "You have proof?"

"Not yet. We're working on it."

"Where's the leak?"

"ATF. We're not ruling out others."

A pained expression crossed the president's face. "In other words, I need to stay out of the arrangements for Mercy."

"Yes, sir. I will take care of her. Nothing is more important to me than her safety."

Her uncle looked thoughtful. "I see."

Maybe he did see. Uncle William was an insightful man, a great thing in a president. Mercy wasn't sure how she felt about her uncle's insight into her personal life.

"Are you sure about this, Mercy?"

Nico's hand squeezed hers. Was she sure? No, but she didn't want to run in fear and never find out if she and Nico had something worth fighting for. "I trust Nico." There, let her uncle and the others interpret that statement however they wanted.

"Nico, if I can help, I will. Otherwise, I'll trust you and your team to take care of my niece. Brent, watch your back, my friend. Many people are speculating as to the identity of the team who rescued Mercy. That may lead them back to you. It's no secret Fortress is the best in the black ops business."

"I'll be ready."

A nod. "Keep me posted. I want to know what's happening. Direct communication only."

"Yes, sir."

"Mercy, if you have a chance, call Charlotte. She's worried about you."

"As soon as I leave here, I'll contact her."

When the president signed off, Trace whistled softly. "Nico, you better not screw up, man. I'd hate for Martin to have a target on my back."

He lifted their joined hands and kissed the back of Mercy's. "Totally worth the risk."

Brent's eyes narrowed. "Everybody out except Nico and Mercy."

Zane left the conference room first, followed by the rest of Shadow.

"Something you need to tell me?" Brent asked, his gaze locked on their clasped hands.

"I'm crazy about Mercy and she's agreed to see where a relationship between us goes."

"Are you okay with this, Mercy?"

"Brent." A warning sounded in Nico's voice.

"Zip it, Patch. I won't have one of our principals feeling pressured by an operative."

Nico stiffened, then rose to his feet. He placed his hands on the conference table and leaned toward his boss. "Are you accusing me of brainwashing Mercy and forcing her to accept me?"

His quiet words held a lethal edge that made cold chills surge up Mercy's back. Undercurrents she didn't understand swirled around the enclosed space. There was a story here, but what?

"Sit down," Brent snapped.

"Answer my question."

"You know better than that. This is not about you, Rivera. Sit down or get out. Those are your only choices."

His jaw clenched in raw fury, Nico returned to his seat, his gaze locked on his boss.

Mercy breathed easier, feeling as though the possibility of imminent bloodshed had passed for now.

"I'll ask you again, Mercy." He glared at Nico when he growled. "Are you comfortable with Nico's personal interest in you?"

"He didn't pressure me. This was my choice."

"And if I thought it would be better to assign a different team as your protection detail?"

Mercy's heart skipped a beat, then raced ahead in a frantic rhythm. She didn't want Brent to assign her another team. She trusted Shadow. A glance at Nico told her he would refuse to leave her side no matter what his boss thought was best. "Nico?"

He turned to her, eyes glittering. "Brent has the authority to reassign my team. However, if he chooses to use that power, I will take an immediate leave of absence and stay with you and the new team until the danger to you is ended." A cold smile curved his lips as he glanced at Brent. "My guess is the rest of my unit will do the same. That means you'll have two teams tied up with one principal. You can't afford to do that since Durango is out of mission rotation for a few more weeks."

"Resorting to blackmail, Patch?"

Nico shrugged. "Whatever it takes. I'm not walking away from Mercy unless she kicks me to the curb."

Brent watched him for a long beat before shoving away from the table and pacing the length of the room. "One moment of inattention on your part could result in the death of both of you."

"Something you don't have to tell me. I'm aware of the stakes."

"Yeah? You're not the one who would have to answer to President Martin about why his beloved niece is dead." He swung around to face them. "Fine. You stay on the detail for now. But the minute you realize your emotions are affecting your judgment, I want to know about it. I will pull you off the detail. You can be the overprotective boyfriend and stay with her. However, if you interfere with the new team that's assigned, I'll cut you and the rest of Shadow loose even though it would kill me to do it. I'd rather have you alive and gunning for me than dead." Brent stalked from the room.

"Are meetings with your boss always that volatile?"

Nico dragged a hand down his face, his beard stubble already rasping against his fingers. "Not usually." He stood, drew Mercy to her feet, and looped his arms around her waist. "I was honest with Brent. I am crazy about you, Mercy. However, if you need more time to decide, I'll step back." He grimaced. "It might kill me to do it, but I want you in this relationship by choice, not coercion."

Mercy wrapped her arms around his neck and captured his mouth in a kiss that set her blood on fire. "My choice," she murmured against his lips. "You didn't persuade me one way or the other." Another soft kiss, then, "Is there something you need to tell me?" Something that made him react as he had with Brent.

Nico's grip tightened. "Not now. Soon."

Fair enough. She could wait for answers. "What's next?"

"The mall to purchase the clothes you'll need and a bag to pack them in. After that, I think it's time for a road trip."

She'd been afraid he would say that. Nico was taking her home.

CHAPTER TWENTY-FOUR

Nico parked in the lot at Cool Springs Galleria. When Mercy reached for the door, he caught her arm. "Wait." He scanned the area for unusual interest in them. Nico saw nothing to set off his internal alarm.

When his teammates approached, he circled to open Mercy's door. On the way into the mall, Nico and Mercy were surrounded by the rest of Shadow.

Mercy's gaze darted this way and that, fear draining the color from her face.

"Relax, kitten," he murmured. "It's our job to worry. Plot your purchasing strategy."

She flashed him a faint grin.

Not as much of a smile as he wanted, but he'd take it. "You have an hour to purchase what you need."

Mercy stopped on the sidewalk. "Nico, I don't have money. I left everything except my license and passport in Kentucky. I was afraid to take it to Mexico."

Nico got her moving again. "I'll take care of it."

"Let's just go. I have clothes in Sherwood."

"You saw what those clowns did to your house. You don't know if they left your clothes intact."

She swallowed hard. "You're supposed to reassure me the bad guys didn't have time to destroy my wardrobe."

"Don't all women want new clothes?"

"Shopping is not my favorite pastime. I limit my time in a store."

Yet another reason to be entranced with this woman. "Focus on what you need for one week. We'll buy more if the people who broke in trashed your wardrobe."

Inside the department store Mercy selected, she and Sam headed for the racks while Nico trailed them and the other members of Shadow kept watch around the women's clothing area. Trace, Ben, and Joe garnered a fair amount of interest from the ladies who were shopping.

Although prepared to wait more than the allotted hour, Nico was pleasantly surprised to find himself at the checkout counter in forty-five minutes. He didn't blink at the price the sales associate quoted him, just handed over his credit card.

"I'll pay you back," Mercy whispered. She looked distressed.

He dropped a quick kiss on her lips and gathered the bags in one hand when the transaction was complete, leaving his gun hand free. "It's lunchtime. I'd rather wait until we're out of town before stopping."

Mercy nodded. "Thanks for taking me to the mall. At least I have clothes no matter what we find at my house." She slid him a sideways glance. "Shopping with you was fun."

Nico grinned. "You expected me to be impatient."

Her face flushed. "I did. I'm glad I was wrong."

Once he tucked her inside his SUV, he turned to his teammates. "I want Mercy out of town before we stop for food. Suggestions on a place to stop?"

"Darlene's Diner off Interstate 65," Ben said. "Wide variety of food for Mercy to pick from."

The rest of them didn't have problems eating in the middle of stressful situations. Mercy might need something light, especially after the conference room scene. Nico scowled. What had Brent been thinking to get in his face like that with Mercy in the room? He'd upset her needlessly, a point he'd make to Brent at a later time.

"You don't like the idea?" Joe asked. "Choose somewhere else if that famous gut of yours says Darlene's isn't a good option."

Nico shook his head. "It's not the restaurant. I'm still angry at Brent." He hadn't had the time and privacy to discover if his boss had scared her off.

Trace shrugged. "He's looking out for your girl's best interests."

More like messing in Nico's business. Of all people, Brent should know that Nico would never take Mercy's choices from her, not after what happened to his sister. The ache in his chest at the thought of his sweet baby sister intensified. "Let's go," he said, his voice gruff.

He climbed behind the wheel and drove from the mall with his teammates tailing him in their SUV.

"What's going on, Nico?" Mercy asked.

He glanced at her. "We're stopping at Darlene's, a diner in Hendersonville. The restaurant has a wide variety of good food."

"I saw the sign for the diner when I drove down here a few weeks ago, but I didn't have time to stop."

"You were in town?" Why didn't he know this?

"I was a guest lecturer in a fine arts class at Middle Tennessee State University. I drove down for the class and went right back home since I was working on the pictures for Sean."

He grimaced at hearing the senator's name from her lips. "Wish I'd known you were in town. I would have loved to sit in on the lecture and met you under better circumstances."

Three hours after lunch, the caravan arrived in Sherwood. Nico liked the look of the town. Old-fashioned charm would be the best way to describe the place. A few traffic lights, flowers and trees planted everywhere, awnings fluttering in the spring breeze. As they drove through town, pedestrians turned their heads to watch their passage.

Good to know they noticed strangers in town. Would they have noticed the people who broke into Mercy's house? "How long have you lived in Sherwood?"

"I grew up here. I met Aiden in college and became a military wife who traveled from one base to another after we graduated. When he died, I came back home. People think I took a step backward, but moving home was right for me at the time. I needed a place to heal and rediscover who I was without Aiden."

"Are you open to moving away from Sherwood?" He felt Mercy's gaze on him. He shouldn't have asked this soon, had promised himself he wouldn't push. Nico couldn't help himself.

"If I had a good reason."

Would she consider him a good reason? He'd make the commute as long as she needed but would burn many hours driving to and from Sherwood. While on call, Nico couldn't be more than an hour from Nashville which drastically cut down on time to spend with her.

Man, he was in over his head. No question about it. His only hope to survive with his heart intact was if her feelings were as tangled about him as his were about her.

"Take the next right. My house is in the middle of the cul-de-sac."

When Nico parked, he evaluated the bungalow. The small yard had an abundance of flowers and shrubs, none too close to the house which was good for security. He could see her living in this quaint, well-loved space. Small and beautiful, like Mercy. Maybe it was petty, but he was glad she moved from the home she shared with Aiden, giving Nico hope she had healed enough to move on. Perhaps with him.

Mercy twisted in her seat. "I don't have keys. We'll have to break a window."

Amused, he shook his head. "I'll take care of it." Nico located lock picks in his Go bag and helped Mercy from the vehicle.

"I hope the rest of Shadow arrives soon. Based on the pictures you showed me, I have a lot of cleanup to do."

"We'll help. Remember, we can't stay here for long."

"The person who broke in must be gone by now."

"Perhaps."

"Way to encourage me, buddy."

He chuckled as they reached the sidewalk leading to the porch.

"I want to check my backyard garden. When you open the door, unlock the French doors at the back of the house for me." She frowned. "If the burglar didn't destroy my door."

Although he was reluctant to let Mercy out of his sight, he couldn't chain her to his side. From the looks of her door, manipulating the lock wouldn't take long anyway. "If something makes you feel uneasy, even if you can't see what's causing the unease, call out."

With a nod, she disappeared around the side of the house.

Nico dropped to his haunches and inserted the lock picks. He scowled when the lock gave within seconds. Mercy needed better locks. Hers wouldn't deter a determined child much less a terrorist or burglar.

He made a mental note to contact Zane. Once Nico evaluated her security, he'd ask the Fortress installation teams to install their best system. He returned the lock picks to his Go bag and jogged to the porch.

Since the police had already been on scene, Nico didn't bother with rubber gloves. The knob turned easily in his hand.

Inside the home, chaos reigned. He blew out a breath. Cleaning Mercy's place would take more than the allotted hour, even with six of them working together.

Picking his way through the debris, he crossed the living room and dining room to the French doors where Mercy waited. The French doors were still intact.

Nico unlocked the door for Mercy and moved aside.

Even though she'd seen the photographs, Mercy gasped when she stepped inside. "Look at this place. My insurance company will have a fit when they see the damage."

"We need to document everything before we clean." He eased Mercy into his arms and hugged her. "We won't be able to finish in the time we have available. We'll return after you're safe and help."

"Won't you have to go on another mission?"

He'd take a few days to help Mercy get her life back in order before he went after the Scorpions. "We're overdue for a break. Brent called Shadow because your uncle asked for me specifically."

Mercy leaned back to look into his eyes. "Why?"

Before he could answer, Nico heard movement in the living room. Not his teammates. He spun, weapon in hand, placing his body in front of Mercy's.

"Police! Drop your weapon!"

CHAPTER TWENTY-FIVE

Nico slowly placed his Sig on the table and backed away, careful to keep his body in front of Mercy's until he was sure the nervous cops wouldn't pull the trigger. He needed to get this situation under control before his teammates arrived. Four more armed strangers would add to the tension in the kitchen.

"Flat on the ground, now."

"Wait," Mercy protested. "You don't understand. This is my house, and Nico is my friend."

"What's your name?"

"Mercedes Powers."

"Back away from him, Ms. Powers. Nice and slow."

Nico sank to his knees, eyeing the policeman. "Mercy, do as he says."

"This isn't right. You didn't do anything wrong." She sounded as though she was on the verge of tears.

"He'll come to that conclusion soon enough." He hoped. Nico laid flat on the floor, arms spread, controlling a grimace when his stitches pulled tight. Yeah, this patrolman wouldn't be happy when he found the backup weapons and Ka-Bar. Looked like his time in Sherwood might be longer than an hour.

"Nico."

"Everything will be fine, kitten. Trust me. Go sit at the breakfast bar. He'll be able to see you while he cuffs me. It's standard procedure until he realizes I'm no threat to you or him." Well, not to Mercy at least. As long as the cop didn't make a threatening move toward Mercy, he was safe.

Nico kept his eyes on the twitchy cop as he cautiously moved closer. Not more than twenty-five, the red-haired officer's gaze shifted between Nico and Mercy and back.

"Don't move." Red holstered his Glock and searched Nico for more weapons. He found Nico's backup weapon and Ka-Bar. He missed the second knife in his combat boot and a few other surprises as well. "Hands behind your back."

With a sigh, Nico complied.

A siren cut off on the street. A moment later, Nico heard another cop ordering his teammates to back up.

Red assisted Nico to his feet. "Sit at the table and don't move."

He considered refusing but didn't relish a trip to jail. Nico chose the chair closest to Mercy.

A second patrolman came into the kitchen with his weapon drawn.

Red inclined his head toward Mercy. "Check her for weapons."

"No." Nico glared at Red. "She's not armed."

"Keep your mouth shut." Red's hand rest on his holstered weapon. "Do it, Fletch."

Gritting his teeth in anger, Nico shifted his weight, preparing to intervene and wondering if he would have another bullet wound to add to his collection.

Fletch cast a wary glance in Nico's direction. "On your feet, ma'am."

Nico watched Fletch's every move as Mercy slid from the stool and turned to place her hands on the breakfast bar. The cop felt along her legs, then moved to her torso and paused when he felt the bandage on her shoulder. He poked at it, causing Mercy to catch her breath.

Scowling, Nico surged to his feet.

"Sit down," Red ordered, his voice filled with tension.

Mercy glanced over her shoulder at Nico. "I'm fine. Please, Nico."

With a warning glare at the ham-handed cop who had hurt his girl, he returned to his seat.

"What's the lump?" Fletch asked Mercy.

"A bandage. I was injured a few days ago."

"Got proof?" Red asked.

"I was treated in Texas at a private clinic."

Although he didn't look convinced, Fletch turned to his friend. "No weapons."

A nod from Red. "Sit down, ma'am." He turned to Nico. "Name?"

"Nico."

"Nico what?"

He stared at the policeman. If he wanted more, he'd have to arrest him and try to run his prints through the system. He wouldn't get anything.

With a huff, Red said, "A neighbor reported seeing you break into this home."

Mercy groaned. "Mr. Stonebridge. I asked Nico to help me get inside the house. I was in Mexico for a funeral and was taken hostage. That's when I was hurt. I don't know what happened to my purse and keys."

Red looked skeptical. "How did you escape from your supposed kidnappers?"

"Nico and his friends rescued me."

"Pretty far-fetched story, lady."

Mercy gave a shaky laugh. "True enough. I can provide proof of that at least. Do you have a cell phone?"

Narrowed eyes. "Why?"

"Write your number down for me, please. You can have the paper after the phone call you're going to receive."

Still suspicious, he yanked out a small notebook and scribbled his number.

"Mercy, tell the officer what you plan to do so he won't think you're pulling a weapon his buddy missed." Like Red had missed some of Nico's weapons.

She blinked. "I'm getting my cell phone from my pocket."

Hand on his weapon, Red said, "Take it out, slow."

She glanced at Nico who nodded. Mercy placed her call. "Uncle William, I need you to call a police officer in Sherwood, Kentucky. He thinks Nico broke into my house and doesn't believe my story about the kidnapping." She rattled off the number. "I'd rather my protection detail stay out of jail. Thanks, Uncle William."

In less than a minute, the policeman's cell phone rang. He frowned as he stared at the screen, showing it to Fletch. "It's a blocked number."

Nico raised an eyebrow. "Are you going to answer it? Trust me, you don't want to miss this call."

With a suspicious glare Nico's direction, Red answered his phone. "This is Officer Adam Gates." He listened. His face paled as he straightened and remained silent for a few minutes. "Yes, sir." A pause. "I understand, sir." He swallowed audibly. "Thank you for calling, Mr. President." When Gates's hand dropped to his side, he stared at Mercy, shell-shocked. "Your uncle is the President of the United States."

She smiled. "I know. Will you remove the handcuffs from Nico's wrists now?"

Fletch groaned. "We are so screwed."

"Of course." Gates retrieved the key and unlocked the cuffs.

Nico flexed his wrists. "Any other questions, Gates?"

"When did you arrive in town?"

"Fifteen minutes ago. I'm sure the folks downtown will corroborate the time. They turned to stare as we drove through town."

"My apologies for inconveniencing both of you."

Mercy slid from the barstool and moved to Nico's side. He wrapped his arm around her, able to draw a free breath for the first time since Gates and Fletch had arrived on scene.

"Thanks for the quick response," Mercy said. "I appreciate your service to Sherwood."

Relief flooded his face. "Thank you, ma'am." With a nod to Nico, he turned on his heel and left, followed quickly by his friend.

Soon, the rest of Shadow walked into the kitchen. Trace set bags from a local store on the table. "We leave you two alone for fifteen minutes, and you get in the faces of the local cops."

"I don't think they'll bother us again." Nico holstered his weapons and helped Joe set out cleaning supplies and trash bags. "President Martin had a talk with one of the officers. Otherwise, I think Officer Gates intended to haul me to jail. Let's split up. The house isn't that large. I'll help Mercy with her bedroom. The rest of you choose a room and get started. Document the damage first before staring the cleanup. No more than forty minutes."

He escorted Mercy down the hall to her bedroom. She paused at the doorway.

"Oh, wow." She eased past him to stand at the foot of her bed and turned in a slow circle, surveying the damage.

Nico moved behind her and drew her against his chest. "I'm glad you weren't here." Based on what he saw, the people who broke in would have hurt or killed Mercy if she had been there.

Nothing was left untouched. Even the mattress hadn't escaped the blade of a knife. Her wardrobe was in shreds. Good thing he'd insisted Mercy buy clothes for a week.

"I need to check my drawings." Mercy's voice sounded choked. "They're in the second bedroom along with the safe."

"Go ahead. I'll start in here." Nico took pictures of the room from every angle, then started filling trash bags. If he thought an item salvageable, he set it aside for Mercy to evaluate. By the time she returned with her camera, the saved pile he had accumulated was small. "Did your art survive the break-in?"

Mercy frowned. "Months of work is gone."

"The perps destroyed it?"

"No. They took the art with them."

Huh. Not what he'd expected to hear. "Did you find the memory card?"

She handed it to him. "I don't understand what they wanted with the studio artwork."

"We'll figure it out, learn who stole the drawings, and return them to you. Do you have a list with descriptions?"

"I took photographs of the finished work. I would show you on my laptop, but they stole that, too."

"We'll use mine when we're in a secure location. Here." Nico handed her empty trash bags. "Let's see what's left of your wardrobe, if anything."

They worked in silence for a few minutes. Finally, Mercy said, "They slashed everything, even my shoes. Who does that?" She walked from the closet with a disgusted look on her face.

"People furious with you. Anyone besides the Scorpions have a reason to hurt you?"

"I'm not a social butterfly, Nico. I don't go out much. My biggest outing each week is to the grocery store or church. I didn't think I had enemies until this happened."

Joe appeared in the doorway. "Nico, company."

"More cops?"

"An older man and two other men just parked in the driveway."

"What are they driving?" Mercy asked.

"A black Silverado."

"It's my father and brothers." She hurried from the bedroom with the two operatives on her heels. When Mercy reached for the doorknob, Nico caught her hand.

"Let me."

"They won't understand why you're here."

"Safety first, always." He urged her to stand at the hallway entrance. Mercy's family could see her from the doorway, but she wouldn't be in a shooter's line of sight.

The doorbell rang.

He flicked a glance at Joe who shifted to stand in front of Mercy. Nico opened the door. Three men eyed him with varying degrees of hostility and suspicion.

"Where's my sister?" the tallest man demanded. "If you've hurt one hair on her head, you're a dead man."

"I'm here, Chris."

The three men stared at Mercy. "Why didn't you answer the door?" her father asked.

"It's not safe for her." Nico allowed Mercy's family inside the house and locked the door behind them.

"Who are you?" the second brother asked.

"Nico. These are my teammates Joe, Sam, Ben, and Trace. We're Mercy's bodyguards."

"Friends who happen to be trained security specialists," Mercy corrected. She turned to Shadow. "This is my family. My father, Patrick, and my brothers Chris and Wyatt."

"Why do you need the protection of five people?" Wyatt asked.

Nico gestured toward the kitchen, the only place with furniture left undamaged by the perps. "Long story. Sit and we'll explain why protection is necessary."

Someone rattled the door knob, cursed, and pounded on the door. "Police. Open up."

He scowled. Again? Nico checked the peephole and unlocked the door. He stared down at the uniformed officer who took a step back when he saw Nico looming over him.

"Where's Mercy?"

A popular question this afternoon. Nico inclined his head to the hallway where Mercy stood with her family.

Relief flooded the cop's face. "Mercy. Thank God. I was so worried about you." He strode across the living room, pushed past Mercy's brothers and tried to sweep Mercy into a hug.

Joe inserted his body between Mercy and the cop.

"Get out of my way unless you want to find yourself behind bars, mister."

The operative grinned. "Can't arrest me for refusing to let you hug a woman who's injured and hasn't indicated she wants to be touched by you."

Mercy's family spun toward her demanding an explanation about the injuries as did the cop.

Nico held out his hand to her. Ignoring the clamors for an explanation, she pushed through the men standing between them and clasped his hand. He squeezed her fingers. "Come on. You should sit while you explain." Silence fell when he dropped a quick kiss on her mouth. Yeah, he was staking his claim. Nico didn't like the way the cop looked at Mercy.

She sent him an amused look.

When her family and the cop were seated at the table with Mercy, Nico positioned himself behind her chair. Although her family didn't pay attention, the cop noticed that Shadow surrounded the occupants of the table, each one within easy reach of men who might be a threat to Mercy.

Mercy explained the events in Mexico and her rescue, including the gunshot wound in her shoulder.

The cop frowned. "You had it treated, right?"

"Of course, Max. Nico and his friends have taken good care of me."

"How do you know these thugs aren't the ones who orchestrated your kidnapping?"

"My uncle sent them for me."

"Who's your uncle?"

Pat sighed. "William Martin."

A snort from Max. "Right. Mercy's uncle is the president?"

Mercy's father shrugged. "My wife's brother."

The cop's gaze shifted from one person to another. "You're serious. How did I not know this? You sure you're okay, Mercy?"

"I had great medical care and I'm recovering well. What do you know about the people who destroyed my house?"

"Not enough to make an arrest. Stonebridge got a picture of the guys as they left, but it was too grainy to be of use."

"Who has the picture?" Nico asked.

"Stonebridge. Like I said, it didn't help."

The Sherwood Police Department might not have the equipment to do something with a grainy photo, but Fortress did.

CHAPTER TWENTY-SIX

Mercy hugged her neighbor. "Thanks, Mr. Stonebridge. You've been a big help."

The octogenarian smiled. "I'm glad. The cops weren't interested in my picture. You sure you can use it?"

"I work for a private security company, Mr. Stonebridge," Nico said. "We have better equipment than your police department." He held out his hand for Stonebridge's cell phone. "May I?"

"Of course." He seemed disappointed when Nico sent the picture to his own cell phone. "Well, then, young lady, are you home to stay?"

"Not yet. Soon, though." Except if she came home soon, she would see much less of Nico, and Mercy wasn't ready to do that.

Her heart skipped a beat. Oh, goodness. How deep were her feelings for the dark-haired sexy warrior?

Nico slid his phone into his pocket. "Thanks for looking out for Mercy. She's important to me."

Stonebridge studied Nico's face a moment, nodded. "You have good taste in women, Nico. You'll protect her?"

"With my life."

A ball of ice formed in Mercy's stomach. Nico meant exactly what he said. He would do anything to protect her, even take a bullet. She shoved her morbid thoughts aside, stood on tiptoe, and kissed the old man's cheek. "I'll see you later, Mr. Stonebridge."

Nico's teammates waited for them at the SUV. "Let's go," Nico said. "We've been here too long."

Trace nodded. "My skin's crawling. I'll take point."

Mercy's family stood on the porch. She couldn't leave without saying goodbye to them. "I'll be back in a minute."

Instead of staying behind with his teammates, Nico walked with her.

Stubborn man. Mercy's family wouldn't hurt her. Mercy hugged her father, breathing in the familiar scent of his spicy cologne and favorite soap.

"Where will you go from here, sweetheart?"

She glanced at Nico and caught his slight head shake. Not because he didn't trust her father, but because he wanted to protect him in case the thieves returned and confronted him, she realized. "I'm not sure, Dad." And it was true. Even when they arrived in Washington, D.C., Mercy didn't know where they'd stay. Nico had made arrangements for a safe house. "I'll be fine. Fortress is the best in the business. Uncle William wouldn't have sent them for me if they weren't."

"We can protect you," Chris said, glaring at Nico. "We're always armed."

"The men after Mercy don't care who they hurt," Nico said. "This is what we do, Chris. We're well-trained. Mercy is our top priority."

Her father was silent a moment, his gaze locked on Nico. "You know what she's been through. Don't make her go through it again."

Stunned, Mercy stared at her father. He was the most compassionate, kindest man in town. This Pat Garwood was a fierce protector. Did her father suspect Mercy was falling for the handsome warrior by her side?

"No, sir. I won't."

"When my daughter is safe, I'll expect to see you."

"Absolutely."

"Dad." Mercy's face heated. "I'm not a child anymore."

"You'll always be my daughter, Mercedes." He kissed her forehead. "Be safe."

After hugging her brothers, Mercy climbed into Nico's SUV and they followed Trace from Sherwood. Mercy couldn't stand the silence between them any longer. "Are you planning to return to Sherwood when this is over?"

Dark eyes locked on hers for a moment before he returned his attention to the asphalt ribbon in front of them. "It's where you'll be, and Fortress owes me time off. I'm taking it with you."

The coldness in her stomach melted. "You want to spend your vacation here?"

"I want to be with you, Mercy, whether here or somewhere else."

Mercy studied his profile, butterflies flying in formation in her stomach. She was either making the biggest mistake or best decision of her life. "Do you like the beach?"

Another glance her direction, surprise in his eyes. "Sand and surf, fresh seafood, parasailing, scuba diving. What's not to like? "

"Would you like to go to the beach for a few days? If we rented a house, your teammates could come, too. If you don't mind and if they wanted to enjoy sun, sand, and the other things you mentioned."

Nico's lips curved as he activated his Bluetooth. "Ask them."

Trace answered the call. "What's up?"

"Mercy had a suggestion."

"Shoot, Mercy."

"After I'm safe, I thought renting a house at the beach for all of us to enjoy might be fun." Why were they so quiet? Mercy cleared her throat. "It's fine if you and the others would rather spend time with your families. It was just a thought." She clamped a hand over her mouth to stop herself from babbling.

"Sounds like a great plan," Trace said. "We'll ask Zane for suggestions on the safest beach and the best house rentals. Thanks for including us in your plans."

Thrilled, she said, "You don't mind vacationing together?"

"Of course not," Ben chimed in. "We often take breaks together. Spending time together away from missions is how we bonded so fast as a unit. Besides, running on the beach and swimming in the ocean is not a hardship."

"Is anybody surprised by that statement? Ben's a Navy SEAL. We'll have to plan the food," Joe said. "The house rental needs to have an outdoor grill. That's a requirement. I can't cook squat in the kitchen, but I can grill with the best of them."

"I'll come up with menus that capitalizes on your skill set."

Nico said, "Trace, I have a tango on my six."

Mercy twisted in her seat to stare out the back window. A large red truck behind them was closing fast. "What can I do to help?" she asked.

"Trace, can you drop back?"

"Nope. Got two tangos inbound. Classic Pincer move. We'll take care of the clowns in front of us, then drop back to take care of the other one."

"Do you have extra weapons?" Mercy asked Nico.

"In my Go bag in the cargo area. Why?"

"Aiden made sure I could protect myself while he was deployed. I can hold off the truck behind us." At Nico's skeptical look, she said, "I can handle weapons, Nico. You asked me to trust you. Now it's your turn to return the favor."

"Go."

Mercy scrambled over the seat and into the cargo area, wincing at the tug on her shoulder. She scooted to Nico's Go bag and unzipped it. She peered inside and goggled. Holy cow. He had an arsenal in there. The bag had to weigh a ton, yet he hauled it around like it was easy. "What should I use?"

"Ever fired an AR-10?"

"Yes."

"Grab it and the Sig. The AR-10 is your best bet for longer distance. If it's too awkward, switch to the Sig. There are more magazines for each in the bag."

She spotted the magazines and grabbed a couple for each. "Got them. Is there a switch back here to raise the hatchback?"

"I have controls up here for the hatchback and window. I'll lower the window partway to keep you protected as much as possible. The glass is bullet resistant and the exterior is reinforced. Stay low. I'm growing quite fond of that pretty head of yours."

"Sweet talker." Mercy went through the safety checks Aiden had drilled into her. When she was satisfied, she glanced out the back. "Lower the window, Nico. I'm ready."

"Aim for the windshield, kitten."

"Aye, aye, Captain, sir."

He laughed. "I'm a Marine. The correct response is 'copy that.'"

"Copy that, sir."

As soon as the glass slid partway down, she lined up her sights for the middle of the windshield. Hopefully, these guys would back off if their target returned fire.

She took a deep breath as the truck zoomed closer, exhaled half the air, and squeezed the trigger. The driver of the truck swerved and slowed.

"Keep firing, Mercy."

Jazzed now, she repeated the process twice more before the creeps in the truck surged closer and one of them leaned out the passenger-side window with a handgun. Not as much range. With luck, the wind blew in the direction of the truck and would throw off their accuracy.

Trusting the SUV's upgrades to keep her safe, Mercy fired a steady barrage of bullets. When the magazine was empty, she dropped lower and replaced it with a fresh one.

"I'm going to straddle both lanes," Nico called back. "We're moving into a heavily populated area. We need those goons off our tail. The windshield's gone now and they're still coming. Aim for the grill. If enough bullets hit the truck engine, it will lock up."

"One tango in front down," Trace said. "Going after the second one."

"Nico, lower the window all the way." Mercy got into position and commenced firing at the approaching truck's grill. After five shots, the vehicle veered off the road, hit an embankment, and rolled onto its side.

"Yes! You are seriously amazing, Mercy Powers." Nico hit the button to raise the window. "Come back up here."

"You better hang onto that woman, Nico," Ben said over the Bluetooth connection. "She's one in a million."

"Trust me, I know. I have no intention of letting her get away."

Startled at his statement, Mercy returned the AR-10 to the Go bag along with the extra magazine. She kept the Sig and two magazines in case they ran into more trouble. She could hide the gun in the glove box if local law enforcement stopped them for some reason.

Scrambling over the seats, she slid into the front passenger seat again.

Nico captured her hand and brought it to his lips. "Excellent job."

Mercy gave a huff of laughter. "Right. It only took me one magazine and one quarter of another one to stop the truck."

"You didn't panic and got the job done. That's what matters. While I'm off, I'll work with you to hone your shooting skills."

"I'm out of practice," she admitted. "I haven't been to the gun range since Aiden died. Going there reminded me too much of him."

He squeezed her hand. "I'll teach you to shoot like a Marine." A smile. "Of course, I'll have to steal kisses between magazines. You'll think of me and my kisses every time you go to the gun range."

"Hey, that's too much information," Sam complained although her voice was filled with amusement. "And I'm seriously jealous about the pending kisses. I haven't been kissed in a long time."

"If you want volunteers to help you break your dry spell, I'll get in line," Ben said.

"Shut up, Ben," Joe snapped. More rifle fire came over the Bluetooth connection.

"Tango two is down," Trace said. "We're clear."

"Injuries?" Nico asked.

A snort from Joe. "Not on our part."

"Good. Stick with the plan. I don't want to be in D.C. without our reinforced rides. Zane reserved a suite for us at the Horizon Inn and Suites in Palmira."

"Copy that. Let me know when Mercy needs to stop." Trace ended the call.

During their conversation, Mercy started to shake. Stupid adrenaline dump. She tried to keep the trembling from Nico. He glanced at her, then turned on the heater in the passenger seat and warmed the temperature in the SUV.

"Would you like me to find a coffee shop and buy you hot tea? Might help."

She shook her head. "Thanks for the offer, though."

"Go to sleep when you need to, okay?"

The way Mercy felt right now, she wouldn't be sleeping for a week. The buzz would drop her like a rock before long, she knew. And the heat felt heavenly. She might survive after all.

Nico threaded his fingers through hers.

After a few more miles, the shaking subsided and fatigue set in. She fought to stay awake, but her eyes grew heavy. The next thing she knew, Nico was stroking her cheek with his rough fingers.

"Mercy, we need to walk for a few minutes. Sam's orders."

"Can't defy the medic."

"I'm not stupid. That woman works with sharp instruments. I know not to make her mad."

He came around the hood of the SUV and opened her door. Nico brushed her lips with his, then lifted her from the cab and set Mercy on her feet.

The small caravan had stopped at a truck stop off the interstate. After visiting the facilities with Sam, the women joined the others in the convenience store.

"Are you hungry?" Nico asked her. "They have a sub shop here."

Mercy assessed how she felt. Yeah, she needed to eat. Something light, though. "A chicken sandwich would be great."

"I'll take care of it. Find snacks and drinks we can take with us. Sam, what kind of sandwich would you like?"

"Turkey."

"Toppings?"

Mercy and Sam told Nico their preferences, then wandered around the convenience store in search of snack food and drinks.

Fifteen minutes later, they were back on the road. Mercy unwrapped Nico's sandwich and handed it to him. At ten o'clock, Nico and Trace parked at the back of the Horizon Inn and Suites.

"Stay here until I'm sure it's safe." Nico exited the SUV.

"I'll check us in," Trace said. "Ben used his card in Nashville. Let's keep your name off the Scorpion's radar as long as possible." After obtaining his team leader's agreement, he loped off.

In short order, Shadow and Mercy were ensconced in the Presidential suite. Nico placed Mercy's bag on one of the double beds in the first bedroom. "You and Sam will share a room."

"What about you?"

"I'll be on the couch in the living room. The rest of the guys will share the second bedroom."

"Why not you?"

"I don't want to be that far from you."

How was a woman supposed to resist a man like Nico Rivera? "Thank you."

He kissed her, long and deep. "Rest, kitten. Tomorrow will be a long day." Nico nodded at Sam as he passed her.

Mercy watched him walk away and prayed they found answers before Nico or his teammates were hurt.

CHAPTER TWENTY-SEVEN

Nico sat up when Mercy's door opened. He glanced at his watch and frowned. A few minutes after midnight. Sam stepped out and closed the door behind her. "Everything okay?" he asked.

She shook her head. "Mercy is restless. Nightmares or memories from the abduction."

He stood. "I'll make her some tea."

"Nico, I think she needs you."

Joe turned from the French door where he was keeping watch, his eyebrow raised. "What are you suggesting?"

"He could watch a movie or a television show with her until she fell asleep."

A smile curved Nico's mouth. "I planned to do that as well as ply her with tea. Tell Mercy to join me. Joe, go rest. I'll take over."

His teammate shook his head. "I'll sit on the balcony to keep watch. Focus on your girl. Sleep if you can."

"I'll bring you coffee and join you," Sam turned on her heel and returned to the bedroom.

Nico considered saying something to Joe about Sam and decided the timing was wrong. Soon, though. His teammate was crazy about the medic. He didn't know what held Joe back, but he needed to wise up. Operatives from other teams had noticed Sam and knew she wasn't involved with anyone. It was only a matter of time before Sam gave up on Joe and turned to someone else.

By the time the microwave signaled the end of the heating cycle, Joe had settled into a balcony chair with his back to the suite. A moment later, Sam left the bedroom with Mercy trailing behind her.

Mercy looked sheepish. "I'm sorry, Nico. I told Sam I was fine."

"Come here." He set the tea on the counter to steep and opened his arms. He drew Mercy against his chest and held her while Sam poured two mugs of coffee and went to the balcony. Then he and Mercy were alone.

"This will be the first of many sleepless nights," he murmured against her ear as he trailed his hand up and down her back. "Different things will trigger nightmares. You have an excellent reason to be sleepless. The ambush set you off this time. Testifying before the Intelligence Committee will probably stir emotions and memories, too. We can set up another video chat with Marcus if you want." The longer he talked, the more Mercy melted against him. "Want to watch a movie with me?"

"If you don't mind."

Nico carried her tea to the couch where he sat beside her and draped a blanket over her lap. Warmth would help her become sleepy. Sitting on the couch the rest of the night would be well worth the discomfort to help Mercy rest.

Grabbing the remote, Nico found an action-adventure movie with a romance thread he thought Mercy would like. He draped his arm around her shoulders and tucked her against his side.

When she finished the chamomile tea, Nico urged Mercy to lay her head against his shoulder. Within half an hour, she was sound asleep.

Perfect. Nico turned down the volume so the sound registered as background noise, propped his feet on the coffee table, and settled more comfortably on the couch. Knowing his teammates were awake and on watch, he fell into a light sleep.

He opened his eyes when Ben took over the watch from Joe. The EOD man signaled that everything was fine and for Nico to sleep. With a slight nod, he drifted off again.

When he woke the next time, the sun was beginning to make an appearance on the horizon. Nico held Mercy another few minutes before stroking her cheek to wake her. "Mercy."

She opened her eyes. Mercy glanced out the French doors and frowned. "Nico, why didn't you wake me and tell me to go to bed?"

He tipped her chin up and kissed her. "The whole point was to help you sleep."

"But not at your expense."

"I slept more than I usually do." And that was a surprise. He hadn't expected to sleep much himself. Nico had been afraid for Mercy when she'd shot at the gunmen pursuing them. All he could see in his mind's eye was her falling in the cargo area with a bullet in her head. Maybe having her safe in his arms allowed him enough peace to sleep himself.

"I still feel guilty."

"Don't. I enjoyed holding you." He stood and extended his hand. "I'll order room service while you're getting ready."

After Mercy disappeared into her bedroom, Nico stretched and went to the kitchen to make another pot of coffee. While he dumped the grounds into the basket, Trace wandered in from the balcony.

"When do we leave?" he asked Nico.

"No more than two hours. Sleep. We'll save you breakfast."

With a salute, Trace returned to the bedroom he shared with his teammates.

Nico perused the room service menu and called in a large order, then grabbed his duffel bag and headed for the bathroom. With a signal to Joe to take over the watch, he made quick work of showering and dressing. He considered shaving, but growing out his beard would be safer while he was in D.C. The media hounds would be all over Mercy when they learned she was in town. Since he didn't plan to leave her side, his face would be splashed all over television, newspapers, and tabloids.

Back in the living room, he clapped Joe on the shoulder. "Thanks. I'll take the watch now." He studied his teammate's face and didn't like Joe's troubled expression. "Want to talk?" he asked.

"What's the point?"

"I make it a policy not to stick my nose into my team's personal business."

A sour look crossed Joe's face. "But you're going to make an exception in my case."

"I don't have a problem if you want to date Sam. I will have a problem if your feelings for each other interfere in Shadow unit's cohesiveness, and it's starting to."

Joe looked stunned. "Wait. Sam is interested in me?"

"Are you dense?" Nico murmured. "Open your eyes before you lose your chance with her."

The bedroom door opened and Sam stepped out. She paused when she saw Joe, then continued into the living room. "Good morning."

Joe cleared his throat, darted a look at Nico before turning back to Sam. "Morning. Thanks for the coffee and company last night."

The medic smiled. "You're welcome." She turned to Nico. "Mercy looked well rested. Your tea and movie must have done the trick."

"I'll be back," Joe said and walked into the other bedroom.

Nico went to the French door to take up the watch. "Breakfast should arrive in thirty minutes or so."

Once Ben and Joe showered and changed, they joined Nico and Sam in the living room. When the knock on the door came, Joe pulled his weapon and checked the peephole. "Room service," he said as he slid his gun into his holster.

Two bellhops delivered carts loaded with food and juices. Not long after they left, Mercy emerged from her bedroom, cheeks pink and her hair damp. She was dressed in jeans and a long-sleeved shirt and tennis shoes.

Nico eyed her critically. Sam was right. Mercy looked better. Good. She would need every bit of strength she possessed over the next few days. He handed her a plate. "Choose what you want. The rest of you need to leave enough for Trace."

Two hours later, they pushed the carts into the hallway, checked out, and loaded the SUVs. This time, Ben opted to ride with Nico and Mercy in case they ran into more trouble.

After a long day of driving, Nico and Trace parked behind a colonial-style, two-story house. As soon as they turned off the engines, a broad-shouldered man dressed in black opened the back door and stepped onto the deck.

Nico relaxed when he recognized the Fortress operative. He should have realized Maddox would think four or five steps ahead.

"Is that Eli?" Mercy asked.

"It is." Nico climbed from the vehicle to open Mercy's door.

"Need help with your gear?" Eli asked.

"We'll handle it. Do you mind showing Mercy around?"

"Glad to. Come on up, Mercy. I'll show you where you and Sam will stay."

Jon walked onto the deck. He nodded at Mercy as she passed him. Once she and Eli were inside the house, he bounded down the steps from the deck and reached into the cargo hold to grab Nico's duffel bag. "Heard you had some trouble on the way here. What happened?"

Nico summarized the events since he'd last seen the SEALs.

Jon whistled. "Your girl is one tough lady. Did you know she could shoot?"

"Had no clue." He smiled. "She was ticked off it took her a magazine and a half to take out the truck."

"You'll train her?"

He nodded. "I'm taking time off after we dismantle the Scorpions. I'll work with her then."

Jon's lips twitched. "Does Maddox know?"

"I told him last night." Before Mercy had come to him. "Shadow needs a break. We were two days into a break when Maddox called us in to rescue Mercy. I'm glad we were available." Thinking of what would have happened to her if they hadn't been tore him up inside.

"When is the hearing?"

"In two days. Jeffries wants to talk to her tomorrow." Something that didn't make him happy. The only advantage in talking to the senator a day before the hearing was it gave Shadow a chance to scope out the setup before the media circus began.

A nod from Jon as he hefted Nico's duffel bag onto his shoulder. "Eli and I will keep watch tonight."

"Thanks. We'll work out a rotation for tomorrow night." He followed the sniper inside the house. "Where will Mercy sleep?"

"Second floor, corner bedroom, east side. It's the most secure room in the house." Jon sent a pointed glanced over his shoulder. "We put you in the room across from hers. Figured you'd want to be close."

Jon dumped Nico's bag on the bed in his room, then left him alone. Nico set his Go bag on the floor near the bed and walked across the hall. He leaned one shoulder against the door jamb. "You okay?"

Mercy turned from the window. "Shoulder hurts some," she admitted.

"Are you hungry?"

"Not really, but I should have something on my stomach before I take the pain meds."

That she'd even mentioned taking the medicine told Nico how bad she was hurting. "Let's find out what Jon and Eli brought in for us."

He started to follow her downstairs when his cell phone rang. After a glance at the screen, Nico motioned for Mercy to go on as he answered the call from Zane. "What do you have for me?"

"Cops in Sherwood filed a report of multiple gunshots. They found three vehicles abandoned, all of them stolen. No sign of the drivers or passengers. However, the cops ran their prints and got multiple hits. From the evidence they gathered, the Scorpions sent nine men after Shadow and Mercy."

Nico scowled. "They know she has a protection detail. Any inquiries on our names yet?"

"On your real names, no. They ran the aliases from Trace and Ben."

"They're tracking us." How had they managed to do that? A tracker on the SUVs? "We'll check the vehicles again, see if we missed something."

"Good idea. We've used the Garden Hotel before, but the most likely explanation for the attack there was the government leak."

"I'll buy that. What about the ambush outside Sherwood?"

"If you don't have a tracking device on your vehicles, I'd consider a bug or hidden camera in Mercy's house. The thugs who broke in had plenty of time to wire the place. With that much chaos and very little time to search, you might have missed both."

Nico blew out a breath in frustration. "Send someone to Mercy's house. Call her father and have him meet an operative to let him inside the house. Mercy has a neighbor who keeps an eye on the area. He called the police who cuffed me within fifteen minutes of arriving in town."

"I'll take care of it. We'll let you know what we find."

After he ended the call, Nico walked into the kitchen. "Joe, with me."

His teammate rose and followed him outside. "What's up?"

"Check for a tracker." The thought that he might have missed one made Nico's stomach burn. Had he led Scorpion to Mercy's safe house?

CHAPTER TWENTY-EIGHT

Nico pulled an electronic scanner from his pocket, turned it on, and circled his SUV. Nothing. Still not satisfied, he grabbed a flashlight from his vehicle and crawled underneath to check for anything amiss.

Minutes later, he stood and brushed off his clothes. Nothing. "Clear," he said to Joe.

"Same. What made you think we had a problem?"

"Ambush outside Sherwood and the attack at the hotel in Murfreesboro."

"Government leak?"

"For the Murfreesboro incident. Zane thinks there might have been a bug or camera, maybe both, at Mercy's house."

The spotter flinched. "We were so concerned with protecting her and sorting through all the debris we didn't think about the bozos leaving something behind." He leaned back against the SUV and sighed. "We're slipping, Patch."

"I've already told Maddox as soon as Mercy is safe we're taking a month off."

"The beach trip?"

"Maybe not the whole month." He smiled. "No offense, but I'd like to romance Mercy without my teammates watching every move."

"I don't know, man. I might learn something from the master."

Nico got him in a headlock. After tussling with his friend for a minute, the men returned to the kitchen.

"Problem?" Trace asked.

Nico shook his head. "Double checking that we didn't have a tracker on one of the vehicles." He turned to Mercy. "Zane is going to call your father. We want one of our operatives to go through your house to search for bugs and cameras."

She set down her partially eaten peanut butter and jelly sandwich. "That's how those vehicles ambushed us. We could have taken three or four different routes from Sherwood, but they were on the one we chose."

"Yeah, but we talked about taking Highway 10 while we were inside your house."

"What did Zane discover about the clowns who attacked us?" Ben asked.

"All three vehicles were stolen. The cops ran the fingerprints. Turns out these guys were associated with the Scorpions."

"Big surprise," Ben muttered.

"Was anyone hurt?" Mercy asked, her voice soft.

Nico sat in the chair beside hers. "Doubt it. No one was around to ask."

Relief filled her eyes.

"Finish your snack so you can take your meds." When she resumed eating, he looked at Eli. "How is Brenna?"

"As beautiful and amazing as ever. I'm one lucky man."

"Is she working on another book?"

A snort from Eli. "She's always writing another one. My wife takes two or three days to do whatever she wants between books, then jumps back into writing. She says if she takes a long break, it's too hard to resume a regular writing schedule."

"Ask him why Brenna is writing like a crazy woman right now." Jon smiled.

"This sounds good." Sam folded her arms and leaned on the table. "Spill."

A broad smile curved his lips. "Brenna is pregnant. She's writing fast so she can take two months off with the baby before she writes while our son or daughter is napping."

After a round of congratulations and back slaps, the talk turned to favorite vacation spots. Nico deliberately steered the conversation away from anything to do with Mercy's situation. He wanted her well rested for the interview with Jeffries. He had a feeling she wouldn't be sleeping much once the circus started.

When she and the others finished with their snacks, Nico held out his hand to Mercy. "I'll walk Mercy to her room, then we have plans to make."

Jon stood. "I'll get my laptop."

With a nod, Nico clasped Mercy's hand and walked upstairs with her. At the doorway to her room, he cupped her nape and drew her in for a kiss that heated his blood. He was in so much trouble. Nico was addicted to Mercy's touch and taste. No other woman would do for him anymore. Mercy's rejection would kill him. "If you need me, I'll be across the hall after we finish planning. Eli and Jon will cover the watch tonight. Promise you'll come get me if you need me."

"I don't want to impose."

He brushed her lips with his. "Holding you while you fall asleep is not an imposition. It's a privilege. Promise?"

Mercy hugged him tight. "I will."

"Good." Knowing he couldn't stay any longer, Nico nudged Mercy inside the room and closed the door before he gave into temptation to stay with her longer.

He followed the rumble of voices to the kitchen and stopped by the coffee pot to fill a mug before joining his team.

"So, your girl took out a carload of terrorists." Eli leaned back in his chair. "The boss may try to recruit her."

Nico sipped his coffee and considered her worry that she'd hurt someone by her actions, the distaste he'd seen on her face. "I don't think that will be a problem. Mercy doesn't have the heart for this kind of work." He sat beside Jon. "Let's get to work."

They spent the next two hours looking at schematics and routes to and from Capitol Hill. Nico pointed to one room. "This is where Jeffries wants to meet with Mercy tomorrow."

"Too many access points," Trace said. "Worse, we won't be able to carry our weapons in the building."

"I brought ceramic knives that will fit in your combat boots." Jon shrugged. "Not as good as a firearm, but it's better than nothing."

Nico grinned. Of course Jon brought a weapon undetectable to metal detectors. All of them were lethal without weapons. However, a weapon upped the odds of survival.

"Why does the senator want to see her tomorrow?" Sam asked. "Shouldn't he wait until Mercy is before the committee before he peppers her with questions?"

Nico had wondered the same thing. Why wasn't the senator concerned about being accused of impropriety? Maybe he had enough power to sweep away the accusations. "He wouldn't tell Mercy why he wanted to meet with her. Guess we'll find out tomorrow." Nico didn't like it. Wouldn't be the first time he'd worked without full intel. He glanced around the table. "Everybody satisfied we've covered all bases?"

When no one spoke up, he sent his teammates to bed. He eyed the SEALs. "Concerns?"

"Your objectivity is shot." A smile curved Eli's mouth. "For good reason."

Like that was news. "Other than that?"

Jon closed the lid of his laptop. "I don't like her being in this town. If it were Dana, she wouldn't be out in the open, especially near Jeffries. Mercy is already a target. Bringing her here is like throwing meat in front of a starving lion."

Nico stiffened. "You think I don't know that? I hate this arrangement more than you do. I don't want Mercy in the same state as that man and his father, but I can't keep her a prisoner."

"Won't help if the committee sends law enforcement after her for refusing to appear to answer questions," Eli pointed out. "Mercy isn't Dana. She's already shown herself to be one tough lady and she didn't face the same problems."

Jon looked at his partner. "Only because Shadow arrived in time to stop it. Look, Nico, there are too many players in this thing and we don't know any of them aside from the Jeffries, and Hector and his boss. If the Scorpions get their hands on Mercy again…"

"They won't." He wouldn't let them take her again, and if giving his life to protect her prevented it, he'd do it without regret except for missing his chance at a life with her.

Nico's heart skipped a beat before starting again in a frantic, pounding rhythm. Couldn't be. He swallowed hard. It wasn't possible this fast. Was it? Unable to process the new revelation with the two SEALs watching him with growing concern, Nico turned toward the sink and dumped what was left of his coffee down the drain.

He braced his hands on the edge of the sink, staring out the window into the darkness. Nico drew in a deep breath and accepted the truth. He was in love with Mercy Powers. How could this happen in a few days' time? With the loss of her husband, she would be wary of his fast-developing feelings. Although she was attracted to him, Mercy might never fall in love with him. She might be too afraid of losing another man she loved to a terrorist's bullet or an IED to give her feelings a chance to develop to their full potential.

Nico's heart ached. He wouldn't blame her if she refused to take the risk. He wasn't in the safest profession. Would he leave Fortress if Mercy asked? He didn't know. Protecting innocents was what he was trained to do and it was in his blood. The restrictions faced by law enforcement would bind him like an ill-fitting suit.

Eli leaned against the counter beside him, facing the hallway. "Jon's doing the security round. You look like you need to talk."

"How long did it take you to realize you loved Brenna?"

The SEAL chuckled. "I fell in love with Brenna the minute I saw her face off with a slime ball on a downtown Nashville street. Took me less than a week to figure it out. In my defense, the week was intense." His smile faded. "When human traffickers had her in their clutches, I was terrified we wouldn't get to her in time. She still has nightmares."

"Mercy couldn't sleep last night for the same reason."

"The nightmares fade. Brenna doesn't have them often. Holding her while she calms down is a sweet privilege."

Nico remembered the night before on the couch with Mercy in his arms. Although he hated the reason she woke, he was glad he'd been close to comfort her. Falling asleep with her in his arms and waking in the same position was worth the sore muscles from sleeping sitting up. He'd never forget that experience.

"Does Mercy know you're in love with her?"

He shook his head. "She's a widow. Lost her husband in Afghanistan to an IED. She just agreed to date me two days ago. It's a little early to be declaring my love for a woman who met me for the first time when I sprung her from a cave in Mexico."

Eli turned to look at him. "Give her time while you win her heart."

Some of the tension eased from Nico's muscles. Eli was right. He and Mercy had time. She'd already expressed interest in spending more time with him after she was safe. He'd convince Mercy he was worth the risk. The alternative was unthinkable.

"Rest." Eli clapped him on the shoulder. "Jon and I will keep your team and Mercy safe."

"Wake me if anything happens."

"Copy that."

Nico trudged upstairs and got ready for bed. Within minutes he was sound asleep. Early the next morning, he rose before the sun came up. He glanced at Mercy's closed door. She didn't wake him. He hoped that meant Mercy had been okay through the night. He walked to the kitchen, poured himself a mug of coffee, and went in search of the SEALs.

He found them both on the front porch, sipping coffee themselves. "Morning. Any problems overnight?"

"Nothing." Eli stretched and stood. "Zane called a few minutes ago and said no one went to a hospital in or near Sherwood with a gunshot wound. No bodies have turned up, either."

"Anything new on the Scorpions' search for Mercy?"

The SEALs exchanged glances.

Oh, man. "Tell me."

"The bounty has increased by another million," Jon said.

He gritted his teeth. "Not what I wanted to hear."

"Gets better. The person offering the money also put a bounty on her family. He or she wanted them captured alive." The sniper held up a hand. "Maddox already has them covered. He dispatched Adam Walker's team to search the house. They'll provide protection for her father and brothers and their families."

"They were planning to use the Garwoods as leverage to bring Mercy out of hiding."

"Wasted effort." Jon turned to stare at Nico. "She'll be in the open in a few hours."

"Maybe they don't know that."

"They want her to panic and run scared. If she ditches her security detail, they'll have her with no effort."

"She's too smart for that."

"Make sure she knows that." With those words, the SEAL rose and walked into the house.

"No offense meant, Nico. Jon's worried about her. Her situation reminds him too much of Dana's troubles with the human traffickers," Eli said and followed his partner into the house.

Nico sat on the cushioned wicker couch and sipped his coffee as he scanned the area. Jon wasn't the only one worried about Mercy. Everything in Nico said this trip to Washington, D.C. was a bad idea. On the other hand, he didn't want Mercy on law enforcement's radar for refusing to testify before the committee. He couldn't protect her if she was in jail.

When he finished his coffee, Nico returned to the kitchen for a refill and grabbed his laptop. He heard someone stirring upstairs and hoped it was his teammates rather than Mercy.

After booting up his computer, he retrieved Mercy's memory card and copied her photographs to his hard drive.

Nico spent several minutes scrolling through the images, amazed at her photographs. He frequently took pictures of landmarks around Nashville and sent them to his mother. None of them had the same quality as Mercy's shots. If she wasn't an artist, Mercy could be a photographer.

He scanned hundreds of photos before he heard someone coming down the stairs. Nico looked up in time to see Mercy walk into the kitchen. He abandoned his laptop and went to her. "Morning." He cupped her nape and kissed her. "Sleep okay?"

"Until a few minutes ago. Where are Eli and Jon?"

"Asleep. Want tea?"

"I'd love some. How long have you been awake?"

"Almost an hour." He filled a mug with water and placed it in the microwave. When the machine signaled the end of the heating cycle, Nico dumped a bag of chamomile mint into the water.

"What's wrong?"

"We need to talk."

CHAPTER TWENTY-NINE

Mercy's stomach threatened to revolt. *We need to talk.* To hide her sudden pain and fear, she teased him. "Are you breaking up with me already?"

Nico looked startled. "No, of course not. I'm crazy about you. Why would I be stupid enough to let you slip away from me?"

"Isn't that always what men and women say before they dump their boyfriend or girlfriend?"

He cupped her face between his palms. "That's not what's happening here. I have information you need to know." Nico turned away and grabbed her mug. He led her to the living room. "Let's sit while we talk."

"That bad, huh?"

"It's not good," Nico admitted. "I don't want to hide anything from you."

What had him so worried? A horrible possibility occurred to her. Mercy's hands clenched around the mug, and she felt the blood drain from her face. "My family."

"They're safe." He wrapped his arm around her shoulders and drew her tight against his side. "The Scorpions raised the bounty on you by one million dollars and placed a bounty on your family. The orders are to capture them alive. Hector and his buddies want to use your family to bring you into the open."

She set her mug on the coffee table and got to her feet. Her phone. Where was her phone? With such turbulent emotions pinging around inside her, Mercy had a hard time focusing on the immediate need. Talking to her family. "We have to warn them."

"Fortress has a team protecting them." Nico tugged her back down beside him and pressed the mug of tea back into her hands.

"Are they good?"

"All of our teams are good. This team is one of the best. It's also the team I planned to ask to protect you if we were called back into the field before you were safe and when Shadow went after the Scorpions."

Her eyes widened, inexplicable hurt twining through her. Her emotions were raw right now. Nico wouldn't just hand her off to someone else. Would he? "You planned to have someone else take over my protection?"

"I had to make contingency plans, Mercy. Shadow is the team Maddox sends after victims taken by human traffickers."

"He can't send other teams in?" Did he and his teammates always have to face the worst people the world had to offer?

"Of course. But that kind of mission is our passion. We're always his first choice if we're available."

"Nico, that can't be good for Shadow."

"That's the reason we're taking a month off after you're safe. Those missions demand a high price from us."

Mercy sipped her tea, grateful for the warmth that eased the knots in her stomach. "I understand the need for your work. But why is rescuing victims from human traffickers a passion for you and your team?"

For the first time since she'd met him, Nico broke eye contact with her, pain filling his gaze.

What hurt him so much? "It's okay, Nico. You don't have to tell me."

He shook his head. "You need to know. It's part of what drives me to the point of exhaustion." And still he wouldn't look at her.

"Turn out the light." She set her tea mug on the coffee table again as he frowned at her.

"Why?"

"Please." When he complied, Mercy snuggled up to his side and wrapped her arm around him. She pressed a kiss to his jaw. "Talk to me. Start wherever you need to and tell me as much or as little as you want." Although curiosity might kill her if he didn't tell her everything.

He was silent a few moments. Maybe Nico was gathering his courage or simply trying to figure out where to start. Mercy didn't press him. He'd start when he was ready. If he could tell her. The pain she glimpsed in his eyes might be too great to share with her today. She hoped he would unburden himself someday if not today.

Nico pressed a kiss to her temple. "I have two sisters and one brother. When I was eighteen, I enlisted in the Marines. My parents were proud that I chose to serve my country." He gave a wry laugh. "The truth was I didn't want a job where I had to work behind a desk, and I didn't have an interest in going to college. I'm not much for school. Anyway, while I was in boot camp, my fourteen-year-old sister disappeared along with several other girls about her age in our neighborhood. The cops were convinced Marta and her friends ran away." Another kiss to Mercy's temple. "She was the sweetest, most content kid in our family. Marta didn't have a rebellious bone in her body."

Oh, no. Tears stung Mercy's eyes. She already knew where his story was going.

"My baby sister didn't run away. Neither did the other girls who were taken. Marta and the girls were friends. They went everywhere together. The girls had similar qualities. Young, innocent, and beautiful, qualities irresistible to a human trafficker. The police eventually quit looking. My parents burned through their retirement money to pay for a private detective to find Marta. The detective called late one night months later and told my parents he had a lead on Marta and he was going to Mexico to follow up."

"Did he find her?"

"I don't know. While he was in Mexico, he disappeared. No one heard from him after that." He fell silent again.

Mercy thought about what he'd said and more importantly what he hadn't. "You've been looking for her."

He sighed. "It's foolish. After fourteen years, I know in my head Marta is dead. Women and girls in the hands of human traffickers don't survive that long. It's a hard, ugly life. However, my heart won't give up hope."

"Do you have any proof human traffickers took your sister?"

"While I was enlisted, I made contacts in the military and black ops community. I even had Zane dig into Marta's disappearance. He confirmed there was a large human trafficking ring working that part of California at the time. Two of Marta's friends were found dead at the Mexican border. Each girl had a brand on her ankle, an infinity symbol which was the symbol used by the trafficking ring. The traffickers had dumped their bodies on the side of the highway."

"Oh, Nico, I'm so sorry. No wonder you're the first to go after human traffickers. What about the rest of your teammates? Are they invested in the missions because of you or do they have something personal against traffickers?"

"Each of them has their own personal story."

In other words, he wouldn't divulge their tales himself. Fair enough. If they wanted her to know the details, they would tell her. "Thank you for telling me about Marta."

Finally, Nico looked at her. "You needed to know."

Time to change the subject. "Will you answer another question for me?"

"If I can."

"Why do your teammates call you Patch?"

He grinned, his expression lightening. "It's my military nickname."

She thought about that. Aiden's nickname was Boston because he'd loved the Boston Red Sox. "Why Patch?"

"I learned how to fly Cobra helicopters in the Marines. However, my favorite chopper is the Apache. A friend from the Army taught me how to fly one. My battle buddy, Harry, shortened Apache to Patch. The moniker stuck."

"Hmm. You're a man of many talents, Mr. Rivera. Are your parents Hispanic?"

"My great-grandparents are Hispanic. From there, the family bloodline was diluted." He studied her face. "Does my heritage bother you?"

"Does it bother you that my ancestors are from England?"

"Nope."

"Same with me."

Footsteps sounded on the stairs. Trace walked into the living room, dressed in what Mercy had realized was the standard Fortress attire.

"Any news?" Trace asked.

Nico brought him up to speed on the higher bounty on Mercy and the new one on her family.

"Man, these guys don't want to give up, do they? Have you had a chance to check the memory card from Mercy's camera?"

"I downloaded the pictures to my laptop. It's on the kitchen table if you want to scroll through them. I haven't finished looking at them yet."

"I'll grab some coffee and take a look." Trace turned to Mercy. "How did you sleep?"

"Better."

With a nod, he turned and went to the kitchen.

"Are you hungry?" Nico asked.

She nodded.

"Good. Let's see what we can find before the others wake." He pulled Mercy to her feet.

"How soon do we have to leave?"

He grimaced. "With D.C. traffic, no later than nine."

Mercy poked around in the refrigerator and pantry. "Do you like French toast?"

Both men perked up. "Who doesn't?" Trace asked.

With a laugh, she told the operatives what items to gather while she found two bowls that would work. Between the three of them, they established a good assembly line. By the time the rest of Shadow descended the stairs, they had two platters of French toast plus a mountain of scrambled eggs, coffee and juice.

"Be still, my heart," Joe said, delight on his face. "French toast? Please tell me you taught either Nico or Trace how to make this. It would be a flat-out shame not to recreate this on another protection detail."

Mercy smiled at the operative over her shoulder. "They're great students."

"Yes!"

Nico rolled his eyes. "Sit down before you drool on the food, Joe."

"You don't have to tell me twice."

After they set aside enough food for the SEALs, finished breakfast, and cleaned the kitchen, Mercy sat with Nico and Trace at the breakfast bar with the laptop.

She scrolled through the pictures until she found the shots of the Jeffries estate. "This is the first picture of the senator's estate. The barn has twenty horses stabled inside. I understand they bred a couple of Kentucky Derby winners. They have an eight-car garage. This is the ranch house for the hands."

She moved to the next picture of a building in the distance. Mercy had been after the rolling hills, the stream, and trees. She'd used that in one of the pictures she'd drawn.

"What building is that?" Nico asked.

"I don't know. Sean's aide, Theo, said it was an old spring house and refused to take me closer to shoot pictures. He said it wasn't safe. Something about sinkholes in that part of the property."

Trace studied the picture, frowning. "Do you have your mouse?" he asked Nico.

The operative thrust his hand into a computer bag and pulled out a wireless mouse, then handed it to his friend.

Mercy watched in fascination as Trace highlighted a particular section of the picture and magnified it. She frowned, not sure what she was seeing. He did something else with the mouse and the magnified section of the picture became sharper.

Three men stood in front of the spring house. Mercy didn't recognize one of the men, but she did the other two. Her breath stalled in her lungs. What did that mean?

"Mercy." Nico's hand covered hers. "What do you see?"

"That's Sean Jeffries and his father. I don't recognize the third man."

"Trace, focus on the third man."

After working a couple minutes, he said, "That's the best I can do. Zane might be able to finesse the picture a little more."

"Send it to him. I want Z to run the face through facial recognition and see if he's in the system."

"Safe bet." Trace shot off an email to Zane with the picture attached. "Done. Want to look at the rest of Mercy's photos?"

Nico motioned for him to keep scrolling. Mercy pointed out various buildings around the estate and told them about the rooms she'd been allowed to photograph inside the massive mansion. "That's only a handful of the rooms in the house. A whole football team could live in that place, and there would still be plenty of room for everybody."

"Did you like the house?"

"It's beautiful."

"But you didn't like it."

"I wouldn't want to live there. You saw my house in Sherwood. I love the cozy feel of the place. Sean's home feels impersonal."

When they finished studying the pictures of the Jeffries estate, Trace turned to Nico, eyebrow raised. "We have another two hours before we leave. What's the plan?"

"Sam and Joe are on shift. Ask Ben to dig up anything he can find on Jeffries Industries. You take the senator's father. Mercy and I will look into the senator's background."

With a nod, Trace left to find his teammate.

"Do you think Sean is responsible for my abduction?" Nausea boiled in her stomach at the thought.

"I don't know, kitten, but we have to look into the possibility."

"Maybe we shouldn't go today. Take me somewhere with your team. I can call Sean again and tell him it's not safe for me to come to Washington today."

"You could. You will still have to talk to him and the committee. If you don't, they'll send law enforcement after you."

222

She scowled. "So take me out of the country."

"A fugitive life is not what you need. Eventually, you'll make a mistake, and they'll have you. If I think there's no choice, I'll create a new identity for you, and we'll relocate to another country."

"We?" Mercy turned toward him. "You would go with me?"

"I won't let you go on your own. Fortress offers a private witness protection program. If I determine that's the only way to save your life, I'll adopt a new identity and go with you."

How could she protect her heart against a man like this one? Strong, valiant, noble, caring, kind, and deadly when he needed to be. Mercy pressed her mouth to his and felt her heart fall, hard.

She drew in a shaky breath. Oh, man. She was in so much trouble. There was no turning back now. If he didn't come to love her, she was doomed to another heartbreak of epic proportions.

Nico gripped her upper arms and nudged her back. "What is it?" Concern filled his gaze.

Mercy didn't want to lie to him, but she also wasn't ready to talk about her revelation, either. "I'm not ready to talk about it yet."

He looked deep into her eyes for a moment. "Will you tell me at some point?"

"Yes." Eventually, she wouldn't be able to hold the truth inside. "It's not bad, Nico. I'm just not ready to share." Mercy cupped his jaw, unable to resist rubbing her fingers across his beard scruff.

Nico captured her hand and pressed a gentle kiss to the center of her palm. "All right. Ready to tear Sean Jeffries' life apart?"

"I hate to invade his privacy."

"In an investigation like this, there are no secrets. Everything will come out."

She glanced at the handsome operative by her side, wondering what he would think when he knew her secret.

CHAPTER THIRTY

Nico followed another link in his and Mercy's search through Sean Jeffries' life and skimmed through the article. Nothing new, he decided. More about Jeffries' rise to political power.

"Nothing," Mercy said, sounding disgusted. "I thought we'd have better luck. The tabloids love to spread gossip about everybody. Why not Sean? I've heard all this news in the mainstream press."

He gritted his teeth at her continued use of the senator's first name. Yeah, Nico needed to get over it. He couldn't act like an overbearing, jealous boyfriend every time she mentioned another man's name even though jealousy burned inside when he thought about her interaction with Jeffries. "The man has money. Maybe he greased palms to keep unsavory items out of the headlines." Tough to squash all of it, though. Most tabloids would create scandal if they couldn't unearth any on their own.

He logged into the Fortress website and clicked on one of their search engines.

"What's that?"

"A search engine Zane created that surf's information on the dark web, too." He typed in the senator's name. A moment later, the search produced thousands of hits.

He checked the time. They had thirty minutes left. "I'll start reading while you gather what you need. Bring your sketch pad." He didn't want to stay in D.C. overnight, but plans could change, depending on what happened in the city.

"Should I pack everything, Nico?"

He kissed her. "To be safe, yes. If we have to go on the run, I want to stay out of stores to avoid surveillance cameras." Shadow would take their gear as well.

With a nod, Mercy slid from the barstool and went upstairs.

While she was gone, Nico clicked on the first link. The senator was Dwayne Jeffries' golden boy. The second son, Mark, became hooked on cocaine in high school. Jeffries cut his son off financially when he turned twenty-one, refusing to support his drug habit. Desperate for money to buy his next hit, Mark broke into houses and stole money and jewelry.

Six months into his criminal career, he chose the wrong house. The homeowner, a third-shift worker, was sleeping in the master bedroom at the time. The Army veteran heard Mark rummaging through his belongings in another room and confronted him with a gun. The kid charged him with a knife. The vet took him down. No charges were filed against him despite Dwayne's threats to do just that.

Sean, on the other hand, appeared to be the perfect son. Excellent student, top notch athlete in football, and voted most likely to succeed in high school. He earned a full ride scholarship at Harvard and graduated with a law degree. After practicing law for a few years in a prestigious New York City law firm, Sean ran for senate and won. Rumors said he was the favored pick for the next presidential run.

Nico frowned. No mud anywhere. Everybody had a past, including the golden boy senator. He clicked on another link from the dark web, skimmed the first few paragraphs, and sat up straighter. Perhaps the golden boy had a smudge on his halo after all.

He changed the parameters for his search and read more. Nico rubbed his jaw, the beard stubble scraping against his fingers. Not sure what to make of the information, Nico sent Zane a text, requesting him to dig deeper. If Z didn't have time, the research geeks at Fortress could handle it.

When Mercy descended the stairs, Nico took the bag from her hand. "How's the shoulder?"

"No need for pain meds this morning."

"Might change after the drive into D.C."

"I can take something if I need it." She motioned toward the computer. "Did you find anything?"

"A couple things I'm having Zane check before I say anything. The rumor mill says Sean Jeffries is the favored pick to succeed your uncle."

Mercy frowned. "He's a power player, but I don't see him as presidential material."

"People with money and power are grooming him for a run." Nico set her bag by the back door. "How much do you know personally about Jeffries?"

"Almost nothing. He's a pleasant dinner companion. Very attentive, polite."

"Do you know if he's involved with a woman?"

Her cheeks colored and she glanced away. "I don't think so."

Interesting reaction. "Mercy." When she didn't turn his direction, Nico tipped her face up to meet his gaze. "Jeffries is interested in you, isn't he?"

"Sean asked me out several times, yes."

He considered her words and reaction. "You turned him down."

"Every time. I didn't think I was ready to date again. Even if I had been, I wasn't interested in him. He's too slick for my taste and he always paid attention to who noticed him while he was with me. He considered me a prize to be shown off rather than a treasure. Besides, I have zero interest in Washington social life."

"What's your idea of the perfect date?"

Surprise filled her eyes. "I don't know."

"Think about it and tell me." He'd do his best to fulfill her dream date.

His teammates arrived in the kitchen, bags in hand. Nico tossed his keys to Joe. "You and Trace check the SUVs to be sure we don't have surprises while I grab my gear."

"What about Jon and Eli?" Mercy asked.

"They'll stay here to keep the house secure unless we tell them we're on the run." Nico squeezed her fingers and took the stairs two at a time. Soon, he returned to Mercy and the others. He set his bag on the floor and distributed the ceramic knives Jon had brought for them, keeping the last one for himself. "SUVs are clear?"

"They're clean." Trace turned off kitchen lights as Shadow hoisted bags to their shoulders.

Nico picked up Mercy's bag as he spouted off the name of the parking garage a few blocks from the Capitol. "Maddox arranged parking passes at the ticket booth as we drive into the garage."

Ben scowled. "Jeffries insisted Mercy come in a day early, but didn't bother to provide secure parking for her? Some friend he is."

Nico agreed with his teammate's assessment although he refrained from commenting. Jeffries didn't know Mercy was accompanied by a security team. Didn't say much about a man who wanted a relationship with a woman yet didn't provide basic security for her when he knew what she'd been through in Mexico. If he thought she might be in danger from the Scorpions, he should have insisted law enforcement escort her to the Capitol building. Unaccompanied, Mercy was an easy target. "Time to go."

Nico drove from the house with Trace on his six. Hopefully, they wouldn't run into trouble today. Mercy had almost reached her limit of tolerance for disasters and emergencies.

This time, Joe and Sam rode with Nico and Mercy. Although they kept the conversation on neutral topics, Nico sensed Mercy's uneasiness growing by the increasing tension in her shoulders.

"This is a waste of time." Mercy glanced at Nico. "We're spending all this time driving into D.C. so I can tell Senator Jeffries I don't know anything. I could have told him that on the phone if he'd bother to talk to me personally. Instead, he pawned me off on his aide, Theo Morris."

"Not a waste of time." He threaded his fingers through hers. "He'll be answering questions, too."

"I hope he knows more than I do."

Two hours later, he and Trace parked the vehicles in the parking garage. "Wait here." He exited the SUV along with Sam and Joe, and scoured the row of vehicles near his own, looking for signs of something that didn't belong or someone who paid too much attention to the anonymous black SUVs from Fortress Security.

Nothing set off his senses beyond his growing unease. Nico opened the passenger door and extended his hand to Mercy. "We have ninety minutes to kill before your appointment. Are you hungry?"

"A little."

He smiled when his teammates brightened at the mention of food. "I know a nice cafe two blocks from here. It's a hole in the wall, not a place the political bigwigs enjoy frequenting. The food's great and the owner is a friend."

"Sounds perfect."

Nico walked with his arm around Mercy, his teammates surrounding them in a loose circle. When they walked into the Blue Moon Cafe, Nico's friend, Ace, spotted him and exited the kitchen with a huge smile on his face.

"Patch! What are you doing in D.C.?" He dragged Nico into a one-armed hug and pounded him on the back.

"Working. Let me introduce you to some people. My teammates. Sam, Joe, Trace, and Ben." He turned to Mercy. "And this is Mercy Powers. Ace O'Brien."

The gunnery sergeant held out his hand to Mercy. "Let me know if Patch doesn't treat you right. I'll set him straight."

She smiled. "He treats me like a princess."

"Glad he paid attention to the lessons I taught him about wooing a lady while we worked together." Ace winked at her, then turned to Nico. "You stopping in to visit or eat?"

"Both." He glanced around at the full tables. "Looks like you're packed, though."

Ace grabbed a handful of menus and motioned for them to follow him. He led them through the dining room to a hallway at the back of the cafe. Ace turned into a break room with a large round table and chairs along with vending machines, refrigerator, and coffee maker. "Have a seat and check the menu. I'll be back in a minute for your orders."

An hour later, the group left Blue Moon with full stomachs and an admonition from Ace to stop the next time they were in D.C. They walked the remaining blocks to Capitol Hill. After clearing security, Nico escorted Mercy to Senator Jeffries' office.

"Trace, Ben, stay in the hall. Sam, Joe, with us. Wait outside the senator's office in case we need you." Overkill. Maybe. Nico wouldn't take chances with Mercy's safety.

He glanced at her. "Ready?"

She nodded.

Nico brushed her lips with his, then opened the door to the senator's office. A receptionist smiled as they approached her desk.

"May I help you?"

"Mercy Powers to see Senator Jeffries. She's expected."

"Make yourselves comfortable. I'll tell the senator you're here, Ms. Powers." She turned away to speak softly into the phone as Nico led Mercy to the seating area.

Sam and Joe sat, eyeing the senator's staff. When Mercy showed no inclination to sit, he wrapped his hand around hers and memorized the office layout and the entrances and exits.

Ten minutes later, a door to one of the offices opened, and a tall, slender man with dark hair and eyes stepped out. His gaze swept over Mercy. "Ms. Powers, Senator Jeffries will see you now."

"Thank you. It's good to see you again, Theo. How is your mother?"

Theo smiled. "She's great and sends her thanks for your gift. Mom brags to all her friends about the original MJ Powers drawing hanging on her wall."

"I'm glad she liked it." She walked toward Theo and the door to the inner sanctum with Nico by her side.

Theo held up his hand, his gaze on Nico. "I'm sorry. The senator is only expecting Ms. Powers. You'll have to wait out here."

Nico slid his arm around Mercy and pulled her against his side. "With danger circling her, Mercy isn't going anywhere without me by her side. If Jeffries wants to see her today, he'll do it with me in the room or not at all. If you want to consult with the senator, we'll wait two minutes for his decision. After that time, I'm taking Mercy back to her safe house."

A scowl. "This is a secure building. She's perfectly safe. On top of that, the senator is a very busy man. He can't juggle his schedule to accommodate your demands."

"Clock's ticking, Theo. Talk to your boss or let us pass."

After another hard look at Nico, he reluctantly motioned for them to follow him.

Anticipation hummed in Nico's veins. Maybe they would finally learn some answers.

CHAPTER THIRTY-ONE

Mercy stepped into the office, glancing around at the decor. Nice. Really nice. Leather furniture. Cherry desk. Coffee bar. Several paintings on the walls by famous artists. Plush carpet. Huge windows with a killer view. Great natural light.

Her attention focused on the blond-haired man with a surfer tan and blue eyes who leaped to his feet and hurried around the desk toward her as she moved further into the room.

"Mercy, thank God you're all right." Sean Jeffries spread his arms and went to envelop her in a hug when Nico stepped between them. The senator stopped abruptly and glared at him. "Who are you?"

Nico pushed Sean back a few steps before he clasped Mercy's hand again. "Nico, a friend of Mercy's." He kissed her knuckles. "A very good friend."

The senator shifted his attention to Mercy, his jaw tight. "Care to explain?"

Something about his tone raised her hackles. "Nico and I are dating."

"You weren't dating two weeks ago when I asked you out. You said you weren't ready." His lips pressed into a thin line for a few seconds. "Why did you bring him here?"

"He's the head of my protection detail."

"You're safe. We have security."

"Not safe enough for me to trust Mercy's life to the Capitol police," Nico said, his voice low.

Sean's eyes narrowed as he motioned them to guest chairs. "She's not in Mexico any longer."

"The Scorpions aren't giving up." Mercy sat. "They tried twice to capture me since I've been back in the States, and someone broke into my house in Sherwood and trashed the place. Do you blame me for preferring to trust my own security over a police force spread too thin with more important people to protect than me?"

The senator leaned against the edge of his desk, stunned at her revelation. "I had no idea. Now I understand why you wanted me to delay the hearing. I'm sorry I couldn't accommodate you, honey. The committee refused to wait. National security is at risk and you might have vital information."

Nico scowled at Sean. Mercy laced their fingers together. No doubt he objected to the pet name. She wasn't a fan of that one. Mercy glanced at Nico. It seemed she'd developed a preference for being called kitten.

"Were you hurt in the attacks?" Sean asked.

"Gunshot wound to her shoulder." Nico stared at the other man. "It's only a matter of time before she is hurt unless I stop them."

"You can't think the attacks will continue. They failed. The gunrunners should move on."

Mercy blinked. What did a United States senator know about gunrunners and their behavior patterns?

"That would be smart," Nico agreed. "Based on the continued attacks, they aren't shifting to an easier target. Mercy has a price on her head, and so does her family."

Blood drained from Sean's face. "The Scorpions put a hit on you? This is insane. There's no purpose."

"She knows something," Nico murmured.

If anything, Sean grew paler. "What? What do you know? You must tell me, Mercy. I'll authorize more protection for you than your friend can provide. I know important people. I'll make sure you have the best protection the US government can provide."

"The same government that has more leaks than a sieve?" Nico huffed. "No, thanks."

Mercy shook her head. "I don't want anyone else watching over me. Nico and his friends are amazing."

Startled, he turned to Nico. "Friends?"

"We're a team of five."

"Overkill, isn't it? Unless you aren't as good as Mercy thinks you are."

"It's not overkill. What do you know about the Scorpions, Senator?"

He shrugged. "They're thugs. What's to know?"

"They're a bunch of well-armed thugs, gunrunners with an almost unlimited supply of weapons at their disposal. You know anything about that?"

"Why would I?'

Mercy blinked. Sean was answering every question with a question. What was going on with him?

"Family connections, Senator Jeffries."

A frown. "Jeffries Industries is an import/export company. We don't deal with gangbangers and terrorists."

"Get real. Your company does business with anyone with the money to pay for your service or product. What product or service from Jeffries Industries interests the Scorpions?"

"Careful." A cold smile curved his lips. "I'm still licensed to practice law."

Nico shrugged. "Stating facts. What do you know of your father's recent activities?"

Sean scowled. "What is this? I didn't ask Mercy here so I could be interrogated."

"Answer the question, Senator, then you can ask Mercy whatever you want to know."

"I'm too busy to keep up with my father's social calendar. I know he traveled out of the country on several occasions recently. I haven't seen him for weeks."

Nico stared at Sean. "You sure about that?"

"Are you accusing me of lying?"

He reached into his pocket and extracted the picture Mercy drew. "While Mercy was in the hands of the Scorpions, she saw someone who wasn't part of their organization. I asked her to draw his face." Nico handed it to Sean.

Sean glanced at the drawing and froze. "You're saying Dad was down in Mexico in the Scorpion's compound?" He turned to Mercy. "You're mistaken. You must have seen Dad somewhere else and thought some other man resembled him."

Sympathy filled Mercy at his obvious distress. "I have a good memory for faces. Besides, I haven't met your father."

"I'm telling you he wasn't in Mexico. However, I'll ask when I see him to be sure."

Mercy didn't know Sean, but she knew him well enough to know he was lying about more than one thing. He might not want to admit why his father was in Mexico, but he suspected the reason and didn't want to tell them.

"Ask your questions," Nico said.

Sean turned to Mercy. "Tell me what happened in Mexico, honey. Don't leave out any details."

Mercy tightened her grip on Nico's hand and told Sean about the abduction at the funeral, the cave, and her sessions with Hector and his merry band of thugs. When she mentioned the threats of rape and white slavery, Sean looked sick.

The senator dragged a shaking hand over his face. "I need a drink," he muttered and shoved away from his desk. Sean crossed to the other side of his office to a cabinet. He yanked open the doors, grabbed a bottle filled with amber liquid, and poured three fingers worth into a tumbler.

After tossing back the contents, Sean coughed slightly, closed the cabinet again, and faced Mercy. "How were you shot?"

"Hector's men opened fire on us as we ran to the plane."

He scowled at Nico. "You should have protected her better. I'm tempted to have her put into protective custody since it's obvious you can't do the job."

"Try it," Nico said, his voice soft. "I'll find her and we'll disappear. You'll never see or hear from her again."

Sean eyed him, then turned to Mercy. "He can't do that. You shouldn't trust your life to this man."

"Nico will do exactly what he says."

"He'd send you away without any protection? That's crazy."

"Nico would go with me. He'd never set me up in a different place and walk away."

"How long have you known him? Were you seeing him two weeks ago? Is that why you turned me down?"

"I don't belong in your world. I have no interest in the Washington political scene. I like my quiet life where no one cares what I buy at the grocery store or what I wear to yoga class, where I ate dinner and who I was with."

"You would be the perfect first lady, honey. Just give me the chance to prove it to you. Dump this loser and let me show you the finer things in life. You deserve better than this clod."

Nico growled.

"First, I would be miserable in a fishbowl like the White House. Second, who said you're going to win the nomination for your party much less win the national election? Third, I married Aiden because I was head-over-heels in love with him. If I marry again, I won't settle for less. I refuse to be anyone's trophy wife."

"One day you'll see Nico for the lowlife he is." He glanced at his watch and scowled. "I have a meeting in five minutes. Where are you staying? How can I contact you again?"

Nico rose and held out his hand to Mercy. "Get word to President Martin. He knows how to contact Mercy."

"I need to see Mercy tonight."

"Why?"

"I'm presenting her drawings to my father tonight at his birthday party. Mercy needs to be there."

"No, she doesn't. You do remember that she's in danger from the Scorpions, right?"

Sean brushed aside Nico's concern. "The party is at the Jeffries estate. It's well guarded. We have extensive security." He turned to Mercy. "You know my father is a huge fan of your work. This would make his night."

"I don't want to disappoint him, Sean, but your parties are notorious for being packed with people. I'm not a security expert, but that doesn't sound safe for me."

"Why would gunrunners crash an old man's birthday party? Please. You've already told me everything you know and it's not worth killing you over."

And that was supposed to make her feel better? "Maybe you should tell the Scorpions that. I don't think it's wise, Sean. I'm sorry. Please express my regrets to your father."

"There's another reason why you must come tonight. My father is leaving in the morning to go overseas. He won't return for six weeks. If you want to talk to him about his presence in that Mexican compound, you'll have to talk to him tonight."

Oh, man. Couldn't the man stay in the country more than a few days at a time? Mercy sighed. "All right. What time?"

"Mercy." Nico turned her to face him. "It's too dangerous."

"We need answers, Nico. We'll bring your team." She placed her hand over his heart. "I'll be safe with the five of you watching over me."

Mercy glanced over her shoulder at Sean who observed their interaction with rapt attention. "You don't mind if I bring my security detail?"

"Of course not."

His expression and body language said otherwise. Mercy didn't care if Sean liked the arrangement. Taking Shadow to the party was the only way Nico would agree to let Mercy attend.

While she dreaded the coming evening, she would regret missing an opportunity to find information to stop the Scorpions.

Nico stared at her, anger simmering in his eyes. "What time, Jeffries?"

"Seven o'clock. Need directions?"

Nico shook his head. "My team and I will be armed. Warn your security. If they stop us because of the weapons, we'll turn around and leave."

"Understood." Satisfaction and relief gleamed in his eyes.

"We won't stay long," Mercy warned him. "No matter what's on the party agenda, if you want me to help you present the pictures, you'll have to present them as soon as we arrive."

"After I introduce you to Dad, we'll unveil the pictures."

Nico pressed his hand to the small of Mercy's back and guided her to the door.

"Wait. What time should I expect you? I need to tell the gate guards."

"No, you don't. See you tonight, Jeffries." He opened the office door and ushered Mercy from the room.

CHAPTER THIRTY-TWO

"I'm sorry, Nico."

He turned to look at Mercy's beautiful face as they strode down the hallway surrounded by his teammates. "Try again, kitten."

"Okay. I'm not sorry about agreeing to go to the party. I am sorry I upset you."

"Party?" Sam glanced over her shoulder at them. "What party?"

"Senator Jeffries is throwing his father a birthday bash. He's insisting Mercy attend. We'll talk about the situation later. Right now, we need to leave D.C. and find a clothing store."

He stifled a laugh at the scowls on his teammates' faces and the low-voiced complaints. On the walk to the SUVs, Nico remained silent. When Mercy repeatedly sent worried glances his direction, he wrapped his arm around her shoulders and pressed a kiss to her temple. "Don't worry. We'll work out the details so you're safe."

"Will you yell at me when we're alone?" she murmured.

His gaze locked on hers. "I don't have a reason to yell."

"But you don't want me to do this."

"No, I don't. I understand your reasoning, but it's risky."

"Attending that party is the quickest way to discover what Dwayne Jeffries knows."

"Maybe. We won't have a chance to interrogate him in a crowded party."

"What if we ask to talk to him in a quiet room?"

Nico squeezed her shoulder. "We'll try." If the senator's father was involved with the Scorpions, he doubted the man would agree to a private interview. He breathed a sigh of relief when he tucked Mercy into the passenger seat of his SUV with Joe and Sam in the backseat.

Once Nico headed out of D.C., he called Trace. "There's a shopping center with a clothing store halfway between here and the safe house. That's probably the best bet to purchase what we need for tonight."

"Please tell me we don't have to dress up in monkey suits," Ben grumbled.

"Not if I can help it." He wasn't a fan of tuxedos himself. The high collars and tie choked him.

"What about me?" Sam asked.

Nico glanced in the mirror and grinned. "No tuxedo for you, either."

"Ha ha. If I wear a fancy dress, my movements will be hampered. And the shoes?" Sam gave a mock shudder. "I'm not running after a gun slinging terrorist in high heels."

Mercy twisted in her seat. "What about black pants and a black shirt or sweater along with black ankle boots? You'll have full freedom of movement if you need it, and you'll blend into the surroundings."

"That sounds perfect. Great suggestion."

"You have fashion advice for the rest of us, Mercy?" Trace teased.

"Sorry. I'm fresh out of suggestions for the day."

The operative chuckled. "We're on your six, Nico." He ended the call.

An hour later, Nico parked near the entrance to the clothing store. "Will this work for you, Mercy?"

"I'm sure I can find something."

He escorted her into the store, then trailed Mercy and Sam. His teammates hustled to the men's department, figuring they'd be finished with their purchases long before the ladies were.

Turned out, they finished at the same time. Since Trace knew Nico's sizes, he'd picked up what Nico needed.

Taking Mercy's selections to the checkout counter, Nico paid for her purchases. He found it interesting that Joe did the same for Sam although the medic had an intense whispered discussion with him about it. The spotter prevailed.

Back in the SUV with their packages, Nico called Jon. "We're thirty minutes from the safe house."

"You're clear. We haven't had any activity on site."

The ball of ice in Nico's stomach melted. "Good. I need information on Senator Jeffries' estate."

"Why?"

"Jeffries is throwing his father a birthday party tonight and plans to present Mercy's pictures to him. He insists she attend."

"And you're allowing her to go?" Jon's icy question had Nico stiffening.

"I want to," Mercy cut in before Nico could defend his decision. "Sean's father is leaving the country tomorrow and won't return for more than a month. This is our only opportunity to question him about his presence in that compound."

"It's not safe and puts your security detail in the crosshairs. Did you think about that in your campaign to get answers, fast?"

"Jon." Nico's hands tightened around the steering wheel. "Enough."

"I'll see what I can find out about the estate before you arrive." Jon ended the call.

Joe whistled softly. "What's eating him?"

"He's worried about Mercy." Nico clasped her hand. "I think her being kidnapped and transported to Mexico reminds him too much of his wife's situation."

"Dana was taken by human traffickers," Sam pointed out.

"They were both ill-treated and threatened with rape and sex slavery. This operation brings back bad memories. He thinks I'm irresponsible for allowing Mercy into the open."

If a SEAL of Jon Smith's caliber thought Nico was making a mistake, he had to consider the possibility that he was dead wrong in his decision, a decision which might cost Mercy her life if he'd miscalculated.

"It's my choice," Mercy reminded him. "I want to spend my time getting to know you, not running from terrorists who think I know something important. If going to this party moves me one step closer to that goal, I'll follow through with the idea. I know you have to go to another assignment eventually. I don't want to watch over my shoulder for trouble as I go about my day while you're gone. I also don't want to worry whether or not you're distracted when you leave."

Leave her while she was still in danger? Nico drew in a careful breath. He didn't think he could do it. Yeah, Nico had made plans to hand off her protection to a team he trusted. Now, that team was protecting her family. More important, leaving Mercy was no longer an option. She meant too much to him to walk away from her while there was a possibility of trouble finding her.

Maddox wouldn't be happy if Nico refused to deploy with Shadow, especially if this situation with the Scorpions couldn't be resolved soon. He squeezed her hand. "We'll figure it out."

When Trace and Nico parked the SUVs at the house, Eli was waiting for them at the back door. "Trouble?" Nico asked.

"Mercy okay?"

Ah. Eli must have been listening to the phone conversation with Jon. "She has a mind of her own. I can't keep her locked up."

A slow smile spread across Eli's face. "Dana and Brenna don't let us get by with caveman tendencies, either. Believe me, we try."

Nico chuckled as he circled the SUV to open Mercy's door, then helped Joe with the bags. He kept an eye on Mercy as Eli left the porch and swept Mercy into a one-armed hug. The SEAL talked to her a moment, his voice low enough that Nico couldn't hear the conversation.

After a moment, Mercy nodded and went inside the house.

As Nico and the others approached, Eli shifted into their path. "I thought you would visit the senator and hustle our resident artist back into protective custody. Looks like you made a surgical strike through a store."

"What are you doing?" Nico's eyes narrowed.

"Giving Jon a minute to eat crow without an audience. What's in the bags?"

"Not cargoes and t-shirts, unfortunately." Joe leaned against the side of the house. "Jeffries' party will be attended by the Washington elite. We settled for black dress pants, jackets, and tailored shirts."

Eli winced. "Ties?"

"No, thank goodness," Ben said.

After a quick glance over his shoulder, Eli stepped aside. "Thanks," he murmured to Nico.

He led his teammates inside. When he didn't see Mercy, Nico took the stairs two at a time and dropped off her bags in her room, then took his jacket, pants, and shoes into his own room.

That done, Nico searched for Mercy. He found her in the office on the first floor with Jon, sitting in an arm chair, listening with rapt attention to the SEAL. Not wanting to intrude, Nico turned to go when Jon called out.

"Join us, Nico." The operative vacated the chair next to Mercy's and motioned for Nico to take his place. Jon leaned back against the desk, arms folded across his chest.

"Finish your story, Jon." Mercy reached for Nico's hand. "You have me curious. You can't stop now."

"Not much more to tell. Eli and I and two Fortress teams invaded the island, rescued Brenna and Dana, and dismantled the human trafficking ring."

"What about the girls who had been taken and sold?"

"I tore apart the traffickers' computer records. We tracked down and freed those who were still alive."

"How many did you lose?"

"Too many." Jon's eyes looked haunted.

"How long did Dana make you wait until she married you?"

Nico captured Mercy's hand and pressed a kiss to her knuckles, grateful she'd read the pain in Jon's eyes from the losses of the girls and turned the conversation to a topic guaranteed to lighten the SEAL's mood.

Jon chuckled. "Not long. She married me in a small, private ceremony six weeks after we rescued her and her sister. In fact, we married the same day as Brenna and Eli."

"Sweet."

The SEAL flinched. "Not sweet. Logical. The women are close. It made sense to marry on the same day."

"Thanks for telling me," Mercy said. "I'm glad to know about you and Dana, but I wasn't angry at you, Jon. Nico told me you were worried about my safety. How can I be angry when you're looking out for my best interests?"

His lips curved. "Wish my wife was as reasonable."

"She's independent?"

A look of pride filled Jon's eyes. "She's getting there. It's a constant battle for me to balance giving her freedom and protecting her. Dana also struggles with repercussions of her captivity. One day she's fine going out on her own to buy groceries. The next, she's afraid to leave the house for anything unless I'm with her. I'm thankful those days are growing farther apart."

"Has she talked to a counselor about what happened to her?"

"Yeah, Marcus Lang. He's great with her. She likes the fact he's in Otter Creek and she can talk to him about painful things without Marcus being in the same room. The separation is better for her. She's still uncomfortable being in the same room with a man unless I'm with her or Eli.

"Nico set up a counseling session with Marcus for me. Talking without dealing with another man in close proximity helped."

Nico's gaze shifted to Mercy. Had he made her uncomfortable by being in the room when she talked with Marcus? Mercy asked him to stay with her. Maybe he should have left anyway.

Jon stood. "Nico, I have information on the estate. Where do you want me to set up?"

"The kitchen is the easiest place to gather. Mercy and I will be there in a few minutes."

With a nod, the operative left.

Nico tugged Mercy to her feet. "Come on. I have a few things to give you."

She frowned. "But you've been with me constantly since you rescued me in Mexico. I don't need gifts, Nico."

He turned and faced her, curious. "What do you need?" She was silent a moment, watching his every move. Finally, she said, "You. I need you."

CHAPTER THIRTY-THREE

Nico cupped Mercy's cheek and planted a gentle kiss on her lips. "You have me, kitten." More than she realized. Maybe more than she was ready for. "Come on." He wrapped his hand around hers and led her upstairs to his room.

He opened his Go bag and pulled out the box Zane had given him at Fortress headquarters. Opening it, he dumped the contents on his palm. Oh, yeah. This was perfect. He'd have to send his friend a case of root beer, his favorite beverage.

Mercy's jaw dropped. "Jewelry."

"Not just any jewelry. The ring, earrings, and watch have tracking devices embedded in them. If you insist on attending this party, you're going to wear all of them. I don't care if it goes with your dress or not."

She rose on her tiptoes and kissed him. "You're worried about the Scorpions capturing me again?"

"Until the organization doesn't exist anymore, I'll be concerned for your safety."

"I don't mind wearing them."

Nico eyed her. "I hope you don't because I'll want you to wear them any time we're apart, especially when I'm on missions. I need the reassurance that my co-workers can find you if there's trouble while I'm deployed."

He fastened the watch on her wrist, slid the ring on the fourth finger of her right hand, and motioned for her to remove the earrings she wore and replace them with the new ones.

A moment later, she turned to let him see. "What do you think?"

"You're beautiful." He dropped a quick kiss on the bridge of her nose. "Then again, you're always beautiful to me."

A smile lifted the corners of her mouth. "You make me feel beautiful."

Nico lowered his head and captured her mouth with his, the kiss hot, deep, and possessive. A short time later, he forced himself to let go of the addicting woman and stepped back. "We need to join the others." Before he moved too fast and crossed a line neither of them was ready to cross.

His team and the SEALs waited in the kitchen. They had laid out supplies on the breakfast bar to make sub sandwiches for an early dinner.

"Grab a plate," Trace said. "Jon's ready to give us a rundown of the Jeffries estate."

Once Mercy made her sandwich, Nico signaled Jon to begin the briefing while he put together his own meal.

"The estate is located outside Knollwood, a city an hour north of D.C. Two hundred acres of prime real estate, rolling hills, a creek, extensive landscaping. You already know they breed prize horses. Although the place is beautiful, the estate is a security nightmare. Jeffries hired Westgate Security to keep an eye on everything." His lip curled. "There's no way to secure that property, Nico, even if Westgate had been anywhere close to the skill level and quality of Fortress. Sure, it's fenced for the horses. Doesn't stop a person from climbing through the fence and sneaking into the buildings."

"Security arrangements?"

"Cameras and motion sensors. Guards at the gate. Roaming guards at night."

And a lot of holes where intruders could slip through undetected. He glanced up after he shoved a mug of water into the microwave to heat for Mercy's tea. "Dogs?"

"Negative. Jeffries tried. Apparently, the dogs scared the horses and employees."

"House security."

"Cameras, motion detectors. At night, the guards do rounds inside the mansion and outside twice an hour."

"Clockwork?" Trace asked.

"What do you think?" Scorn filled the SEAL's voice. "They roam on the hour and half hour in the same pattern."

Idiots. When the heating cycle finished, Nico dumped a bag of tea into the water to steep and placed it in front of Mercy. "You said there's extensive landscaping."

"Yeah." Jon frowned. "Too close to the house. Too many places to hide in the shadows. It's not safe for Mercy."

"Jon." Although Eli's tone was mild, his eyes warned his friend to back off.

The sniper held up his hand. "Stating a fact, not pronouncing judgment."

Nico checked the time. "We have two hours before we leave. Time to come up with a plan to keep her safe and give us the best chance of getting answers from the senator's father."

By the time Mercy left to prepare for the party, Nico's team had hashed out a plan and memorized several escape routes. He pointed out a spot on the map half a mile from the estate. "If we're separated, this will be our rendezvous point. No matter what, we can't allow the Scorpions to take

Mercy again. As desperate as they are to capture her, Mercy won't survive a second encounter with Hector and his friends."

He and his team scattered to change clothes. As he slipped on his jacket and made sure his weapon was easily accessible, Nico's cell phone rang. He checked the screen. "What do you have for me, Zane?"

"You were right. Sean Jeffries was involved in an affair that led to the birth of a daughter named Georgia two years ago."

Did that information have anything to do with Mercy's situation? "What about a connection between the Jeffries and the Scorpions?"

"Still chasing leads. So far, I've struck out. Rumors are rampant about a connection between Dwayne and the Scorpions, but I haven't uncovered a link. I also can't find a link between that group and Sean. Just a lot of speculation about a connection."

Nico rubbed his jaw, frustrated with the lack of concrete evidence against the two men. He'd been sure they were at the root of the danger to Mercy. "All right. Expand the search to the senator's staff and Dwayne's management team. There has to be something, Z. I feel it in my gut."

"I'll keep looking. One other thing. I've searched for the information leak. The leak is outside the ATF."

"How can that be? The ATF agents indicated their raids were sabotaged. That information has to come from inside."

"Not necessarily. You're in D.C., Nico. That place is a hotbed of secrets and intrigue. If someone in power knew the right people, he could find out anything he wanted."

"Jeffries?"

"It's possible. He's in the right place and has his hands on sensitive information. I'll let you know if I find proof. In the meantime, keep a close eye on your lady."

"We're escorting Mercy to Dwayne's birthday party. Sean is presenting his father with Mercy's pictures tonight and insisted she attend."

Zane sighed. "Let me guess. The senator invited everybody he knows to attend the party and security is lousy."

"You got it."

"What do you need from me?"

"She'll be wearing the jewelry you provided."

"Ah. Want me to activate the trackers?"

"Please. I'm praying this is overkill, but I'd rather be safe. The Scorpions are determined to get their hands on Mercy. I just wish I knew why."

The sound of keys clicking on Zane's keyboard came through the phone's speaker. "Done. Her trackers are active. Let me know when you're back at the safe house and I'll deactivate them."

"Copy that." Nico ended the call and left the room. Since Mercy's door was still closed, he joined his unit in the kitchen. He smiled at the sight that greeted him.

"What?" Ben groused, tugging at his collar.

"Us. We're all dressed like penguins except for Sam and the SEALs."

Eli chuckled. "That's the advantage to being the backup rather than on the main security detail. Jon and I will wait at the rendezvous point and swoop in to save the day if you and your team run into trouble."

Shadow protested Eli's assertion.

Upstairs, a door opened, then shut.

Nico walked to the foot of the stairs while his teammates traded insults with the SEALs and waited for Mercy to appear. His eyes widened when she descended. Good thing he would be armed tonight. The way she looked in the sparkling champagne-colored dress, Nico would be hard pressed to keep suiters away from her.

He held out his hand as she reached the last steps. "You look incredible, Mercedes Powers. You'll outshine every woman at that party tonight." Nico kissed the back of her hand.

Mercy's cheeks flushed. "Thanks."

He led her into the kitchen. Wolf whistles broke the sudden silence that fell in the room.

"Sugar, you look drop-dead gorgeous," Eli murmured. "Poor Nico will have his hands full keeping other men at bay."

"Let's load up." When Nico pulled out his keys, Joe held out his hand.

"I'll check your ride." He and Trace walked out the back door, scanners in their hands. When Joe returned, he said, "We're clear."

Nico walked with Mercy to the SUV, lifted her into the front seat, and handed her the seatbelt. A moment later, the three SUVs headed toward the Jeffries estate.

When they arrived at the front gate, Nico lowered his window. "Mercedes Powers and her security detail. The second half of my team is in the SUV behind me." The SEALs had turned off the main road a half mile back and parked in the shadow of a clump of trees.

"ID?"

"Take Mercy's picture and send it to the senator for confirmation. You have one minute. If you don't confirm by then, we're leaving."

The guard, a beefy guy with a high-and-tight haircut, scowled at Nico. When Nico refused to back down, the guard freed his phone from the holder on his belt, snapped Mercy's picture, and shot off a text. Two seconds before Nico told Trace to turn around, the guard signaled to his partner to open the gate and moved aside.

Nico and Trace parked at the edge of the driveway near the side of the house. Shadow exited the vehicles and scanned the area. Nico took his time circling around to

Mercy. When he was satisfied, he nodded to his teammates and opened Mercy's door. "We're entering the house through the kitchen. Less people around to worry about. The party is in the third-floor ballroom. We're taking the stairs."

"Right." She smiled. "No place to go in an elevator."

Nico scooped her from the seat and set her down. "Straight to the door, kitten." He hustled her across the open space, surrounded by his teammates. "Smart idea wearing flat shoes."

"In case I have to run."

He hoped it didn't come to that. If it was necessary for Mercy to run, the situation was dire.

Nico moved in front of Mercy. When the knob to the kitchen door turned easily in his hand, he walked inside followed by Joe. As they surveyed the kitchen, the staff and caterers twisted to stare at them with curiosity. No one objected to their presence or made threatening moves. The aroma of food and the clink of china and crystal filled the air.

Satisfied it was safe for Mercy to enter, Nico motioned for her to come inside. She slipped her hand into his. "Stay with me no matter what."

Nico signaled Ben and Trace to go up the stairs ahead of them. Sam and Joe followed Mercy and Nico.

"How do you know where to go?" Mercy whispered.

"Memorized the house layout. We also know the parties on this estate are always lavish and held in the ballroom."

A door at the top of the stairs opened and the noise of the party spilled down the stairwell. Nico swept Mercy behind him and pressed her against the wall, blocking her from view with his body.

A man and woman with slurred speech laughed at some private joke and stumbled their way past the Fortress operatives. Once they exited into the kitchen, Nico and the others resumed their trek to the third floor.

They exited the stairwell into a crowded hallway outside the ballroom. Ben and Trace led the way through the glut of people. Nico wrapped his arm around Mercy's shoulders and tucked her close to his body, assessing every person who came near her as a potential threat. Sam and Joe kept pace behind them, protecting their backs.

Inside the ballroom, Nico spotted Senator Jeffries standing beside his father. The men were surrounded by a bevy of men and women, laughing and talking to the Jeffries and each other.

Great. They stood on the opposite side of a room teeming with people. Nico envisioned a dozen scenarios for their journey through the sea of celebrants, all of them bad.

As Shadow moved closer, the senator glanced up and saw them approaching. Relief flooded his face. He leaned close to his father's ear and said something to him, then pushed through the crowd toward Mercy.

"I'm so glad you could make it, honey." Jeffries took hold of her arm. "Come with me. I'll introduce you to my father. After we get everyone's attention, we'll present Dad with his gift."

Nico clamped a hand over the senator's wrist and squeezed. "Let go. Now."

Sean Jeffries' face reddened. He looked like he wanted to protest, but thought better of it and released Mercy's arm.

"Lead the way." Nico stared at the senator until the man turned on his heel and pushed through the crowd of well-wishers toward his father, jaw set.

Dwayne Jeffries looked up as they approached and broke away from the crowd surrounding him. The senator's father was a distinguished looking man with pure white hair and piercing blue eyes. He clapped his son on the shoulder. "Introduce me to your friends, Sean." His gaze settled on Mercy, speculation in his gaze.

"Dad, this is President Martin's niece, Mercedes Powers."

Nico frowned, not appreciating the senator insinuating Mercy's worth lay in her relation to the president instead of in her own value as a person.

"It's nice to meet you, Mercedes." Dwayne pressed Mercy's hand between his palms.

"I understand you have several of my drawings in your home."

He gave a puzzled frown. "I do?"

She smiled as she freed her hand. "You know me better as MJ Powers."

Delight filled Dwayne's face. "I'm a huge fan of your work. I had no idea you and Sean were good friends."

Mercy slid her arm around Nico's waist, an action which filled him with satisfaction. "This is Nico."

After a cursory nod, the senator's father shifted his attention back to Mercy. "Would you like to see my collection of your art?"

"I'd love to. I'm curious about which drawings you chose for your personal residence."

"Later, Dad." Sean gave a hand signal to Theo, his aide. Seconds later, the musicians stopped playing and the crowd quieted as Sean led his father to the microphone on the raised platform.

Nico guided Mercy forward with his hand on her lower back, Sam and Joe close behind. Trace and Ben moved to the sides of the platform and faced the crowd.

"Thank you for helping to celebrate my father's birthday tonight," Sean said into the microphone. "As part of my gift to Dad, I commissioned a series of drawings by a renowned artist, Ms. MJ Powers. We're honored to have Ms. Powers with us tonight." He held out his hand to Mercy.

Nico reluctantly released her. She stepped up on the platform beside the senator as the audience applauded.

Sean wrapped his hand around Mercy's and tugged her toward the first covered drawing.

Catching her slight wince, Nico had to make himself stand in place.

Together, the two of them unveiled each of the five drawings. Dwayne and the crowd responded with enthusiasm. Nico understood their appreciation. Mercy's work was exceptional.

"Again, thank you for coming. Enjoy yourselves." Sean signaled the musicians and music flooded the ballroom once again.

Nico moved to Mercy's side. "The drawings are spectacular." He cupped her cheek. "I'm glad I had the chance to see them."

"It was a fun project."

"Ms. Powers, thank you for the estate series. I'm overwhelmed." Dwayne captured her hand again.

"I'm glad I could work the series into my schedule."

"Sean tells me you have to leave soon. Would you like to see my collection of your art before you go?"

"I'd love to." Mercy freed her hand again and threaded her fingers with Nico's. "Please, lead the way."

"I'll come with you." Sean grabbed a couple of glasses filled with a clear liquid and fell into step with his father.

The Jeffries crossed the ballroom, stopping frequently to greet guests who detained them with well wishes and congratulations. When they finally left the room, the men led them to the elevator.

Nico squeezed Mercy's hand, a silent reminder about his elevator warning.

"Sean, I'd rather take the stairs. What floor should we meet you on?" Mercy asked.

A frown. "Are you claustrophobic?"

"What floor?" she pressed.

"Second."

"We'll meet you there," Nico murmured and turned Mercy toward the stairs. Inside the stairwell, the noise level dropped dramatically.

Mercy sighed. "I hate to be in crowds that size."

Despite the tension wracking him, Nico grinned at her. "Same for me." Mercedes Powers was a perfect match for him. A good thing since he'd fallen head-over-heels in love with her.

They exited the stairwell on the second floor where the Jeffries were waiting for them.

"That way." Dwayne gestured toward the right wing.

And have this man and his son at Nico's back? Not in this lifetime. "We'll follow you."

With a shrug the older man walked ahead of them until he reached a large room on the right side of the hall. "I wanted to keep the drawings together. The library seemed the most appropriate place to display them as a group." He smiled over his shoulder. "I wanted to keep the drawings all to myself."

Nico held Mercy by his side as he glanced over his shoulder at Ben. The EOD man slipped into the library and did a cursory inspection of the room. When he signaled the room was safe, Nico moved forward with her while his teammates waited in the hall.

She smiled as soon as she saw the drawings. "You chose some of my favorite pieces, and I love how you've displayed them."

Pleasure flooded Dwayne's expression. "I bought a few others. Since you're pressed for time, you'll have to come back to see them."

"I appreciate the invitation." Mercy turned to Nico, eyebrow raised.

He gave her a slight nod in silent agreement for her to broach the topic of Dwayne's presence in the Scorpion compound.

"Did Sean tell you about my kidnapping in Mexico last week, Mr. Jeffries?"

The senator's cheeks flushed and his eyes glittered as he stared at Mercy.

Dwayne's smile faded. "He mentioned it. Were you hurt?"

"I was shot in the shoulder while escaping."

His gaze swept over her. "I would have never known you were injured if you hadn't told me."

"Have you been to Mexico, Mr. Jeffries?"

"Of course. I have many business contacts in that part of the world and many others."

"When were you there last?"

A frown. "Why are you asking me these questions?"

"Answer the lady's question," Nico said. "When were you in Mexico the last time?"

"You're not a cop. I don't have to tell you anything."

"No, you don't. You will, however, be answering questions for the feds in a matter of hours if you don't tell us what we want to know."

The scowl on his face couldn't disguise the glint of terror in the older man's eyes. His gaze skated to Sean before returning to Nico. "I was there last week. Why does it matter?"

"Where exactly in Mexico?" Nico pressed.

"What are you after?" Dwayne countered.

"The truth, Mr. Jeffries." When he remained mute, Nico continued. "We know you were in the Scorpion compound when Mercy was being held captive. She saw you."

"I don't know what you're talking about."

"Yeah, you do. The question is, why are you lying about it?"

CHAPTER THIRTY-FOUR

Sean Jeffries set the glasses on his father's desk and pulled a cell phone from his pocket. He tapped in a few keystrokes before sliding the instrument away and picking up the glasses again.

Nico frowned as the senator gulped down one of the drinks. His hands were shaking and his face dotted with perspiration. What was wrong with him?

Sean set aside the empty glass and pressed the remaining drink into Mercy's hand. "Here. Have a drink. You look like you could use one."

Muscles tensing, Nico prepared to stop her from taking anything offered by the senator when she shook her head.

"No, thanks." Mercy tried to give the drink back to Sean.

He shrugged. "Your loss." The senator moved to take the glass from her when he tripped and stumbled into Mercy. The full glass tilted toward her and spilled the drink down the front of Mercy's dress.

Nico shoved the senator away from her.

"I'm so sorry, honey. I'm a klutz tonight." Sean dragged a white handkerchief from his pocket as though he intended to blot the liquid from her dress.

"No." Nico eased her back a few steps. "You're not touching her." Not if what he suspected about the senator was true. His eyes narrowed. Who was he kidding? If Nico had anything to say about it, neither Jeffries nor any other man was going to touch her.

"I wouldn't hurt her," Sean insisted. "You're overreacting. There's a bathroom in the suite across the hall, Mercy. You can use towels to dry your dress. I'm sorry, honey. For everything."

Was he admitting to having a role in her kidnapping? Nico glanced at Sam. "Go with her. The senator and his father have questions to answer."

When the women left, Joe slipped from the room to follow them.

Nico returned his attention to the Jeffries. "Let's try this again, Dwayne. Why were you in Mexico?"

"Business," the man snapped. "The kind that doesn't concern you."

"Wrong." Nico jabbed a finger his direction. "Anything that impacts Mercy is my business. You arranged her kidnapping, didn't you?"

"What? You're crazy. I have no reason to harm her."

Interesting that Dwayne didn't deny he'd ever arranged a kidnapping, just that he had no reason to harm Mercy. "You're doing business with the Scorpions."

Another scowl. "It's a legitimate business deal, one I don't have to explain to you."

"You're dealing with thugs and terrorists, Jeffries. Do you know they're a weapons broker?"

"I don't knowingly import weapons from anyone."

The man was lying through his teeth. "The president has a vested interest in Mercy's kidnapping. If he thinks you had anything to do with it, Martin will investigate your son as well. You know Washington politics. People like nothing better than a juicy story, and D.C.'s gossipmongers work overtime 24 hours a day. What do you think Sean's association with terrorists would do to his presidential ambitions?"

Dwayne cursed him, his face reddening in outrage. "You're threatening to leak a false story? I have a team of lawyers who'll sue you into the poor house, then have you thrown into jail."

Nico bared his teeth in a semblance of a smile, one he knew held no warmth or humor. "It's fact, and by the time a court case is finished, your son's potential career would be toast."

"How dare you?"

He moved several steps closer to Dwayne, deliberately crowding the older man against the desk. "Mercy means everything to me. I'll do anything to protect her, Jeffries. Do you understand what I'm telling you?"

After a hard swallow, Dwayne gave a curt nod.

Shots rang out. Nico pivoted as screams and running footsteps echoed through the mansion. As shots continued to pepper the air, he raced into the hall in time to see Trace and Ben sprinting toward the stairs. Joe spun and pounded on the door to the suite where Mercy and Sam had gone.

"Sam, open up. Trouble."

As Nico ran toward him, Joe turned the knob and frowned. "Sam!" A moment later, the operative kicked the door open and hurried into the suite with his weapon drawn, Nico on his heels.

"Mercy." Heart in his throat, Nico glanced around the living room of the suite. Empty. He ran to the bedroom and skidded to a stop at the closed bathroom door. Blood pooled under the door.

Oh, man. Please, no. Had he failed to keep her safe? Nico opened the door only to have it stop after swinging in a few inches. He saw black boots and pants and shoved harder. "Joe."

His teammate rushed into the bedroom. "No. Nico, I didn't hear anything, I swear."

Nico entered the bathroom, avoiding the red puddle on the floor. He scanned the bathroom as Joe surged into the room and dropped to his knees beside his fallen comrade.

Joe pressed shaking fingers against Sam's neck and let out a breath. "She's alive."

"Take her to the closest hospital." Nico tossed Joe his keys. "I'll find Ben and send him with you."

The spotter shook his head as he gently scooped the medic into his arms. "Shadow will be down three. We'll be fine."

"Wait for Ben. That's an order."

"He's got two minutes. After that, I'm leaving with or without him," Joe said flatly and strode from the suite.

Worried over Sam's chance of surviving a chest wound and Joe's reaction if he lost her, Nico shot Ben a text, then went after the Jeffries. The senator's statement rang in his ears. Did Sean know this was going to happen? That would explain his odd apology to Mercy.

Guilt assailed Nico. He'd promised Mercy the Scorpions wouldn't touch her again on his watch and he'd broken that promise. Running into the hall, he spotted the senator talking on his cell phone and saw red. He crossed the remaining distance between them, caught the senator by the shoulders, spun him around, and slammed him against the wall. "What did you do?"

"I'm sorry. I didn't have a choice."

Nico thumped him against the wall once more, pleasure blooming at the satisfying thud of Sean's head against the flat surface. "Try again."

"They have my daughter. She's only two. They threatened to turn her into a sex slave if I didn't give them what they wanted."

"What do they want?"

"Mercy and her memory card. I swear, I don't understand why they want it. I just want my daughter back alive."

"You sold Mercy to them." Nico forced himself to let go and back away before he killed Jeffries. "Who has her, Jeffries?" He needed confirmation. If what he suspected was true, Nico might need more help than just Eli and Jon. His gut knotted. He'd better not need more than the SEALs and Trace. Mercy might not survive until Maddox sent in another team to back up Shadow. "Give me a name."

"I don't know. I only have a cell phone number."

"Give it to me." Nico sent Zane a text with the number and asked him to trace it. He glared at the senator. "What's your father's role in this? Why was he in Mexico?"

"Bargaining for Georgia's life. I didn't know who they were until you told me Mercy saw Dad in the Scorpion compound. I still don't know if that's who kidnapped my daughter. For all I know, they could simply be a go between. I'm sorry," Jeffries muttered. "I never meant for Mercy to be hurt."

Hand fisted around his phone, Nico said, "You better pray nothing happens to her. If she dies, I will kill you after I destroy whoever took her from me."

He turned and sprinted for the stairs. Trace called him from the third-floor landing.

"We've got several wounded up here. EMTs and cops are on the way."

"We need to get out of here." No one was going to stop him from going after Mercy, not even law enforcement.

"Mercy?"

"Someone took her. Don't know who. Sam was unconscious when Joe and I found her in the bathroom. One shot to the chest."

Trace's face hardened. "She going to make it?"

"I don't know." A wry smile curved his mouth. "She could tell if one of us was hit."

The two men hurried down the stairwell, through the kitchen and out the back door. Inside Trace's SUV, Nico called Zane. "Please tell me you have information."

"Sorry, man. It's a burner. I can tell you the phone signal is pinging off cell towers heading toward D.C."

"Keep tracking the signal. Is another Fortress team in the D.C. area?"

"Negative. Why?"

"Mercy's missing and Sam's been shot. Two of my team are with her. I have Trace, Eli, and Jon with me. I'm not sure Jeffries and his father are involved." He summarized the information he'd learned from the senator. "There's another player in the mix, Z. That person wants Mercy's memory card. She must have caught something incriminating when she was taking photographs at the Jeffries estate."

"I'll inform the boss, then look closer at the photographs you sent me. Want Fortress to mobilize another unit?"

"Put them on standby for now. Don't pull the details from Mercy's family or Sorensen."

"Copy that."

Nico ended the call to Zane and placed the next one to Eli. "Trace and I are headed to you. Mercy's missing and Sam's down. The others are headed to the hospital."

"We'll be ready."

That done, he activated the tracking program and keyed in the information to track Mercy. His fist clenched. The signal showed she was headed into D.C. The person holding Sean Jeffries' daughter hostage either had Mercy or was heading to meet with the people who took Georgia. If Nico and the others couldn't get to her fast enough, Mercy would die.

CHAPTER THIRTY-FIVE

Mercy woke to darkness again. For a moment, she feared she was back in a dank Mexican cave. Then she realized she was sitting up in a chair, hands restrained, and the air smelled of dust and water. In fact, she could hear water sloshing close by.

She frowned. A boat? No, she didn't feel like she was moving. Maybe a house near the water. Her heart sank, realizing that she must not be on the Jeffries estate, close to Nico and the rest of Shadow. Sam. Mercy's stomach twisted. So much blood had poured from the medic's chest wound. Sam had been wounded trying to fight off the three gunmen who had emerged from seemingly out of nowhere to take Mercy.

They'd hit her with something. Not a shot of nasty drugs, thank goodness. This time, pain had flooded her system and her muscles had simply quit responding. The way her head ached, she must have hit the counter or bathtub when she fell because she didn't remember anything else.

How did the men enter the bathroom? Joe wouldn't have let anyone into the suite with Mercy and Sam inside. That meant the suite had a hidden entrance.

A sick certainty filled Mercy. Sean and his father knew. They had to know about the entrance. Did that mean they were complicit in her second kidnapping and perhaps the first one? A weird mix of anger and sadness weighed on her heart. What had she done to either of them to elicit this kind of violence?

She thought about calling out to them and decided to wait. She'd know soon who was desperate enough to pull off such a bold stunt in the middle of a large birthday celebration when she was surrounded by a team of bodyguards.

Mercy remembered multiple gunshots and prayed there weren't any injuries other than Sam's. A door opened, bringing with it a gust of fresh, cool evening air permeated with the scent of water.

She sat still, waiting. If the person calling the shots was in the room, Mercy didn't want to give him or her the satisfaction of knowing she was terrified. All she had to do was wait, she reminded herself. Her jewelry had trackers in them. Nico would come for her. But would it be in time to save her life?

If the creep who took Mercy killed her before Nico arrived, the operative would never forgive himself. After losing his sister and his buddies on various battlefields, Mercy's loss would scar the warrior on a deep level.

Footsteps drew near. A moment later, a bright light blinded her. Squinting against the glare, Mercy saw a strip of black cloth on the ground. A blindfold. No wonder she hadn't been able to see anything.

Once her eyes adjusted, Mercy glanced around. She was in a deserted warehouse. Her gaze locked on the man dressed in a black tux, waiting for her to acknowledge him. "Theo. I don't understand. Why are you doing this?"

His dark eyes glittered at her. "You're a threat. You know too much, Mercedes."

Confused, she said, "I don't know anything. You're my contact with Sean." Mercy stopped. "Sean's to blame for this?"

A scoffing laugh from the senator's aide. "You think the future president is going to jeopardize his election chances by dipping his hands in dirt? Oh, no. He's too ambitious to take that risk. No, this is all me."

"What have you done?"

"Nothing some other enterprising soul wouldn't be doing. I'm selling information to the Scorpions. My employer has access to a lot of classified information. All I have to do is throw around Jeffries' name and information falls into my lap. I pass it along to my boss and the Scorpions for a nice fee."

"How can you do this? Your enterprise is costing innocent lives and compromising our nation's security."

"Do I look like I care?" He moved closer, hands fisted. "Where is it, Mercy?"

"What are you looking for?" She needed to stall to give Nico time to find her.

"The memory card. Where is it?"

Mercy stared. Memory card. "You know what I do for a living. I have many memory cards."

Theo backhanded her. "You try my patience. You're a danger to my plan and I'm not having it. Where is the memory card with the pictures of your visit to the Jeffries estate?"

She waited for the blackness at the edge of her vision to clear. Man, she was getting tired of blows to the face. First Hector and his goons, and now Theo.

Mercy considered what was best for her and Nico. The man she loved had the memory card. If she admitted as much to Sean's aide, he wouldn't have a reason to keep her alive. That would also set Theo on a direct course for Nico.

"I took a lot of pictures on my visit to the estate. You were at my side for most of them. I don't see how those pictures would compromise you or your operation."

"This is your own fault," he snapped. "I escorted you to your car when you said you were finished. Instead, I looked up to see you on the hillside overlooking the estate, taking more pictures of the area where I was meeting my contact.

Mercy frowned. "But you said Sean wasn't part of this. He's involved with a terrorist and doesn't know it?"

"That's right. He thinks the Scorpion soldier is an aide to the Mexican president who's interested in forming business ties to Jeffries Industries."

"Aren't they worried about Dwayne Jeffries connecting this man to the Scorpions?"

He shook his head. "My contact made himself scarce when the old man came into the Scorpion compound to beg for his granddaughter's life. He didn't know who he was meeting. The senator's innocent of everything except selling you to me."

Shock rolled through Mercy. "Sean has a daughter?"

"A two-year-old blond beauty."

Sick to her stomach, she whispered, "The Scorpions have the girl?" Just the thought of that possibility made her want to barf. The Scorpions were evil personified.

"Hector and his buddies don't care about the kid. All they want is the information about ATF raids."

"Then who...?" She stopped mid-sentence. "You have her. Why?"

"You said it yourself. Leverage. I needed the brat to force Sean to hand you to me on a silver platter."

"Where is she?"

A smirk. "Here. There's an office on the second floor where she's being taken care of."

In a dirty warehouse? "You didn't have to involve a child in your scheme."

"It's more fun this way. Your bodyguard needed to be brought down. I'm just the man to do it."

If Sean's aide believed that, his opinion of himself was inflated. "You're the one who broke into my house in Sherwood."

"Please. That's what I have the Scorpions in my pocket for. They stole your precious drawings. I might sell them after I take care of you. Maybe I'll just burn them."

Theo wrapped his large hand around Mercy's throat and squeezed slightly in warning. "Where is the memory card, Mercy?"

She stared at him, mute.

The man's eyes gleamed. "We're doing this the hard way?" His hand constricted, slowly cutting off her ability to breathe. "Suits me. I'll enjoy forcing you to talk."

Mercy dragged in a wheezing breath and prayed Nico would hurry. Her time was running out.

CHAPTER THIRTY-SIX

Nico stared at his phone. The marker indicating Mercy's location hadn't moved for the last thirty minutes. Had her captor stripped Mercy of her jewelry or was she being held at that location? He prayed the second option was true. If Mercy was without her trackers, his chances of finding her in time dropped dramatically.

Trace swerved around a slow vehicle and dove back into the correct lane of the two-lane road to the chorus of horns from oncoming cars. "Any change?"

As Nico shook his head, his phone signaled an incoming call from Zane. He jabbed the speaker button. "What do you have for me?"

"I examined the rest of the pictures from Mercy's photo shoot at the Jeffries estate. She took several shots of the estate from a higher elevation than the place where she caught the Jeffries on film. The Scorpion soldier was meeting with the senator's aide, Theo Morris, alone. The time stamp shows the shots were taken thirty minutes after the meeting with the Jeffries and there is no one else around."

"Did you run him?"

"He was one of many people you asked me to run a background check on," Zane reminded him. "Initially, he came up clean. When I saw the photo, I did a deeper, more creative run."

"Hold on. Trace, call Eli so he and Jon can hear this information first hand."

His friend activated the Bluetooth system. When Eli answered, he said, "We have Z on speaker. He has information. Go, Zane."

"I just informed Nico and Trace that Mercy photographed Theo Morris, the senator's aide, meeting alone with the Scorpion soldier on the Jeffries estate."

"He's after Mercy's memory card," Jon said.

"That's my guess."

"You did some hacking?"

"What do you think?"

A chuckle from the sniper. "What did you find?"

"Theo has a tidy little nest egg in an account in the Caymans."

Nico frowned. "He's in bed with the Scorpions?"

"Think about it. The senator has the inside track to a lot of classified information. Wouldn't be a stretch to think he had access to the information about ATF raids. Jeffries plays golf with the top brass at the ATF. I can't connect the senator to the Scorpions aside from Mercy's photo, but I can connect Morris to them along with a hidden account with a large balance. I'd say the mole ratting out the ATF is Morris. If I have enough time, I'll connect the dots for the ATF."

"The senator has a two-year-old daughter named Georgia. He admitted he set up Mercy to be kidnapped again in order to save his daughter." He ignored the stare from Trace. "I thought the Scorpions had her. Is it possible Morris kidnapped her?"

"Mercy's trackers are still showing her at the same location. I'll check the security and street cams in the area and see if I can spot the child. I'll text you if I find evidence she's in the same place as Mercy. Otherwise, contact me when you have her back and I'll give you an update."

Nico ended the call.

"The senator has a daughter?" Eli's voice sounded strained. "Guess that explains his actions."

"He should have asked for help. If Morris has the girl and learns the information he wants from Mercy, he won't have a reason to spare either of them. In fact, he has quite a motive for not leaving witnesses behind. If they live and identify him, his whole money-making scheme goes out the window." A man who was cold enough to use a toddler to blackmail her father wouldn't hesitate at killing her or Mercy when he got what he wanted.

"How close are we?" Eli asked.

"Fifteen miles. We'll park two blocks away and gear up. The kidnapper is desperate and we can't afford to skip the precaution." Even though he desperately wanted to rush in and find the woman he wanted to marry soon if she'd have him.

"Copy that."

As their SUV covered the miles, Nico kept an eye on the position of the tracker while he checked his weapons. Once they stopped and suited up, the operation would execute fast. Didn't have a choice but to move without complete intel. Mercy had been in the kidnapper's hands too long.

By the time they reached their destination, Nico's iron control had worn thin. As soon as the SUV cruised to a stop, he threw open the door, glancing into the deep shadows where Trace and Eli had parked to be sure they were unobserved by hostiles.

He grabbed his Go bag and donned gear to protect him while he searched for Mercy. Two minutes later, the

Fortress warriors moved toward the address where they hoped Mercy was being held.

One block from their destination, Nico's phone vibrated. He held up his fist in a silent signal for his team to stop and checked the screen. Relief swept through him. Zane had hacked into the traffic cams around the area. Georgia had been taken into the warehouse when Jeffries started pressing Mercy to appear before his committee, and the little girl had never left.

"Georgia's in the warehouse, too."

Jon growled. "A stray bullet might hit the child. We have to take these guys down hard and fast."

"Agreed." Nico signaled the others to move forward. They prowled down the darkened street with silent steps. When the Fortress operatives were close enough, Nico retrieved his night-vision glasses and scanned the warehouse.

Six people in the warehouse. The small body at the south end of the building had to be Georgia. One person was with her.

Two people roamed the building. Two others were in a room on the north side. The person seated must be Mercy. The other person in the room stood over her, hands wrapped around Mercy's throat.

Nico hissed. "He's choking her." His muscles bunched, ready to ram his Sig down the throat of the person hurting his woman. Trace grabbed him.

"Use your head. If you race to the rescue, we'll alert them to our presence. Mercy's life isn't the only one at stake, Patch."

He knew his friend was right. Didn't make it easier to hold himself back. Nico reigned in his emotions and focused on what he needed to do to save Mercy, then nodded at Trace. "I'm ready."

He glanced at Jon and Eli. "Georgia is on the south end of the building. One tango guarding her. Two roaming guards. Take care of the guard on your end of the building. Trace and I will go after Mercy and the man with her plus the second guard."

The SEALs split off from them and melted into the night. Nico and Trace circled to the back of the building and found an accessible window. Nico peered into the room. Empty. Perfect.

Nico raised the window, breathing easier when it moved without resistance. Hoisting himself over the sill, he slid silently into the room, weapon up, ready to protect Trace as he entered the building.

Seconds later, his teammate stood beside him. Nico approached the door leading to a hall. Mercy was about two hundred feet to his right, at the end of the hallway. The only thing standing between him and the woman he loved was the roaming guard.

He eased the door open a crack. The guard was just making the turn at the end of the hall to come this direction. Nico signaled Trace to be ready.

The sniper moved into position. As soon as the guard passed the room where the operatives hid, Trace stepped behind the guard and clamped a hand over his mouth.

Nico raced to the end of the corridor. At the door, he heard a male voice taunting someone who was coughing.

"You think your blockheaded friend will rescue you?" Harsh laughter. "He won't find you until it's too late, Mercy. Make it easy on yourself. Tell me where the memory card is and I'll let you go."

Theo Morris was a liar. He couldn't let Mercy live. She would identify him as her kidnapper and possibly more. Nico tried the knob. It turned easily under his hand.

"I won't tell you anything."

A crack filled the room as Nico entered from the hallway. Fury exploded in him as Morris reached back to strike Mercy again. Nico sped across the room, yanked Morris away from Mercy, and threw him against the wall.

The aide slammed against the surface with a satisfying thump and lost his weapon. He spun and dove for the Sig but wasn't fast enough. Nico kicked the gun to the opposite side of the room.

With a roar, Morris lunged for Nico.

He used the aide's momentum against him and shifted just enough for the other man to race past without touching Nico's body. He tripped Morris. When the other man hit the floor, Nico dove on top of him.

Morris swung out with a right cross, cursing.

Nico blocked the punch and landed one of his own, a powerful fist to the nose. Cartilage crunched, and the other man's howl of pain filled the air.

Methodically, Nico rained blows on Morris's face and ribs. He didn't bother to pull his punches. He saw and heard nothing but his fists plowing over and over into the man who would have killed the woman Nico adored.

Two sets of hard hands grabbed Nico and pulled him off Morris. He tried to shake them off.

"Patch," Eli snapped. "He's finished. Let the feds have him. Take care of Mercy."

Mercy. Nico's head whipped her direction. His vision cleared as he threw off the restraining hands of his friends. Nico pulled his Ka-Bar and sliced through the restraints binding her wrists.

She gasped as the strain on her arms disappeared.

Nico caught her arms and slowly lowered them to her sides. He frowned at the spot of blood on her injured shoulder. A new injury?

He circled around and dropped to his knees in front of her. "Where are you injured, baby?"

"Nico, he kidnapped a toddler. We have to find her."

"She's safe," Eli said. "Jon has her. No one will touch her."

Mercy shuddered. "Thank God."

Nico cupped her battered and bruised face between his palms. "Where are you hurt?"

She gave him a wobbly smile. "I don't know. I hurt everywhere. Theo used me for a punching bag. He wasn't happy when I wouldn't tell him where the memory card was located."

"Why didn't you?" It was good she hadn't cooperated, but Nico was curious about her motive in refusing to talk.

"He would have gone after you. I couldn't take that chance."

Nico's breath stalled in his lungs. She'd endured a beating to protect him. "Mercy." Was it any wonder that he was in love with her?

Jon walked in with a beautiful blond-haired, blue-eyed toddler nestled in his arms. The little girl had her arms wrapped around the SEAL's neck. "Feds will be here any minute. Unless you want to be stuck in this warehouse for hours, we need to leave now."

"Go," Eli said to Nico and Jon. "Trace and I have this covered. Take the ladies to the hospital."

Suited him. Nico hated dealing with the feds. "I'll have to carry you, Mercy. We parked two blocks away to prevent Morris's men from spotting us." Without waiting for her to agree, Nico scooped her gently into his arms and strode from the dirty warehouse.

CHAPTER THIRTY-SEVEN

Nico paced the hospital corridor outside the examination room where a doctor was examining Mercy. What was taking the man so long? He'd been in the room for nearly an hour.

Maybe Mercy had extensive internal injuries. Nico's gut knotted. If she required a long recovery period, he'd have to postpone his mission to dismantle the Scorpions and take a leave of absence from Fortress. He refused to leave her until she'd healed.

He grabbed his phone and called Joe. "Any word on Sam?"

"She's still in surgery. I'm worried, Nico. The surgery is taking longer than the surgeon said it would."

That news concerned him as well. "Doesn't it always? How many times have we been injured and Sorensen took longer than he predicted to complete the surgery?"

"Yeah, you're right. Look, I know you want to destroy the Scorpions, but I'm not leaving Sam while she's recovering. She'll need help, and you know she doesn't have anyone but us."

That meant Shadow would be down a medic and a spotter. "I understand. I don't know how soon we'll go after the Scorpions. I'll be with Mercy while she heals. I want to know the minute you hear anything about Sam."

"Yes, sir." Joe ended the call.

"You'll wear a path in the floor if you keep pacing," Jon said. His lips curved as he watched Nico.

"You wouldn't be patient, either, if Dana was behind that door."

A shrug. "I'd be in there with her so I'd know what's going on."

"You're married to Dana. I can't demand entrance into Mercy's examination room." Yet.

"How soon will you remedy that?"

"If I had my choice, today. I still have to convince the lady to take an even bigger risk by marrying me."

The door to the examination room opened. "Nico?"

He moved toward the doctor, heart in his throat. "I'm Nico."

"Ms. Powers is asking for you."

"How is she?"

"She has cracked ribs, deep bruising to her face, arms, and torso. I replaced three stitches from her gunshot wound. The stitches broke during the abduction and beating. Ms. Powers will fully recover. She needs to take it easy for a couple weeks and follow up with her doctor. I'm admitting her for observation tonight and gave her pain meds so she will be sleepy. However, she can leave tomorrow."

"I'm staying with her." He dared anyone to try to throw him out of Mercy's room. They'd lose. "I'm also her bodyguard. My teammates and I will be armed." Nico wasn't convinced the danger to Mercy was in the past. The Scorpions had a score to settle with her. Mercy had cost them their mole.

"I'll make sure the appropriate people are notified. An orderly will arrive soon to take Ms. Powers to her room." With a nod, the doctor left.

"I'll keep watch," Jon murmured. "Focus on Mercy."

Without glancing back, Nico pushed open the door and walked into the room. Mercy lay on the bed, face swollen in places and already beginning to bruise. The sight of her injuries made Nico want to hunt down Morris and inflict more damage.

When he wrapped his hand around hers, Mercy looked at him. Relief and something he couldn't identify filled her gaze. "How do you feel?"

"Like a bus ran over me." Her words were slurred and her eyes looked glazed.

Amusement outweighed the fury inside him. "Hate to tell you this, kitten, but you wouldn't pass a sobriety check right now."

"I'm a lightweight when it comes to medicine."

Jon peered into the room. "Orderly is here. I checked his credential. He's legit."

Nico nodded and helped Mercy sit up and swing her legs over the side of the bed. Jon held the door open for the orderly to push the wheelchair inside the room. Ten minutes later, Mercy was ensconced in a new bed on the fifth floor.

"Will you stay with me?" she murmured as her eyelids drooped.

He squeezed her hand. "I'm not going anywhere. If I step out of the room for a minute, one of my teammates will be with you." He pressed a kiss to her knuckles. "Rest. I'll be here."

Mercy scooted over with a grimace and patted the bed beside her. "Would you mind holding me?"

"You know I don't mind, but I don't want to hurt you."

"Please, Nico. I need to feel your arms around me."

Who could resist that request? He eased onto the bed beside her and gently gathered her against him. "Tell me if I hurt you."

She settled against his side with a sigh. A moment later, she was asleep.

With Jon on watch, Nico allowed himself to drift into a light doze. He woke when Mercy jerked and moaned in her sleep. He rubbed her arm. "Mercy, you're safe."

She stilled. "Nico?"

"Right here. Do you need a nurse?"

Mercy shook her head slightly. "Just need you."

He kissed her forehead, a place he knew wasn't bruised. "You have me, Mercy. Always."

She relaxed against him and snuggled closer. "Love you," she whispered.

Nico froze. "What did you say? Mercy?"

No response.

Great. She was asleep again. Did she mean what she said or was that the meds talking?

Two hours later, a light tap sounded on the door and Maddox eased into the room. He nodded at Nico, then settled in a chair at the foot of the bed.

Eyebrows winging up, Nico stared at his boss. What was the Fortress CEO doing in D.C.?

Maddox signaled that everything was fine.

Unwilling to wake Mercy by asking questions, Nico relaxed and slept, knowing he and Mercy were safe.

At four o'clock, a commotion in the hallway outside the room had Maddox on his feet with a weapon in hand and Nico on alert.

Trace walked in and inclined his head toward Mercy. "She has a visitor."

Maddox strode to the doorway, peered out, then glanced back at Nico. "It's the president."

"Give us a minute."

The door closed as his boss greeted the most powerful man on the planet in soft tones.

Nico turned his attention to the woman still snuggled against his side. "Mercy."

"Mmm."

"Your uncle is here."

She opened her eyes as Maddox returned with President Martin on his heels. Two Secret Service agents trailed them.

Martin flinched when he saw Mercy. "Oh, sweetheart."

"I look that good, huh?"

He looked at Nico. "Injury report."

"Cracked ribs, a lot of bruising. Needed three stitches replaced in her shoulder. Her voice is raspy because Morris choked her out more than once. She'll recover, Mr. President."

"Federal law enforcement is filing multiple charges against Theo Morris. He'll be an old man before he's released from prison."

"Is he the reason I was kidnapped in Mexico?" Mercy asked.

Martin shook his head. "The Scorpions do want their leader released and planned to kidnap the US representative at the funeral regardless of who it was. They bagged an unexpected prize when they kidnapped my niece. Dwayne Jeffries being in the Scorpion compound at the same time you were was a coincidence. Morris and the Scorpions had a mutually beneficial business arrangement. When Morris needed muscle for his dirty work, they provided assistance in order to keep their mole in place."

"And Sean?"

"He and his father didn't know they were negotiating with the wrong people to save the child."

"How is the girl?" Nico asked.

"She's fine. The woman who watched over Georgia gave her allergy medicine to keep her docile. The pediatrician said although the medication wasn't necessary to treat allergy symptoms, the nanny was careful to give the toddler the correct dosage. Georgia's with Senator Jeffries and her mother right now."

President Martin curled his hand around Mercy's. "I'm glad you're safe, sweetheart. I don't suppose you'll be willing to take another diplomatic mission for me after this."

"Only if I'm with her." Nico refused to let her leave the country again without him by her side.

Martin turned his gaze to Maddox, silently questioning if that was possible.

"I'll work it out."

"Excellent." He leaned down and kissed Mercy's forehead. "I apologize for visiting so early this morning. I leave for Europe in an hour."

He held out his hand to Nico. "Thank you for saving Mercy. I knew I could trust you with her life."

"She will be safe in my care."

Martin's eyebrows rose. "I see. See that you treat her right, son."

"Yes, sir."

The president turned to Maddox. "Walk with me."

In less than a minute, the room was empty except for Nico and Mercy.

"What did you mean by that?" Mercy asked, her voice soft.

"What did it sound like?" Nico's heart rate sped up.

"That you plan to be in my life permanently. Do you?"

"Yes."

She studied his face a moment. "As a friend?"

He cupped her chin and brushed his lips over hers. "As your friend, your lover, your husband." He punctuated each statement with another soft kiss. "I love you, Mercy. Before I met you, my life was empty. You awed me with your courage in Mexico, and I started to fall in love with you the moment I saw you in the cave. I know I'm not your first love, but I want to be your last."

"Oh, Nico." Mercy reached up with a trembling hand, cupped the back of his neck, and kissed him. "I love you, too. I've been afraid to tell you. I thought you wouldn't believe I knew my own heart."

Nico pressed his forehead to hers. "I want a family with you. A home filled with kids and a couple pets. Will you do me the honor of marrying me, Mercedes Powers?"

"I would love to be your wife, Nico Rivera."

"Soon?"

Mercy smiled. "As soon as we can. I know you'll want your teammates to be there. How is Sam?"

"She's in ICU. Joe said she's resting easily. The doc says she'll recover, but it will take a while."

"What if Brent calls Shadow for a mission?"

"I'll ask another medic to take her place until Sam's ready to roll."

That brought a frown. "Only the best. I want you and the others to have the best medical care if you need it."

He dropped a quick kiss on her mouth. "I know of two or three other medics I trust as much as I do Sam. They're as good as she is."

Nico cupped Mercy's nape. "I promise to take every precaution. I won't take unnecessary risks. I have too much to live for, and I don't want to cause you fear or grief."

"When will you leave?"

"When you're healed. For my peace of mind, I need to know you've recovered. After that, I'll plan the mission, secure a medic and spotter, and tap operatives I trust at my back."

"Who is your spotter?"

"Joe."

"Of course. I should have guessed."

"I need to talk to your father."

Mercy blinked. "Why?"

"I want his permission to marry you."

"I've been living on my own for years, Nico."

"Doesn't matter. I want his blessing before I make you mine."

After another light tap on the door, Maddox entered the room and returned to his seat at the foot of the bed.

"I'm surprised to see you in D.C.," Nico said.

"I thought you could use a hand since the other units are tied up. Looks like I arrived too late to do much." He folded his arms across his chest. "I want in when you go after the Scorpions and so do several other operatives."

"I want a list." He'd promised Mercy to take care. He didn't intend to break that promise.

"You'll get it. How long before you're ready to move on the Scorpions?"

"Probably two weeks. Depends on Mercy's recovery."

"We'll start gathering intel. By the time we're finished with those clowns, they'll be nothing but a bad memory."

CHAPTER THIRTY-EIGHT

After Sam was released from the hospital in Joe's care, Nico drove Mercy to Sherwood to help her with the mess the Scorpions had left behind and to spend time with her family.

She was careful to keep large sunglasses perched on her nose to shield her face from the curious busybodies as they drove through the center of town toward her home. If she didn't, the gossips would speculate about Nico's role in her bruises.

Walking inside her house, the chaos stole her breath once again. "Those creeps don't mess around when they want to send a message, do they?" she murmured.

"We'll repair or replace everything." Nico rested his hand against her lower back. "Call your family and tell them you're in town before they show up unannounced and have an unpleasant shock. I don't want to fight my future brothers-in-law and father-in-law before we have a chance to explain what happened."

Right. She needed to prepare her father and brothers for the sight of her colorful face. Otherwise, they might gang up on Nico.

She called her father first and told him about the second kidnapping. "I'm fine, Dad. I have facial bruising, though. Morris wasn't happy when I refused to talk."

"I want to see for myself that you're all right."

"Why don't you and the boys come over for dinner tonight? We can order take out."

"I know what you like. I'll pick up dinner for everyone. We'll see you tonight at six."

Mercy and Nico filled multiple trash bags until he insisted she rest for a while. Although Mercy didn't think she would sleep, she woke a few minutes after six to the sound of the doorbell.

She slid her feet into her shoes and walked to the living room. All conversation stopped. Her father and brothers moved closer, scowls on their faces.

Her father glanced at Nico. "Tell me you did something about this."

"The man who hurt Mercy has a concussion, a broken nose and cheekbone, and four fewer teeth than when he laid his hands on your daughter. He'll be using a walker when he's released from prison."

"Good." He inclined his head toward the kitchen table loaded with bags from Mercy's favorite hamburger joint. "Let's eat."

"Should have killed him for what he did," her oldest brother muttered.

"I agree." Nico seated Mercy, then sat in the chair beside hers. "I didn't want your sister to visit me in prison."

After dinner, Nico said, "Mr. Garwood, will you join me on the porch? I want to discuss something with you."

When the two men left, her brothers turned on Mercy. "What's that about?" Chris demanded.

"Nico wants to marry me."

The men exchanged glances. "The feeling is mutual?"

She smiled. "I love Nico and can't imagine my life without him." Didn't want to imagine it.

"Where will you live?"

"Nashville. That's his home base. Nico works for a private security firm. He has to train with his teammates on a regular basis. He can't do that if he lives here."

"Are you sure, Mercy? Aiden's death devastated you," Wyatt said. "Nico's job is more dangerous than Aiden's."

"I loved Aiden with my whole heart, but he's gone. He wouldn't want me to mourn him the rest of my life. I think Aiden would have like Nico. Be happy for me, not worried. Nico's a great man with a heart of gold. It's time for me to live again."

The next two weeks passed in a blur of activity. During that time, she and Nico made trip after trip to the dump to get rid of things the thugs had destroyed, and he completed repairs around the house and repainted the interior.

And then it was time for him to go. Early in the morning, Nico grabbed his Go bag and his duffel, and carted them to his SUV. After he closed the hatchback, he wrapped his arms around Mercy and tucked her against his chest.

"I don't know how long I'll be gone. It could be a few days or a few weeks. We can't afford to let any of the Scorpions escape, kitten. If we do, they might come after you, and I won't allow that to happen."

Mercy slid her arms around his waist. "I understand. Promise me you'll be careful."

"Always, my love. I'll call you when I can. Don't worry if I miss a day or two. When we hunt, we don't watch the clock. If you need anything, call Zane. He'll take care of it."

"I'll be fine. My father and brothers are here."

"Call Zane, too. He can provide things your family can't."

Seeing the worry in his eyes, Mercy tightened her arms around him. "All right. I'll call your friend. How will I know if something goes wrong on your mission?"

Nico cupped her face. "You're the first person on my contact list. Either Maddox or Z will contact you immediately." He captured her mouth for a series of blistering kisses. "I have to go. I'm missing you already." More kisses before he released her. "Go inside so I know you're safe before I leave. I love you, Mercy. I'll return as soon as I can."

"However long it takes, I'll be waiting, Nico. I love you." With tears blurring her vision, Mercy forced herself to turn away from him, walk to the house, and lock herself inside. She stood at the window until his taillights faded from view.

Wiping the wetness from her cheeks, Mercy went to the room she used as an art studio. With the house back in order, she turned to drawing to keep her mind busy.

She smiled wryly. The next few weeks could be productive ones as she sought activities to distract herself. After a three-hour session, Mercy worked the kinks out of her back, wondering if Nico was close to Nashville.

That line of thinking wouldn't help the days pass. She walked to the kitchen and filled the tea kettle. She needed something positive to think about while Nico was away.

The wedding. Nico's only request was for a simple wedding. She liked that idea. Her wedding to Aiden had been an elaborate affair. He'd wanted a huge celebration.

An idea popped into her head. The more she thought about it, the more the idea seemed doable if she had assistance from Nico's teammates and friends. Knowing Trace and Ben would be awake, Mercy sent them a text, explaining what she needed and swearing them to secrecy. Their reply was immediate and enthusiastic. Nice.

Next, she checked the time. Zane was probably awake by now. Just in case he wasn't, she sent him a message, detailing what she needed. The communications guru called her less than a minute later.

"This is going to be fun," he said, laughter in his voice. "I can't wait to see Nico's face."

"You'll tell me when he's coming home, right?"

"I will although I figure you'll know before I do. We'll have everything ready on our end. Send me the list of what you want me to do, and I'll get it done. What about your family? Will they be comfortable with this?"

"As long as I'm happy, they'll go along with it. Thank you, Zane."

"No problem. I'll be in touch soon."

Satisfied that the plans were in motion now, she poured hot water into her mug and dropped an herbal tea bag in the water to steep. She needed paper to start the list. After that, she had some searching to do on the Internet.

Two hours later, her phone rang.

"I'm in Nashville and getting ready to board the jet," Nico said. "I love you, Mercy. I'm looking forward to the day when I can wake up with you in my arms."

Oh, man. Mercy's heart melted. "I love you, too." Instead of tears when the call ended a short time later, she sat at her computer and got to work.

CHAPTER THIRTY-NINE

Four weeks later, Nico grabbed his Go bag and duffel and hurried toward the jet's exit. If he pushed the speed limit a little, he could be in Sherwood by six, just in time to surprise Mercy and take her out to dinner.

He'd missed her until his heart ached with every beat. The texts and phone calls had been his lifeline during the long, grueling weeks in Mexico. He and his teammates had left the US branches of the Scorpions to law enforcement. The ATF and FBI had been systematically dismantling the groups for the past month.

Nico's teammates all stood near their seats, waiting for him to pass. They had huge grins on their faces. "What?" he demanded.

"Go on," Trace said, clapping Nico on the shoulder. "You have an appointment to keep."

Odd, but he was too interested in going to Mercy to demand clarification. Nico strode down the aisle and hurried down the stairs to the tarmac.

Nico glanced up and came to an abrupt halt. Mercy. He drank in the sight of her, eager to hold her in his arms after such a long time apart. She raced across the tarmac. Nico had just enough time to drop his bags and shift his stance to take her weight when she threw herself into his arms.

He swung her around in a circle, set Mercy on her feet, and covered her mouth with his. Long minutes later, he broke the kiss. "I missed you."

"Good because I missed you, too." She smiled, her eyes glowing in the bright afternoon sun. "I have a surprise for you."

He blinked. "You do?"

Mercy nodded. "I hope it's a surprise you'll like. I've been working on it since the morning you left."

"A drawing?"

"Come on." She tugged on his hand. "If you'll give me the keys to the SUV, I'll drive."

Intrigued, he shoved his hand into his pocket and drew out the key fob. "Knock yourself out." All he wanted to do was sit back and look at the woman he loved.

Two minutes later, Mercy drove them away from the airport. They crossed town to the south side of Davidson County into Rutherford County.

Nico's brow furrowed. Where were they going? She parked in the lot of a church he'd been to before. The parking lot was nearly full. "Why are we here?"

"You'll see. Come on." Mercy led him up the stairs into the vestibule where Zane waited for them, dressed in a suit.

"Z. Good to see you, buddy." He shook his friend's hand. "What are you doing here?"

"Waiting for you. Let's go, man. You need to change clothes." He spun his wheelchair around and led Nico down the hall to the men's restroom. "What you need is in there."

He glanced inside and saw the black suit, shirt, and shoes. Puzzled, he looked at Zane. "What's going on?"

"You're marrying Mercy in twenty minutes."

Shock rolled through Nico. "Are you serious?"

A nod. "Your bride planned everything while you and your team were gone. Mercy said she didn't want to wait any longer to be your wife. Get dressed, Patch. Your family is waiting to greet you." He smiled. "Fortress flew them in on one of the jets."

Pulse jumping, Nico stepped inside the bathroom and closed the door. When he came out five minutes later, his father was waiting for him. "Dad." He dragged his father into a bear hug. "It's great to see you."

"Glad you're home in one piece. You have a special woman in your life, son. You're a lucky man."

"She's amazing." How had she pulled this off in only a month?

"Come into the sanctuary. Your mother wants to see you before the ceremony begins."

He spent the next few minutes talking to his family before he turned to Mercy's father and brothers. "I'm glad you came. Mercy certainly surprised me."

Pat Garwood grinned. "She's been like a kid in a candy store for weeks." His smile faded. "Did you take care of business?" he murmured, his gaze locked on Nico's.

"Yes, sir. Mercy's safe."

A nod. "Good." He looked over Nico's shoulder. "Looks like you're needed."

Nico turned. His lips curved. "Marcus." He shook his friend's hand. "Are you here as a guest?"

"I have the privilege of performing the ceremony."

Nico turned and greeted Marcus's wife with a kiss on the cheek. "Thanks for coming, Paige."

"Wouldn't miss it. I'm happy for you, Nico."

"Thank you."

Marcus squeezed his shoulder. "Let's go. Mercy should be ready now." He led the way to the stage.

"I don't suppose it matters, but I don't have rings for us."

"Mercy took care of it. If you don't like what she chose, you can turn it in for something else. Zane pulled some strings with a jeweler in town."

Incredible. He pivoted to face the double doors at the back of the church, anxious to see his soon-to-be wife. As if on cue, the doors opened, and there she was.

Mercy walked into the sanctuary on her father's arm, a smile on her beautiful face. And her dress? She looked absolutely stunning. The long white dress sparkled as she walked toward him. He couldn't take his eyes off her. Nico didn't know how he'd been so blessed to have her in his life, but he was grateful.

Ten minutes later, Mercedes Powers became Mercedes Rivera.

"Nico, you may kiss your bride," Marcus said.

Didn't have to tell him twice. Nico wrapped his arms around the woman of his dreams and took his time kissing her. When he finally lifted his head, the audience of friends, family, and his teammates broke into applause.

He smiled. "Do you have the honeymoon planned as well?"

"As a matter of fact, I do. We're flying to Orange Beach on a Fortress jet tonight. Your teammates will join us in two weeks."

"I love you, Mrs. Rivera. I'm going to spend the rest of our lives showing you just how much you mean to me." She would never have to question his love for her. Mercy Rivera owned his heart and he intended to cherish her as long as they lived.

Rebecca Deel

ABOUT THE AUTHOR

Rebecca Deel is a preacher's kid with a black belt in karate. She teaches business classes at a private four-year college outside of Nashville, Tennessee. She plays piano at church, writes freelance articles, and runs interference for the family dogs. She's been married to her amazing husband for more than 25 years and is the proud mom of two grown sons. She occasionally delivers devotions to the women's group at her church and conducts seminars in personal safety, money management, and writing. Her articles have been published in *ONE Magazine*, *Contact*, and *Co-Laborer*, and she was profiled in the June 2010 Williamson edition of *Nashville Christian Family* magazine. Rebecca completed her Doctor of Arts degree in Economics and wears her favorite Dallas Cowboys sweatshirt when life turns ugly.

For more information on Rebecca . . .

Sign up for Rebecca's newsletter: http://eepurl.com/_B6w9
Visit Rebecca's website: www.rebeccadeelbooks.com

Made in the USA
Middletown, DE
04 January 2021